I0652498

Black Opal

On Trauma and Redemption

A Psychoanalytic Novel

by

Frank R. Morris

ISBN: 978-0-578-00803-5

\- - - - - - - - - - - - - - - - - -

DEDICATION

To every person who has experienced

a major traumatic experience

and has sought

redemptive solutions.

TABLE of CONTENTS

PREFACE

It has not turned out the way I planned.

After forty plus years of doing psychotherapy and listening to the full range of human difficulties, I felt entitled to a restful retirement. My plan was to read and re-read world literature sitting in a leather chair by a nice warm fireplace in winter and, in summer, walk beside mountain streams picking up interesting million year old rocks.

While no longer actively listening to patients, I keep generating ideas about how to solve people problems. Psychotherapeutic theory has been my lifelong obsession. One day I read several journal and magazine articles about Post-Traumatic Stress Disorder (PTSD). It's a frequent subject in media due to mentally troubled soldiers returning from Iraq and Afghanistan. The subject is not new to me. During my active practice, I saw World War II, Korean War and Vietnam War veterans adjusting to life after combat. While doing therapy next to Skokie Illinois for five years, I saw several Holocaust survivors. I also worked with a number of children-become-adults whose fathers suffered after WW II due to battles in the Pacific Islands (Okinawa and Iwo Jima) as well as campaigns across Europe. Their father's issues were unconsciously and ingloriously passed down to the next generation. Clients and I worked to make sure that the passage of suffering did not continue with their children or children's children.

There were numerous other stories I listened to: stories monumental in terms of mental suffering. There were tragic accidents, children blamed for the death of a sibling, rape cases, advanced physical illnesses as a person prepared for death, misshapen bodies, and a host of physical and sexual abuse victims who struggled to overcome their childhood situations. Dr. Bruno Bettelheim spoke of the psychology of 'extreme situations' that led to massive traumas. That term covers thousands of stories I heard.

On a daily basis I never knew which trauma would come forth during a specified hour.

I found myself arguing with the therapeutic recommendations ensconced in the PTSD material, and, for that matter, other present-day psychotherapeutic literature. Many therapeutic ideas seemed trivial and unworthy of honoring the sacrifices of soldiers and patients in Twenty-First century America. It needs to be said aloud: There has been a crass dumbing-down in psychotherapy caused by the cooperation of pharmaceutical companies and health maintenance organizations. Brief drug therapy financially benefits both organizations. The unfortunate losers are those who have the greatest traumas. I find that intolerable.

I have a practical bent. What actually works with clients? War is not the only factor in major traumas. As I look back over my long career and review recent material, I'm deeply distressed by solutions offered to people who seriously hurt. Pills won't cure deep issues, though, it's true, pharmaceutics may stabilize a person massively traumatized. Bothered by my readings during the week, I went to a troubled form of sleep.

All night long I had a serial dream about a Holocaust survivor who abandoned his young son. The dream was incredibly structured. Deep therapeutic solutions appeared throughout the story unraveling through my mind. Upon awaking, I told my wife that I must immediately go to the computer and write a story that came to me overnight. I was at the keyboard for the next several hours. Breakfast was late.

The morning's insights stretched into over a year's intense concentration and writing. Nothing like this had ever happened in my life. The story and its accompanying analysis poured forth. It was like all the years of tortured accounts I heard in my practice somehow gelled, melted and blended into the accounts of Ezra, Shlomo, Daniel, and Sarah. Embedded in the story are major solutions on how to heal from massive traumas.

Forty-five years of doing therapy taught me that there is both a sameness and uniqueness to each human sufferer. The sameness is best seen in Edvard Munch's painting called The Scream. Each person marked by great personal tragedy has a silent scream deep within the soul; a scream saying both 'Why me?' and 'Why?' There are no corresponding answers because theological questions such as those - natural though they are - encounter a benign universe whispering simply 'Because.' There's no further explanation. Each person is alone with very painful mental anguish.

There is also a uniqueness because, with an infinitude of complex options, no one's story is just like that of another. Additionally, no individual's suffering is less significant than that of another. To engage in mental ponderings that 'my suffering is worse than your suffering' (as some do) is to be hoisted on the petard of Narcissism. It is sufficient to know that one's suffering has a uniqueness that is personal and has no similarity with that of another human. Suffering and the encounter with meaninglessness are all part of the human condition. Life is complex. Suffering is quite personal.

It is with great relief to my moral conscience that nothing in the following story breaks the covenant of confidentiality held tightly across my career. The trust given me has been the Golden Rule necessitating my silence across the decades. I'd be aghast if a single patient I worked with was able to recognize her/himself in the following book. They truthfully and trustingly told me their secret stories. I've maintained their trust. I have always been, and am now, grateful for their sensing me a person of honor worthy of private confessions. I hold their confidential secrets close to my heart. They have been my teachers in the human drama of suffering and recuperation.

This is not a traditional 21st Century novel. In his essay called "French Letters: Theories of the New Novel" Gore Vidal said that the electronic revolution has spelled the end of the serious novel. The utter seriousness of dealing with massive traumas - those mind-numbing negative experiences that cause a human to either implode with debilitating despair or expand to a higher plane of personal redemption - call out for a credible story. Is it necessarily the case that the utter complexity of severe soul-searching journeys through the corridors of suffering exceed any conceivable novel of any proposed length? Is it a fact that the modern world will only allow entertaining novels? Answers, uniquely discovered and uniquely applied, are incredibly profound. And very serious. Humans deeply desire meaning. They do not want to go into the dark oblivion of death without some semblance of having periods of worthwhile life.

My confession is this: While I was told by early readers of the following novel that my story is compelling, I've added italicized philosophical and psychological comments at the end of each chapter. My intent is to make those additions friendly and not get excessive with academic babble. The result is that the book is a hybrid. One part is novel; the other part therapeutic analysis. I reveal how a therapist listens, thinks, values, acts and confronts. This new form allows seriousness while maintaining the interest of a novel. It also frees me to study one person's psychological development from despair to victory - something continually thwarted in my writing by my basic value of confidentiality. The reader is to understand that I present my own thoughts as if characters introduced in the novel have shown up in my office.

Thus, in Black Opal I wed the imagination of fiction with cold psychological appraisal. The process adds huge redemptive options to the adventurous soul intent on solving traumas. Those who have faced great tragedy need many things: emotional release, a new narrative to imbed in the software of their minds, a friend who listens, and straight left brain information. That's my intent with both sections of this book with the given understanding that one can read faster than deep healing can take place.

I recommend that readers read just the story itself before studying the analytical remarks. I think it a good exercise, while reading the novel, to imagine how an Analyst might objectively view the situation. Later, the therapeutic analysis will show how close you were in your thoughts. I think the therapeutically curious and those who have bodily encountered major traumas will carefully study part two. So, too, will those who want to help friends who hurt. There is material for all who are curious about human mental health. My writing goal is to make both sections highly redemptive.

A Word about Writing Style

My vocation has ever allowed many hours per day to read both fiction and non-fiction. My range of interests has been broad - from quantum physics to cartoon books. My personal library is also broad with fiction slightly outnumbering books on therapy, history, biography, science and art. My long acquaintance with literature should have prepared me for writing the following material, especially since I have long written material on psychotherapy.

Unfortunately, my past writing did not prepare me for writing a novel. So, during the course of over a year, I've alternated my writing with reading present-day fiction. This practice, again, did not work. In pursuing the range of modern novels, I found myself skipping sections that did not advance knowledge of the characters. I shared this with my Analyst wife who admitted she did the same thing. This caused self-examination. Why did we both void out what we term “fluff?” Returning to my novel, I kept thinking that the style may appear too abbreviated for modern readers.

Then it came to me. After so many decades of listening to client confessions, I had become accustomed to ‘cutting to the chase.’ During the course of an hour session, long discourses involving major description had to be edited out. As therapist, I had to get to the heart of the matter by incisive questions. I could not allow rambling or be seduced by flowing rationalizations, abundant descriptions, well-thought-out sociological analyses, or clever depictions of other people. My job was to find the meat and avoid the vegetables, fruits and desserts. People were paying me; I had to use the time wisely.

Almost fifty years of listening left me bereft of some of the ordinary tools of the novelist. Understand, I tried. When a published novelist friend told me to add more description, I did in early drafts. Confession: I did not like what I wrote. Why? Because I was writing for people who were hurt core deep and I did not (do not) want to send them off into verbal thickets, flowery though they may be - words that do not get to the suffering center. So, on other re-writes I canned the descriptions and made the novel and its accompanying analyses look more like a therapy hour. With all the re-writing I frequently thought: “How the hell did writers do this prior to computers?”

I don’t fool around in my writing. Certainly, my clients didn’t. Those who were in the bush in Vietnam did not spend a lot of time describing the foliage or battle sounds. They talked about death and their fears. Survivors of the Holocaust did not tell me about the clothes of the Nazi’s; they talked about the humiliation and utter insanity of it all. A Japanese-American who was in the famous 442nd did not talk about fellow soldiers’ discrimination of his group; he spoke about the fierceness and horror of battles in Germany. A battalion cook on Okinawa laughingly related about making jungle juice and getting drunk, but, then, scarcely a moment later, he told me of his fear when he heard a burst of machine gun fire, saw his buddies fall and die as he hid in the undergrowth, and then drove like hell in a jeep to get away. "I got sober fast," he said.

In therapy, you get to it, though - it must be articulated - therapeutic lessons are repeated in subsequent sessions. In both novel and critique: I get sober fast. My goal is not like Tolstoy's War and Peace where he told the history of the war with the French in 1812 and explained the utter craziness and goriness of war. My goal is to speak to the issues of trauma and redemption. My pared down writing is similar to what I heard in therapy sessions - though it must be understood that there is a repetition of solutions handled across time. Therapy is not linear. The material is tough to grasp. Thus, lessons are repeated until the person absorbs it. Those who suffer will understand.

As I release insights in how to overcome tragedies and forge a good life, my former clients-become-friends may stand tall with pride. They figured out, not only how to minimally survive, but pathways to affirm life. My gratitude is forever. This book came from my dream and my writing, but my clients were my mentors.

Chapter One

The Sheriff's Call

Beautiful office. Great view. Successful business. And I still feel like crap. Despite being in therapy, I'm not shaking my main psychological problem. This is the first of the Chicago miserable sunless days which doesn't help. I have a Robert Browning phrase running through my head: "a common grayness covers everything."

Here comes my secretary, Jill. I'm not in the mood for my company's problems. I'm restraining myself from snapping at her: "I don't want to hear it, Jill." Instead, she startles me. "There's a sheriff from Abilene Kansas on the phone with sad personal news. I'm sorry, but he says your father has died." My heart skips a beat. My shoulders tighten. My breathing shortens.

My words to the Sheriff are stiff and rather breathless. "We weren't close." I stumble out the words.

"Sorry about that, son, but the will in his personal lock box says he leaves everything to you and his housekeeper. There is a bunch of mystery here. We can't tell you much because the information is slight."

"I can understand that," I almost stammer.

"We need you to come out pronto and straighten this mess out. We have a man that died of natural causes, a house showing no immediate clues to his life, and a housekeeper that - if she knows anything - won't tell us. In sum, everything is as silent as he is. We know his name is Ezra Loew and your name is Dan

Michelson - according to his will which calls you his son. How soon can you get here?"

Switching to my business voice, I say: "I'll be there in the morning, sheriff. I'll view the body and will need to get a picture of his face. As for the difference in names, I carry my mother's name which is Michelson."

"We'll get it done. Come on by as soon as you get here so we can wrap this up."

I stare at the phone in my hand and then hit 'Off'.' What Churchill said about Russia - "It is a riddle, wrapped in a mystery inside an enigma" - comes to mind in terms of my supposed father, this Ezra Loew. Telling the sheriff we weren't close is the essence of minimalism. I don't know him at all; not even his name. Sure, I know he was substantial and not an overnight fling of my mother's. During my childhood, he mailed a monthly check, later paid for my college, and gave me a very large sum when I initiated my Chicago architectural office. The money came from New York. Outside of that, all I could ever get out of my mother was "He is a good man." Christ! That was never enough.

Mom, who was a very good human, died four years ago in 2003. If she were alive now, I'd tell her to use the past tense: "He was a good man." There was never a negative word or even a positive one other than the repeated prescription "He is a good man". How do I know what kind of person he was? What evidence do I have? I never met the man, never saw him, never received a word from him. He's a ghost figure - a man she married who then disappeared - I knew not where - into silence.

Now I have a place: Abilene, Kansas, not New York City. Isn't that just perfect? All my Chicago friends call that state a "flyover." I've never been there and, if truth be phrased, only know it to be some kind of cow-town with a railroad. Suddenly, in one split moment, Kansas assumes Point Center in my quest for a phantom father. Sure, there's a portion of my brain that contains hundreds of questions. It's not like I'm totally incurious about the man. I don't deny this.

My psychoanalyst says I have a "superego lacunae," a hole in my mind labeled "father figure." Over the years I've secretly adopted teachers and great architects - unbeknownst to them. For awhile I've fantasized some admired figure was my dad. I'd study everything the hero figure said or did until I picked up something solid trying to fill what is missing. To be sure, some of the identifications work around the edges of the "lacunae." The hole that remains is more like a cavernous vacuum stealing a good measure of my energy.

One thing that hasn't worked in therapy is my own willingness to be a father. If a woman I date implies she wants children, I'm gone. Not interested. On the road again. The fatherhood dilemma has me nearing forty without ever standing at the altar. Dates, overnighters, and live-ins come and go - especially go when the word "children" is mentioned. I know of no compromise on that score because I feel trembling anxiety throughout my body at the mere mention of kids. No father in my own personal life has meant an ache causing me to refuse marriage because I have no idea what a father does. I definitely do not want some kid to experience the problem I had and have. Would I be able to play ball with a son? Would I skedaddle like my paternal ghost had done? The thought of having a child causes stomach pains, my mind goes blank, and my feet and legs vibrate as if ready to run. I want freedom from obligation and that means no mommy type woman for me. Pseudo-psychologists might call my situation "a fear of commitment." It is much more than that. Maybe having no soul partner leaves an empty spot also, but it is nothing compared to my fatherhood fears. That is intense and brings back all the loneliness and painful questions from childhood.

Yes, I know: my anti-parent position reveals my failure to grow up. If I didn't know it on my own, Dr. Sidney Rabinowitz, my Analyst, makes it perfectly clear to me. I've enjoyed relationships with some stellar women, women with great bodies and decent souls. I'm as careful with birth control as a brain surgeon operating on gray tissue. Even this minor meticulous obsession with birth control shouts out at me that something is very unbalanced in my psyche. When I walk by a public park where kids are playing, my stomach curdles. I automatically look in the opposite direction. Any distraction is sufficient. Luckily, my profession encourages studying interesting buildings nearby. I hurriedly look away from the park to a building to see if there is any old idea I can build upon, any new idea that will stimulate me to come up with innovative structures. Solid architecture is appealing; the laughter of kids on a playground is not.

All this musing reminds me I have an appointment with my psychoanalyst. We'll talk the situation over. I'll need to cancel some appointments for this necessary Abilene trip. I know he will approve of my voyage since my absent father syndrome has occupied many, if not most, of our sessions. Here's part of our conversation.

"Doc, my dad died. He was in Kansas of all places. I'll be gone for a week or so. I have to get some closure on all this."

"That sounds like a good plan. Take notes on what you feel. Make it a feeling journey into both the present and the past. This is a necessary phase for you to build a future free of old junk."

"Dr. Rabinowitz, are you telling me to be up-front and real? Is this psychobabble necessary when a man's father dies? I may compartmentalize and just go through the motions - as if the damn emotions won't be blasting out all over the place anyway."

"I'm saying: Be real. Cry if you feel like it. Be angry if you are alone and can express it. Own your scare when you encounter something that is bewildering."

"Do you have to give me the Shrink Speak right now? My invisible dad - the mystery nightmare figure who haunts me - just died. Have an ounce of pity."

"Don't do the poor victim thing where I'm supposed to be compassionate when I know you really have no love lost for the man. As for your Kansas trip, being real is what it's all about. Otherwise, you go through life driven by forces from your past and never really grow up. You know this father stuff leads to your poor relationships with women. This is a great opportunity."

"I hope it is one that causes you to forego bills for missed sessions while I'm gone."

"That's cute. Check in as soon as you return. This will be interesting."

That's the essence of my session. I know Rabinowitz is a good guy - expensive but good. I have unloaded some old shit at him - which he calls transference - and he took it well. I know he's not my real dad, but as a listening father figure I've dumped some rage right in his lap. He took it in silence which gave me another reaction to the silence of being invisible to my real father. I remember yelling on one occasion "I'm not fucking invisible!" That's therapy. Four days a week, two-fifty a pop, eleven months a year - August being vacation. Forty-eight grand. He's expensive but worth it if I can shake off the negative remnants from a lonely childhood. I don't want a ghost father haunting the rest of my days. And nights. And relationships. In addition to therapy, I've taken a lot of night courses in psychology. The truth is that I've studied psychology at every opportunity my whole life so I can get some kind of handle on my personal fatherless dilemma. Nothing does it. The soul hole remains.

The Kansas sheriff 's beckoning call hits me at a time in my life when I know there can be no more fleeing, no more abruptly ceased short-term girl friends, no more avoidance of my painful unconscious reality. I have a very sad empty spot in my brain. Hating to admit it aloud, the truth is I long for a real father. I secretly yearn for someone of flesh and blood who can actually see me, know me across the years, and give me a paternal blessing. Otherwise, I'm a walking wounded veteran of domestic failure wars. Knowing I'm not whole makes me very susceptible to an immediate dropping of work with an utter willingness to go to Abilene Kansas. Why, of all places, did my missing father live there? The answer coming to mind is that no one would think to look for him in rural Kansas. Even detectives would never search that locale. My theory: he wanted to disappear and be invisible. He succeeded. But why did the checks come from New York? So many questions and no hint of answers. I have to go. It is time in my life to at least attempt to grow up.

In reflection on the abrupt phone call, my blurted commitment to the sheriff was so forthright I surprised myself. And was I ever cool and analytical! "I want to examine the corpse." Gee. I sounded like a doctor doing rounds at a hospital. "Yes, nurse the man I missed during my entire childhood, the man who left me with a hole in my heart and brain, the man whose disappearance caused me to be a deep relationship avoiding jerk … yes, nurse, I'd like to check out his dead body." Cool. That's me on the outside. Luckily, no one asks for a blood pressure test. My heart is beating like a Salvation Army drum.

Looking around I have different thoughts. My office feels like a sanctuary. I don't want to go to Kansas. Nevertheless, I tell my secretary: "Jill, book me a private plane to Kansas - an airport in the direction of Abilene. "What the hell am I doing? I don't know this guy and he didn't want to know me. Why not just hire a lawyer in Abilene to handle everything, slam the body in the dirt at some unnamed cemetery, and get it over with?"

And yet, I know exactly why I'm going. It's not money. It's not to honor the dead. It sure as hell isn't to be curious about some little mid-Kansas town. The internal thrust to go is larger than my conscious mind. My soul demands it. The lonely little boy within has suffered too long. Further, there are too many unanswered questions. Who was he? What did he do? How could he afford to send us money over the years? What was life like in a small town? Can I learn something about him that might free my soul? Did he have friends? Who is this housekeeper - possibly a live-in lover who cared for him in his later years? Is she a gold digger? Where did he find her? Will she want the full inheritance - if, indeed, there is anything of substance? Was my father really a good man as my mother's repeated platitude stated?

After a lifetime of questions, I'm besieged by dozens more running through my crazy mind. Is this just weak talk? My inner child (and yes, I hate that phony psychology talk even if it does have a measure of truth) wants to see and feel his house. I want to walk the streets he walked. I want to ask the mysterious housekeeper what she knows about him. "Did he ever mention his wife and son? Did he tell her any stories about his own childhood? What did they talk about?" Was mom just putting the best face on a bad situation so her son would not hate him with her good guy rap? Who was the guy, anyway? Maybe he'll look like a Skid Row bum that should be buried in a potter's field.

I also know questions will continue to roll once I see the house, once I experience the community, once I … meet the sheriff and see my father's corpse. This isn't going to be easy. In fact, it might usher in the most difficult days of my life.

****

Therapeutic Analysis

***Initial Interview**: Daniel Michelson is 38 years old, about six feet tall, weighs approximately 190 pounds, and is physically healthy. He has sharp aquiline features with brown eyes, black hair, and an athletic demeanor. His clothes are elegant and his social image is that of a successful man on the rise in Chicago. He is known in the circles of power: a board member of the Art Institute, Harold Washington Library and Northwestern Medical Hospital, attends fund-raisers for important civic causes, has the dream home on the near North Side, and is recognized as notable, rich, and single. The architectural firm he owns builds elementary and high schools throughout the Midwest. His office offers a view of a portion of Michigan Avenue and a slice of the Chicago River. Three times a week Dan begins his day with a competitive squash game at a downtown private club. (In these italicized notes I'll act like Dan is* my *patient. Actually, he is the client of Dr. Rabinowitz.)*

He dates beautiful women and takes them to the Opera and Symphony. His image is that of the cavalier bachelor. Dan's picture is frequently in the Chicago Tribune and the Chicago Sun Times. As is obvious from his pursuit of therapy, the private man and the public image are not synonymous. True enough, he actually is the confident man of the world in business, philanthropy and entertainment. He quakes, however, when it comes to the possibility of commitment and family. Some think him secretly gay; he is not. Some think him having the best of all worlds with his serial sexual relationships. That is the social level of his story; not the psychological level.

Diagnostic analysis. *First, a critical matter: therapeutically speaking, in Dan's case there is no chemical imbalance and no* *addiction to alcohol or drugs. In addition, there is no physical or sexual problem manifesting itself.*

If I were to use a diagnostic label per the Diagnostic and Statistical Manual of Mental Disorders, he'd be placed in the category of Narcissistic Personality Disorder. To a great degree, he is in it for himself. Despite charity work, he is rather oblivious to the needs of others. In the old Greek myth, Narcissus was so captivated by his reflection in a pond that he was unaware of the beautiful goddess Echo who yearned for him close by. In Judeo-Christian terms, pride is the great sin. The two concepts are similar and both fit Daniel Michelson. A word study of his private thoughts reveals that he frequently uses the words I, me, and mine and makes himself the center of every conversation. Freud indicated that we all marry some one or some thing. Narcissists marry themselves.

It appears that Dan's little tastes of power have gone to his head so he thinks himself special. Having no father around to check his brashness, Dan thinks his superego lacunae left him just wishing for a dad; it also leaves him uncontrolled in terms of his arrogance. Each seeming contribution is an avenue to business contacts and contracts. Even an innocuous matter like playing squash at the club leads him to decision makers who deal with local, state and Midwestern school building projects. Business success is the first priority in Dan's value spectrum; not love. It seems that Dan does not know how to really give of himself from deep within. He does have flashes of seeking to be a contributor. Those are moments; not the main fare. Most of the time he's in his head figuring out his next moves to be even more successful. He likes living large.

Two paragraph back I began with 'if' quite purposely because I do not use the diagnostic system designed for insurance companies to pay the bill. My clients pay their own costs for therapy. This allows me to not categorically box a person so I can see a larger picture. Narcissism is but one part of Dan's makeup. I prefer the *Psychodynamic Diagnostic Manual* *that understands people are far more complex. This means that I accept that people have what I call 'modules', or differing neuronal brain firings, each of which has a prepackaged way of thinking, feeling, valuing and acting. In other words, Dan has different sub-personalities with Narcissism but one of them, significant though it is. He is also a searcher intent upon growing. This is critical knowledge for analysis.*

The term "Narcissism" is a value term, meaning that excessive focus on self is wrong. It is only wrong if one buys the notions that sharing relationships are better and that concentration upon one's own self leads to a poorer existence. Narcissism is okay if one thinks greed is good, ability to purchase whatever is primary, and having things is preferable to having a free identity that is aware, spontaneous, and capable of deep love. Dan's appearance in therapy and his initial thoughts reveal that his present course of action leaves him unhappy.

In talk therapy clients are free to converse about whatever crops up in their minds. Within a half hour a person unwittingly reveals her or his value structure. This is not conscious whatsoever. It all revolves around the client's emphases on what is deemed important. Money, power, influence, what others think, education, children, a marriage, nature, art, music, etc. may dominate the hour. It is impossible to hide values because they out very rapidly. This leads therapists to note the Narcissism quotient.

In first sessions I explain that therapy contains value components. I assume that some values are more valid than others; in a total relativistic mode even suicide would be acceptable. That is out of bounds in my value structure. I believe it better to love than to hate, to give rather than take, to be aware of the world rather than be oblivious, to free one's self from injunctions received as a child (said injunctions that limit experiencing), and be able to laugh, share, and love - hopefully, with a partner. For some, the last is problematic; they prefer to live alone. I accept that given the situation.

I particularly note Dan's attitude. My value says that an individual needs to exhibit, or seriously be aimed at, having a realistic positive attitude toward life. This means focusing on beauty rather than ugliness, truth rather than lying rhetoric, justice rather than continuing prejudice, and doing good rather than passively waiting for others to improve the world. This is not naïve optimism; it means choosing to look and work for the light even during dark times. It appears that Dan is ready to look full in the face of tragedy and plow through it to some kind of personal victory. He takes therapy seriously.

I also note that Dan reveals a love for Chicago. Therapeutically this is important because humans need to be tethered to a solid piece of ground. Over the years, clients with the most difficulty had little to no sense of place. Dan is grounded.

***The Therapeutic Contract**.*
My practice is to clarify a matter of integrity: mine and the client's. On my part, I will be faithful in terms of being there when he is in need and in terms of keeping confidences. The other half goes like this: "I need from you a contract based on your integrity. I need you to shake my hand that you will not commit suicide, do anything crazy that imperils your health, and will never murder anyone." If the client is unwilling to contract, I conclude aloud with them that I am not the therapist for their situation. "I give integrity; I expect integrity from my clients." In Dan's case, this is not a problem.

I also contract as to the cost of the sessions. Since this is my major income, he is to pay even if he misses a session. If I am sick and miss a session he does not pay. The regularity of the time is agreed upon. I further explain that I am an empiricist and rely upon explainable data that I will openly share if he so inquires.

It's time to go to work. This means Dan forthrightly tells me everything running through his mind without editing. Specifically, I want to hear the emotion that triggers further thoughts, actions, and values. I challenge most stories as to the initial emotion. That way I trace what actions are propelled by old decisions made in childhood. I also look for feelings that continue an old identification with a parent which the person unwittingly carries. I confront phony feelings used to manipulate. I also check to see if the emotion is appropriate in the here and now. Values and thoughts are also analyzed.

As therapist, I am keen on noting behavior to see if it is soul fulfilling to the client. Many pursuits only provide a life not consistent with the values previously elucidated. We, that is the client and I, sift through emotions and values as to their contributions to the life he or she wants.

***The Presenting Problem or Trauma**.*
Dan explained that his unhappiness was related to his being fatherless during childhood. His father abandoned the family as soon as he was born. Dan has never heard or seen him. He describes how this hurt when he saw other kids have a father show up and support their son at Little League ball games. His mother was always there, but not emotionally close. She meant well, but did not know how to give. In not having a father, Dan has refused to accept any older man telling him what to do. According to him, his whole story winds around the missing father issue.

Script. *I find it startling that clients unwittingly reveal their main psychological difficulty in the very first session. It turns out that a child develops a Primary Script, an unconscious psychological story, that has the capability to ruin both personal identity and intimate relationships in adulthood. Dan's main secret narrative is an abandoning father whom he disliked, a mother who he thought weak due to her being abandoned, and Dan's adaptation which was to be smart and a loner. In therapy speak,* *the old Script has a Strong, but Hated Role, a Weak Role, and the Child's Adapted role. As Analyst, I privately underscore the first Script revelation in the first hour and keep it in my mind across the months. My job is to confront Dan when he plays one of the unconscious roles in his real conscious life. Covertly let me say that Freud was on the right track with his Oedipal analysis, though he stretched the idea too far with his biological sexual theories.*

The Primary Script is too powerful to gloss over quickly because, in all cases, it turns out to be a recurring theme through most, if not all, sessions. It is the heart of the dynamic unconscious. The Adapted role is the first to go in therapy, though it takes major time to unlock its grip. Adaptations cover the gamut ranging from being cute to being rebellious, from being perfect as a child's mind conceives perfection to being a slob, from being the intelligent one to playing stupid, from being sweet and pleasing to being obnoxious, from being a jock to an artist, from being invisible to being a Smart Alec (Dan's role). The options are myriad, the pain to self enormous.

Interestingly, and frequently sadly, after the Adaptation becomes rather stilled in the personality through therapy or staunch conditions in life, the next role taken is that of Hated but Strong. In Dan's case he'd switch from the cool bachelor and scorn his date and abandon her. Understand, he is oblivious to the child origins of the Script. Unconsciously though it's very powerful in terms of avoiding real closeness. The Hated role is quite resistant in terms of therapy, because of the unconscious deep fear of vulnerability which is viewed as the Weak and Feared role - Dan's mom. His three role drama limits options in terms of identity and intimacy.

Therefore, a proof of therapeutic success will be when Dan can love fully. He'll be able to risk utter vulnerability in terms of his partner's possible abandonment and, in older years, her death. Right now, tender vulnerability is terrifying to Dan. He will not risk it. To take the final step of tenderness with a partner will be to know, internally, that he is strong enough to survive if the beloved departs - something that originally wounded him with his father's departure. Thus, there has to be massive identity formation. That's a major reason why analysis takes so long. (Again, you can read this material faster than it can be assimilated.)

Script is preceded by a flicker of scare (frequently labeled 'anxiety.) Dan has a lot of work to do. His father's death presents a big opportunity to grow. We'll see.

Chapter Two

Answers in Abilene

Driving to Abilene from Topeka Kansas presents miles of open land. Jill's maternal suggestion that I not land close to my destination and travel across vacant country seems stupid. I resent it. Some airport must have been closer. I do not need time to absorb the reality of my father's death. He's dead. Let's get on with it.

The flight was okay, but, driving so far over empty land seems insane. Over there is a sign saying 'See the Largest Prairie Dog in the World.' I'm not stopping. Miles further I see a huge billboard almost shouting 'ADULT SUPERSTORE'. O God! The field before the huge porn store has a smaller sign proclaiming "Jesus heals and restores. Pornography kills." Unbelievable. Even closer to the superstore in the same field is another sign saying "The eyes of the Lord are in every place beholding the evil and the good. Proverbs 15:3." Great. I'm in sexual Bible land. When and if I survive this and get back to Chicago, I may post an ad for a secretarial job at my firm. Jill, damn her, got me into this visual ordeal. I'm not in the mood to suffer through this crap.

My friends are right when they say this landscape has no there, there. Correct. There is no here, here. It's a wasteland. I'm hungry and the only thing available is an All-You-Can-Eat Buffet. The overweight cashier asks for ten dollars. I pay. What other choice do I have anyway? Before me are six large counters stacked with fatty foods. I can handle this. My large frame of six feet and near two hundred pounds needs protein. I'll choose carefully. Surrounding me are immense bodies lapping over their chairs. This is Big Ass City. Next to these behemoths, I'm tiny. The men are wearing cut-off blue jeans, Coors beer T-shirts, dirty sneakers and no socks. Their bellies hang precipitously over tight belts. The women have large flower patterns on their blouses or dresses in order to camouflage pendulous breasts and tummy bulges. The camouflage doesn't work.

An elderly farm couple sit at a table nearby. They concentrate upon their food and never say a word to each other. That's what a long-term marriage does to you. I dub them Mr. and Mrs. Grant Wood, the Kansas-American Gothics. Very sad.

Though I'm on the non-smoking side of the restaurant, noxious white clouds drift over polluting the taste of my food. On top of that offense, the baked potato in foil was stabbed by a butcher knife so that silver slivers are lost in the white of the potato - one of my pet peeves. I'm getting a fat boy nutrition education here in the middle of Kansas!

Here comes a woman dressed in the equivalent of a one ton flour sack. In her monstrous flowered dress she waddles along with huge globular ankles wearing only flip flops. Her tray is loaded. This is worth a column in a Chicago paper. She has a plate stacked with mayonnaise-doused salad. As I watch out of the side of my eye, it slips magically down her gullet. Her hips swing powerfully as she returns to the bar and gets a plate full of vegetables. She wolfs it down. She systematically proceeds to the next bar where she loads up all over again. This would make a movie. Where is Woody Allen when I need him? She goes from east to west, counter after counter, munching through calories like a giant voracious locust. Her return to the vegetable bar to get another entire plateful of macaroni and cheese is too much for my mental sanity. I switch tables and look at the cars out the window: green ones, red ones, gray ones. All SUV's - no VW bugs. This is no country for small cars. Or young urban men. I've got to get out of here.

People arriving at the restaurant at the same time I did are still chowing down. I cannot help but glance back to see if the Circus Lady has reached the dessert trough which is laden with cakes, puddings, ice cream and cookies. Wups. She's gnawing through the meat dishes … roast beef, chicken, fish, lasagna, and beef goulash. She must save the sweets for the last. I'm not watching. Makes me sick. Nothing like this exists on the North Side of Chicago. Thankfully.

I need the refuge of my car! I find myself wishing that my stomach churning and mental anguish is due to the calorie binge I just witnessed. Another part of me knows my problem is sheer raw anxiety because I'm nearing Abilene. Despite my excellent education, successful business, and suave urban image, I'm scared shit-less. So this is what therapeutic analysis accomplishes for me - a scared little boy afraid of the truth. I have no mental picture of what is ahead of me in the coming bohunkville.

My mind is whirling. Will the guy on the slab be a puny punk, a scar-faced criminal type, a blimp who daily commuted to the gluttony bar? Will I look like him so much that I'll visualize my own blood free cadaver in some altogether too quick future? Why should I even care what I discover at the funeral home? What did mom see in him? Why did she defend him? Why not call him a "rat" and be done with it? In Abilene there'll be no child-inspiring stories passed down to me by a dead body. It is 38 years too late. I missed that long ago and faraway. Why am I driving out here in the middle of nowhere? I'm all a-tumble and it's not because I, too, ate a portion of macaroni and cheese. Fear grips me. My balls even seem cold.

ABILENE.

My stomach clutches as the sign appears Is that sweat that just popped on my brow? Swinging off the Interstate, I decide to not go north because there is nothing but miles of deserted prairie in that direction. Heading south I'm driving on a typical Midwest middle class street called Buckeye. I'm surrounded by an array of mid-level motels, a rundown apartment building, a car dealership, one story office buildings, Western wear, and several insurance outlets. A sign next to a Mexican restaurant proclaims "colonic irrigations." I may need that place later. I'll focus on any distraction to avoid thinking about looking at a dead body on a slab. Architecture on this Buckeye Street is appalling. Why did my father, Ezra Loew, live here of all places? Good God!

In the first mile or so of this American nightmare street, there's no sheriff's office and no funeral home. I mark McDonald's as I pass it because they do have good coffee. There is also Taco Tico, Burger King, Pizza Hut and Sonic. Any port in a storm. Distracting my brain, I focus on other establishments: Napa, Auto Zone, Dollar General, a pharmacy, a grocery store, several banks, a host of churches, and a gas station. I'll fill the tank just in case I have to make a quick getaway to points North.

Hmm. That's interesting. There are a few nice homes built in about the 1920's or so. Continuing south, I enter the downtown area which has red brick buildings with faded signs on the end walls, angular parking, and an antique five and dime whose windows are covered with hand-written sale items. Folks dress like Nineteenth Century mannequins, but I see no banners proclaiming some kind of Hee-Haw Festival. I guess their plaid cotton clothes are just daily typical. I wonder if the Amish got this far West. Slowing the car and rolling down the window, I overhear corny friendliness typical of people accustomed to pastimes. "Hi. How are you?" "How's the wife and kids?" As if they really give a shit. Where am I? I want Michigan Avenue in my beloved Chicago and here I am in a dusty forlorn frontier

Nineteenth Century town. I'm on a misplaced mission to find some remnant from a runaway father. It's all so stupid.

Suddenly my heart beats furiously: I see a funeral home and the police station and angle in to park. I'm still in the old downtown section. I halfway expected an antique white ball light fixture in front of the cop station with the intimidating black letters proclaiming POLICE. The combined fire station and police station are in a converted old yellow brick building. The building looks okay and appropriate. This does not comfort me. Am I in some kind of hallucinatory state, a weird dream brought on by a Freudian wish, a psychotic episode due to the father hole in my brain? This is definitely a time and place warp and I'm no Connecticut Yankee with hidden resources. All I am is a boy, a little boy in search of a father.

Before I meet the sheriff, I better re-build equilibrium by gaining city/country perspective. Abilene is quaint. Homey. My first encounters call forth a yawn from deep within my body. Everyone strolls along slowly - as if nursing sore feet. They amble. Getting out of my car someone says "Howdy" to me while his face questions why a city slicker wearing a suit and a tie dares to come to Valhalla. Why am I wearing a tie anyway? It's totally out of place. I pull it off and throw it in the car. Then I realize: it's not just the suit, tie, and polished dress shoes that are the problem. It's me. I look different from everyone else. I'm 'city.' I'm also Jewish.

Face it: I don't fit. How the hell did my father (the "good man" of my mother) belong in such a place? Did he have a nervous breakdown at the thought of having a son and regress to being a mental case all his life? At any moment I expect a cattle drive down the main drag. "Get 'em up, move 'em out!" Wasn't Abilene famous for some kind of Western shootout, some desperado shot by Wild Bill Hickok? "Maybe he's still sheriff 'in these parts," I think sarcastically.

I pause in order to get my bearings once more by taking some deep breaths. I may not fit clothing wise, but I'm supposedly a mature man of the world. I look around. Nothing resembles any architecture I admire. This town is a throwback to some ancient episode of cowboy wildness. The mortar is so old it's chinking out between the bricks, said bricks which are weather scarred by sandstorms from the prairie. I see no bullet holes; that's a relief. The fading signs are long sunk into the bricks above the doorways. The copper molding has turned green, something nice and worth money in a Chicago architectural antique store. Is there a place where my father sat on a bench, where he walked and shook hands, where he purchased groceries? Good God, how did he survive here? Five minutes and I've done it. It's time for a cigar and a glass of whiskey. Where are the dancing girls at the honky-tonk? I'm ready for a new adventure down the road, some new food dive further West on the Interstate; some place called Blimp Central where I can watch heavyweights chow down and fat up. The mere thought of driving on black Interstate asphalt with no cracks in it makes a renewed drive appealing. "Mount up! It's time to hit the road again," I want to shout to the kiddies.

But there are no kids to hear, no huge car packed to the gills with camping gear ready for us to tent somewhere in the Rockies. That image fades and I remember why I'm here. It's to fill a hole in my soul. The police station is before me. I may look like a city slicker, but I'm tight all over. I'm scared to my toes. Trembling, I push into the police station. An officer with a ten gallon hat is sitting behind a cracked oak desk. I ask to see the sheriff and identify myself as the son of the deceased old gentleman who recently died and is at the funeral home. He points to a back office.

The sheriff is nice enough. He spouts the typical crap heard at a death, things like "I'm sorry about your loss" and "it's difficult to meet at times like this." He's hatless, has thinning hair, and by the size of the paunch overhanging his wide leather belt, I'm tempted to ask how he likes the macaroni and cheese back at the feeding trough on I 70. Yes, I know: My deleted sarcasm is a mental defense where I'm seeking to get back in control. Instead, I'll switch to rapport skills where I'll match his drawl and mannerisms.

"Well, son, there ain't too much to tell. Your dad died. Natural causes. Found in his bed by his housekeeper. She's nice. A little lost now. They live about three blocks from here. He was the silent type. Didn't overdo friendly. Occasionally hung around on weekends. But not like a homeless guy. Like a curious person. Like a harmless old geezer. 'Scuse me, I mean no offense. Occasionally he walked around town nodding his head. He stared at church goers as if he knew something they didn't know. Spoke as little as possible. When in town on Saturdays and Sundays he drank coffee at the café by himself mid-morning. Because he sat and stared blankly at a wall, no one talked to him. Thought him weird, I guess. Seemed to cut his own hair. Wasn't a drinker. Didn't even use the local bank for checking or saving. But there is a key to a security box we got out of his metal box that belongs to our bank. The key was right next to the will with your name, social security number, phone number and address. He was almost invisible … so much so that no one even knew his name."

"Was his full name Ezra Loew as you said when you called me?"

"Just Ezra Loew, no middle name. Yours is Dan Michelson, right? I hear Loew is a Jewish name, but we don't have any Jews around here. Except him, I guess. We have Catholics and Protestants. No Jews. That's not meant as an insult. It's just the way it is. I guess they'd be welcome. No one ever tested it. Even here at the police department we didn't know your dad was a Jew. I don't know why I'm talking about this because it is no big deal. Just strange. Out here. Why he chose to live here I have no idea. Weird. But let's get on with business. Do you have a lawyer?"

“I just got into town. Who drew up the will? Is he a local guy? Forgive me Sheriff: I’m a bit confused. Will you tell me again how you knew he‘s a Jew … besides his name?”

“Yeah, you’re right: the lawyer on the will is local. As for the Jew thing, he looks different from us. Plus the tattoo on his arm is like photos at the Eisenhower Center.”

“Eisenhower Center?”

“Yeah. The Dwight David Eisenhower Library and Research Center is here in Abilene. Before Ike was President, he was Supreme Commander in Germany during WWII and rescued some folks from German concentration camps. The Center has pictures of Jews with tattoos. Gosh, that’s almost poetic. Jews and tattoos. But let’s get back to business. As for the housekeeper, you won’t get much out of her, boy. She’s almost a mute. Hasn’t said ten words in my presence. Called and said ‘I found him dead in bed. Can you come?’ Nine words. That seemed to be a strain. She let us in. Showed us the body. We checked to see if there had been any foul play. Saw none. Called Wilbur at the Funeral Home and he picked up the body. We said ‘Thank you’ to the woman and left the house. That’s it. Oh, one other thing. She pointed out a metal box in his closet which we pried open and found a will that named you and her. All of this is strange: your dad, the housekeeper, the death, the house, the will. It ain’t the way things happen around here. And, excuse me again, all this on top of us finding out his name and that he was Jewish.”

I feel confused. “A Holocaust tattoo?“

“We called the housekeeper and asked if he was a Holocaust survivor and all she said on the phone was ‘Don’t know.’ That was it. ‘Don’t know.’ I said ‘Thanks’ and hung up. We haven’t even told her that she’s on the will. Hell, we don’t even know where he hid his operating money; maybe in the Bank security box. That's it. Do you have any questions?"

I thought but didn't say 'A Jew grows in Abilene.' As for questions, I bite my tongue in order to keep from saying "only a million or so." "Right now, I don't have any questions sheriff. May I have his metal lockbox and the stuff inside it? Then let's go view the body."

****

Therapeutic Analysis

Therapeutic process: *Early on in therapy, my practice is to let the client talk without me adding much. I am confirming my original thesis of the Script as well as noting everything from bodily behavior (gestures, breathing, left-right brain shifts, etc.) to rationalizing content, so I mainly sit and take notes. Sifting through his remarks, it is clear that Dan has a sense of humor which happens to be a mark of a liberated man. Sometimes in the light of major grief and stressful situations, it is helpful to be able to laugh - Defense Mechanism be damned. It is an understandable human response. It is preferable, however, to laugh at one's self and funny situations and not resort to a ridiculing laughter of others. Still, I like the man's possession of a sense of humor. It's necessary in a crazy world.*

I also find myself relieved that Dan caught that his sarcasm was triggered by scare. Sarcasm is a clear Defense Mechanism as were his mental ruminations about the Buffet. Dan was under stress which led him to be critical of others rather than examine his own emotions. Defense Mechanisms are designed to protect a person from feeling the emotion of tenderness, which, at this point in therapy, would leave him quite vulnerable. In Dan's case, a tender approach to seeing his dead father would cause him to have avalanches of sadness which, in turn, would result in body-wracking sobs. That is against his Chicago image as well as his personal defenses. Deep grief would mean the loss of his heretofore established narrative of who he is and what he feels. It would go against his unconscious Script.

Therapeutic confrontation: *If we were further along in therapy, I'd approach this situation differently. What is not clear in Dan's portrayal of entry into Abilene is a heart felt loss, a loss not only of his absent father, but a loss of being able to have his lifelong* *questions answered by the man himself. Humor consistently covering authentic sadness is not good. It needs to be felt in order to heal from a parent's death. It is better to weep. As he is now in his journey, however, the shock of sobbing would imperil his self image.*

Therefore, I would not confront his ridiculing of the Buffet patrons or Abilene citizens in an early session. Dan is a brilliant urban male. It takes a very mature person to accept the panoply of American people without some form of superiority stance. Honestly, as therapist, I'd let this go for now. If it persists as an "I'm superior" and "I look down on others" I'd confront because it does not serve his long term interests.

A word about Dan's thinking process is in order. The word "think" is non-specific due to the fact that people employ different processes when they are "thinking." Some think in music notes, others mathematical symbols, and some are lost in kinesthetic considerations about how their body feels. Some think business and money. Farmers may think crops and weather. Others - like poets and writers - think words, sentences, and plots. Dan's internal dialog can be seen as one sign of Narcissism. If Dan were married and had children, his process might probably dissipate over time because he'd be frequently interrupted. I have had clients who, despite having a wife and children, remain stuck in their "thinking" mode. They are like zombies in the home.

A worse form of internal dialog (usually called Guilt) is where one part of the mental structure (the Superego or conscience) 'should's' on a more natural childlike part - as in "You should be ashamed" with the other internal voice responding "I'm sorry." That form (Critical Parent vs. Kid) can be such a strong loop that it goes on interminably. For that more pathological option, I, as therapist, have the person do the Gestalt practice of two chairs. The parts are sorted and the person repeats the dialog externally … until they get that this internal self abuse is wasted thinking. The idea is to shrink the Superego. In not having a father, Dan does not have a strong persecuting conscience. Therefore, he entertains himself with his Smart Alec mode.

Many times, actual behavior is far more important than either the internal dialog or actual words of the client. The reality is that Dan, scared though he may be, happens to be in Abilene, is actually on a path to look at his dead father, and is pursuing answers for his major 'Superego lacunae' identity issue. He does not have to be there. He went to a strange locale to pursue answers. This shows that he is willing to face reality and not continue to live in darkness, avoidance or denial. Therefore, he is to be admired. I'd say aloud: "Dan, I admire your going to Abilene in search of answers."

***Emotions**: Therapeutically speaking, it is critical to focus on emotion at every session. Unless a person can catch the microsecond kickoff emotion, unwitting rhetoric and errant behavior overtake a person and lead to all manner of irrationality. Rationalization controls. Without clear emotions, limited psychological freedom, spontaneity, and original thinking occur. To be free, a person normalizes sadness, anger, scare, happiness, excitement, and tenderness. This is not negotiable in psychotherapy.*

During this phase of therapy I privately focus on the issue of the unconscious Script that provides the shadow reality from childhood that hurts Dan's life. Script is like a bell ringing at a prize fight. The contestant hears a certain stimulus and automatically reacts along lines developed decades ago. Dan's unconscious triggering emotion is scare. He is unaware of it. Dan and I will get to it as we go along.

Since Script is a key reality, I'll provide illustrations from other clients.

1. Dorothy was in intense sibling rivalry with her younger sister during childhood. It began with the trauma of the sister's birth which moved two year old Dorothy from being the center of attention to a spectator role. She hated that and began a lifelong process of proving herself superior. She lorded it over her sister during the following 15 years as a child. Dorothy's driving motivation was to prove herself in all areas. Later in life, in all personal relationships, she made sure she was top dog. She graded her own children and had favorites. Almost all events were perceived through the prism of sibling rivalry. Her ramblings in therapy were about how she bettered others. Unknowingly, she placed the therapist in the role of the approving parent. Imagine her surprise when he confronted and her Script was revealed.

2. A child growing up in a combating family may choose humor as his defense. As soon as a form of hostility is sensed, he defuses the situation by telling a joke. Therapy becomes a funny parade as he shows how he manipulates others through laughing episodes. He is terrified of conflict. The scare flicker determines his responses so he becomes predictable. Unfortunately, he is incapable of serious discussion of ideas.

3. If stunned by war, the person may choose the defense of silence and retreat from any family conflict. When a child does something irrational and the Script bell rings (ie. Scare microsecond), the person may become stone-like, thinking, perhaps that he/she is sparing the child the insanity of conflict. Or, he can become brutal.

4. If hit by a tragedy like a sibling's death during one's young years, it can be that any spontaneity triggers the bell's ringing and the person adapts like long ago and faraway. The Script falls into place: cease play! Become motionless. Be invisible to the scrutiny of the blaming parent. Don't ever express joy. Hide your feelings.

5. If designated by the family as the Problem Solver, each later dilemma becomes the trigger for the person to figure out a solution. She is ever in the Controlling Parent place. Older siblings frequently take this role. They are unaware that their Mothering life stance prevents them from really experiencing life.

6. If humiliated by dire poverty on a daily basis during childhood, the person may become super sanctimonious or driven, moment-by-moment, to avoid the very perception of being poor. Making money may become the driving motivation so that no fun is had.

* * *

Scripts develop enormous momentum as time passes due to daily repetition and the weight of history. This happens to be the largest psychological deterministic factor robbing individuals of freedom of soul. If a scientific observer were to know a person's childhood and the resultant Script, it would be shocking to see how each new situation causes still another occasion for a secret re-playing of the old story. Script repetition happens to be the apex of human psychological misery. In much of their behavior humans can become microsecond emotionally driven automatons. This is very sad.

To balance this analysis it must be again noted that Dan plunged into a different world in Abilene Kansas. The trip, in and of itself, has the capability of dislodging his normal Script patterns. It takes a large measure of courage and openness. Quietly, as therapist, I study to see if he plays the same old tunes on a different piano. I have the trauma of his presenting problem in mind, note the roles in the narrative, and carefully note repetitions. I'll confront more in the future as it becomes appropriate.

Chapter Three

Dry Ice

All funeral parlors smell alike: formaldehyde from the back room is mixed with dried eucalyptus leaves in the entry along with flower odors from previous and present funerals all topped with cheap commercial lemon spray. I hate the smell. The mortuary housing my supposed father is dark with small corridors opening into rooms where open caskets hold lifeless bodies. Family and friends of the deceased mill around not knowing what to say, and, if truth be known, not wanting to be there.

The Director says the perfunctory sentences and assures me that he has put my Jewish father on Dry Ice just in case he was Orthodox.

"Dry Ice?" "Yes, with Orthodox Jews there can be no embalming. We iced him in order to keep him below forty degrees. This means he will get the proper Jewish funeral if you want to ship him back to Chicago. Once taken out of the ice, he must be buried within twenty-four hours, un-embalmed, in order to fit Jewish rituals. We assumed he was Orthodox just in order to be safe." I provide him with the name of a Jewish Funeral Home in Chicago to which to send the body.

As I stand there somewhat out of it, the Director makes assurances to me that the Chicago establishment will know what procedures to follow. He also hands me a picture of my deceased father. Everything appears professional and, in my private irreligious thoughts, without meaning whatsoever. Still, I must keep up images and respond appropriately - as if I really give a shit. He's dead. I get no answers. That's the real story.

"I'll make sure that my father is buried according to the Orthodox tradition, though I confess I really don't know his religious sentiments. I'll pass along word to have him interred next to my mother's grave the same day the Jewish mortuary receives his body. There'll be a memorial service later. If there are further questions you have, including your costs, my secretary will be in touch. Here's my Chicago card. If you need to reach me, I'll be around for several days at the Ezra Loew home on Fifth Street."

The Director leads me to a room in the back and, for the first time in my life, I view my father. Like all funeral-prepared corpses he looks rather peaceful. Stiff as cardboard. It is true that Ezra Loew's features do not appear like a regular resident of Abilene. I'm told that the corpse has a major burn scar on his back and appears to have been shot on his left side and left arm. Assured that there is nothing else out of the ordinary, I ask to see the tattoo mentioned by the sheriff. I mechanically write down the numbers, thinking that the Internet must have a catalog of Holocaust numbers that will provide more clues to the man's Death Camp experience.

The Director just left so I can be alone with the man who gave me half my genes. It's all surreal. What am I supposed to feel or do now? I'm numb as hell. With a prickly skin and a tight throat it's difficult to be objective. My curiosity is overwhelming. At one level I'm sad, at another level angry at the entire damn situation. I came for answers and get more questions. Now I find out he is Jewish and has Nazi tattoos, scars and bullet holes. Will there be no end to all the mysteries?

Christ! This guy ... my father ... is lying there in Dry Ice with hands folded on his chest, nose pointed at the ceiling, eyelids tightly closed, and a mouth that will never speak to me directly. There'll be no smiling face directed at me, no encouraging words spoken to drive me forward with accomplishments, no loving pat on my shoulder. We'll never have a conversation about sports, school, homework, community, women or even life. Part of me wants to shake him and yell "Where were you!?" As soon as that thought flits through my skull, I remind myself that it's over … all over … and the old silence is now the permanent eternal silence. It's done. The Father-Son relationship that never happened will never happen. Finis.

Ideally, I guess I'd mouth words of goodbye. How can I do that when my feelings are so mixed? Still, I silently thank him for being financially responsible to my mother during my youth, for my university costs, and for the grant that enabled me to start my business. I search for other words. "Thank you for my genes" comes to mind. This whole scene is weird beyond belief. Another wave of sadness ripples through my chest as I realize, once again, how we never knew each other - will never know each other son to father and father to son. Major grief, however, does not course through my body simply because I did not, do not, know the man. He's a stranger. I look at him with puzzlement. I wish I could cry. Nothing comes forth.

I continue standing there searching my mind and heart for a few more minutes but nothing arises. Paying heed to what my Analyst said, I search for any additional feeling, any new emerging sadness or piece of anger. There are none. I feel flat. It's just over. He's dead. Period. End of sentence and end of the non-existent father-son episode. No answers will ever come forth from that iced corpse to answer my deep questions and heal my soul. I'm, somewhat pissed about that, but, what the hell, it's a wasted emotion. It's hard being angry at an iced dead body.

A surprise feeling bubbles up, however … in terms of my mother … a bit of anger. She could have told me my father was a Holocaust survivor. That wouldn't have hurt her rap - or crap as it were. As for me, it might have introduced at least an ounce of forgiveness. Mom must have loved the guy. I guess. I don't know. I didn't get the chance to love him. And don't feel it now.

Still standing beside the casket, I want to squeeze some feeling out or have some words, some piece of wisdom emerge, but am utterly blank. There are no prayers. Nothing. I don't want this to end this way. This is my one chance. I'll never see him again. "Come on, Dan!," I yell at myself inside. "Come up with something!" Nothing. Not a whisper from within. Nothing. I wonder who is in Dry Ice here: me or him? Me and him is more like it. Him literally; me figuratively.

It's time to leave the funeral home. I studiously look at him one more time in order to seal the image in my mind. It's time to go. God! I'm beginning to feel like Dry Ice surrounds my body. Mentally - almost perfunctorily - for the first and last time, I say goodbye to Ezra Loew. "Goodbye Dad" bursts out of my chest. I leave with a familiar empty sensation in the pit of my stomach. Will there be no end to all the mysterious longing in my soul? "Goodbye" I say again aloud. That's all. I don't look back.

I need fresh air. I'm surprised to see that the Sheriff waited.

"Sheriff, I guess the next thing for me to do is go to the house and meet the housekeeper. When I told you on the phone that my father and I were not close, I was actually editing the real truth. I never knew him. Having seen his corpse really did not stir me. It's stories of how he lived at his house and in this community that intrigue me: the living man. So please give me directions to the house and I'll be on my way."

The sheriff pointed down the street and gave me the house number. It's not far away. There's no need for a car for such a short distance, but I drive the few blocks anyway. I stop in front of the house, and just sit there awhile.

I feel kind of dead inside. The mortuary trip was like some kind of weird science fiction tale. I never imagined my quest would end like this: an iced down body in an antiseptic room in a sterile little Kansas town. Life is, indeed, stranger than fiction. At least

Step One in this ordeal is over. I viewed my dead absent father - no big deal. I saw him though, to my knowledge, he never viewed me. Does that make me more courageous than him? Who knows? The door to my mind hasn't closed though. There is no sense of total completion by just viewing a cold lifeless corpse. That accomplished very little, really. The scars and tattoo simply mean an array of more questions, ones that will probably lead to other dead ends. One thing is sure: I'll never receive any replies from Ezra Loew because the grave doesn't divulge secrets. With my psychoanalytical mind, I ask myself "Am I in denial, the first stage of grief, where no real feelings emerge?" With no Analyst around, I don't know. The first few paragraphs of the Father Quest are just over. That's it. Finis. Over. I'll just have to be my own man like always and soldier on.

And who the hell is this housekeeper? Was Ezra romantic in his old age? He must have been to give her forty per cent. Forty per cent of what, anyway? Some old house and maybe a few bucks in a security deposit box? Nothing is turning out like either I or my Analyst hoped. Or wished. The latter is more Freudian. Perhaps this is simply a trip to a meaningless reality, another blind alley in my life of stupid searches for a nuclear family that never had or will happen. Maybe I should have just stayed in Chicago and handle everything by a local lawyer - just throw the old man's ass in the ground and be done with it. Then, again, I am learning tidbits. Furthermore, what is, is. I'm here.

It's time for Step Two: the house and the woman. Cleaning woman? Cook? Matron? Lover? Maybe she'll be a huge prison matron type who shoulders her way through life like a human whale. Who knows? Who really cares? I have to get this over so I can go back to normal life ... dignified life ... culture... my job ... my city.

I study the rather hidden house facing South on Fifth Street. It's a dignified Victorian white painted building with differing cedar tile arrangements at various places on its sides. Despite my cynical mood, it looks good. Two stories. A large wrap-around porch on the South, West and East sides. A few, almost hidden, comfortable looking rattan chairs are on the porch. A white picket fence with loads of large flowers just inside gives splashes of pink and purple and gold leaking over the slats. There's no gate leading to the front door. That's not typical in this town. Then again, I'm not surprised. A covert little trail is off to the East side. I figure that it only exists to discourage visitors, a ploy I believe was characteristic of my deceased father. At least there's no sign warning of an unleashed wolf hound or pit bull inside the fence. I'll risk it. Hell, I have no other choice.

Still, I pause once again and look at the building with an architect's eye, The interior ceilings must be twelve feet high. The house is well painted and everything seems in order for an early Twentieth Century house. Once again, I wonder why the old man lived in this town. How did he make enough money to buy this house, live his life, and send money to me and mother? "Mysteries! Always god damn mysteries."

Though tired and numb by traveling, puzzled at viewing my deceased father, and possessing a whole new set of questions, I'm ready for Step Two: the house and the housekeeper. I dread this, but I have to do it. Feeling great tension due to a flood of anxiety, I follow the almost invisible trail around the fence, climb the steps and politely knock on the door. Part of me hopes no one is home. That's familiar.

****

Therapeutic Analysis

***Notes on the Unconscious**: Consciously speaking, Dan is unaware that a shift has occurred in his being, his soul, his most inner precious self. The reality is that viewing the cold body of his father virtually frozen in dry ice ... a body where the blood no longer flows, the heart has stopped and the brain ceased to function ... such a viewing stimulates its very reverse: an inexplicable awareness of surrounding life. Though Dan is oblivious of being especially aware due to the circumstances, on the periphery of his vision he carefully marked the interior of the funeral parlor, the flowers, and mourning family members visiting in other rooms. Mental pictures of his father are sealed in his mind. As he emerged from the semi-darkness of the mortuary, trees, grass, cars, buildings and people seem to have developed more color to them: they stand out and imprint his brain. Death has that effect.*

It is a different Dan emerging. With rationalization still ruling his conscious mind, the fact is that a new awareness of the world is coming forth. This is a good sign. As therapist, it is my job to point out when a client like Dan adds a new dimension of awareness. Why?" Because awareness is a major step away from Narcissism, of being so lost in one's own processes that there is obliviousness to surrounding phenomena. The great therapeutic scholar Eric Berne noted that one major step in therapy is when a patient sees, really sees, something like a teapot for the first time. Berne further added that the step of awareness happens to be a major step to the next two major breakthroughs: spontaneity and intimacy. Therefore, I'd point out exactly how Dan has changed in his sensory noticing of the world around him. It's that critical.

To repeat: death of a parent - even an absent father - shakes up one's thinking processes. Eyes are more alert, hearing more intense, smell more acute. Though unaware of his re-orienting changes, Dan breathes differently, carries himself differently, walks differently. The changes are slight and only the most searching of observers would notice, that - small or not - they are real and therapeutically significant.

In therapy - as Dan tells me about the Funeral Home experience - part of my job is to monitor not only his emotions, but the honest encounter with death. Does he flee from reality? Does he get the message that he is the next at bat in the long death parade of humanity? If so, he has opened up another avenue away from Narcissism because death is a grand invitation to include others in one's journey. Knowledge that "I, too, shall die" leads one to want a companion soul to witness "my own life so it is known that I have not lived in vain." In a way, Dan has not fully made this connection just yet.

I also check something else. When death hits, survivors turn the page to a new chapter since the book of life is written by chapters. If unwise, the person craters and begins to live in the past. The wise happen to experience new bursts of creativity which religious philosophers point out as the ironic corollary of experiencing death in all its finality. Viewed best, the awareness of death can spur creativity, innovation, and even new personality configurations. That's why I'm heartened by Dan's architectural re-appraisal of his father's house in Abilene. It's a little matter. Not insignificant.

I'm also watching for another sign of maturity. Those aware of their own approaching demise are stimulated to leave a constructive mark that is redemptive to future generations. The reaper will inevitably arrive and claim one's own body. Thus, death's direct opposite can occur: the desire to live more. And give more.

It sounds almost religious to say it: The impulse from the grave is to better conditions for future inhabitants of this earth. Without the specter of real death, materialistic Narcissism with its gloat of power, money and self-absorbed entertainment just as well be all in all. Some understand this; some never do … until the news of one's own impending death hits full force on a lonely hospital bed. Then it is too late.

In regard to Dan, I have hope. In therapy, my job is to listen and see how he uses his mind to either increase freedom or tighten chains of the past. It's still touch and go.

Script. *Why is Script so unconsciously powerful? The reason is that it has been rehearsed so many times since childhood. Let's review. Children are playwrights who make their worlds predictable by composing three character plays based on the traumatic occurrences in their families. They may see their parents go through unconscious irrational Scripts of their own, said plays that make no sense to a young child. "Why do they do that?" the kid thinks because there is nothing that triggers the ugly incidents. Analysts may know that each generation has leftover negative remnants from childhood; children simply witness the irrationality and are baffled.*

The key matter is that the observing child has viewed parental insanity that is grievous - sometimes every day and possibly in both morning and evening. On some occasions, as that of Dan Michelson, the drama is developed on the basis of small clues such as a mother's depression and a father's absence. Fantasy fills in details.

In the light of this, the child figures out his or her role n the drama. The three roles are fashioned. Why three? The reason is that children tend to think in polarities, blacks and whites, good and bad. Thus, they put one person in the Bad role (which I call Hated but Strong), one person in the meek role (which I call

Helpless and Feared), and that leaves the role of the child which is the Adapted position.

There is no way I can explain in this text the entire variety of chosen Adaptations. That would scan the entire range of criminality to sainthood, from pleasing niceness to being a troublesome jerk, from being invisible to being arrogant and obnoxious. This means that every Analyst has to listen acutely to the role the person assumes in each difficult encounter reported in therapy. In this Dry Ice chapter Dan struggles to get into his protective mode of being a superior sarcastic in-control person. This Adaptation will be watched throughout remaining sessions. That's part of my job.

Now, an important matter. Some think addictions relate to only pathological options such as drug, alcohol, or food consumption. It is important to note that the far deeper and more obsessive matter is that of a continual re-playing of the original Script formed by a child who chose roles on the basis of his/her perceptions. I forthrightly declare that all humans become addicted to a meaning system developed during childhood. That is the major unconscious drama destroying human freedom and real love. I'll keep explaining this in italicized notes in future chapters.

Until the Script be quelled, all major soul fulfillment is on hold.

The Unconscious. *One other matter since there is such major resistance to the thought of having unconscious factors that subtly affect us. The secret is the microsecond stimulus of scare. It blips by the conscious mind and throws on the old Child Drama so quickly that a person has no awareness of what is happening. Rather, he or she roars down the track and structures the present world according to old perceived realities. Any display of questioning from others as to what is happening is met with abundant rationalization. The person thinks himself or herself perfectly justified in the re-play.*

I'm thinking of a client whose mother had no clue whatsoever in terms of how to handle her son's temper tantrums. She simply gave into him, year in and year out. The father had the passive philosophy of allowing his wife manage the home. His mind was in absentia the moment he came home from work. The boy learned to bully his way to get whatever he wanted. His mother was always under threat: either give in or I'll go into a raging tantrum. I trust readers can get the Script in the preceding six sentences.

I'll call the temper tantrum kid Joe. During his courtship of his wife, he only showed minor minutes of his Script. Once married, Joe turned on the Bully Role full time. He wanted his way and the method to gain it was to threaten his wife. She was puzzled. If she stood up to him, he'd escalate to the point of standing over her and being on the edge of hitting. Still refusing to give in, Joe turned to physical abuse.

Now. If you were to confront him, Joe would have rationalizations pour forth like a river. If he were to come to therapy and the therapist was a male, he'd expect (per Script) the therapist to turn a blind eye and deaf ear just as his own father did. If the therapist were a woman, Joe would raise his voice thinking that she, too, would surrender and place all blame on his wife.

In the Joe Drama it becomes clear why Sigmund Freud said that "transference" is a major reality in human relationships. Joe transfers, that is, gives the same emotional reaction, to his wife that he did to his mother. He transfers his father to the male therapist. He transfers his mother to a female therapist. And, tragically, if he has a son, he'd transfer his passive father to his son setting the child in an adapted role. (This is not always automatic. He may make a daughter into a princess and set her adaptation.)

This illustration, which has thousands of manifestations with men who may eventually end up in custody, should suffice to explain miserable marriages and the power of unconscious Script. As to the "unconscious" part, a friend who has served as a judge for thirty years once said this to me. "Frank, it's amazing how criminals almost never admit that they were wrong. They regret being caught. That's about all. In their minds, they remain innocent."

Innocent. Self-justified. That's the way the unconscious and conscious mind fail to cooperate. The conscious mind is a master at re-defining and rationalizing each issue. The unconscious mind simply continues its irresistible replaying of Script. Dan, too, will do that interminably unless there is a therapist who knows how to decipher the childhood drama and confronts. Or extraordinary circumstances of love and tragedy intervene.

Please note: *Therapy does not work in a straight line. Matters of personal growth are covered time and again until the client gets the lesson. Therefore, in my analytic notes I return to ideas repeatedly. Why? Novels can be written as if matters are horizontal - a lesson encountered is a lesson learned. Not so in therapy. Not with major psychological issues. My plan is to deepen the moral by successive expanded repetition.*

Chapter Four

The Mysterious Amelia

When the housekeeper answers the door, I see a woman of approximately my age who uses her auburn hair to mask her face. Still, I discern that she has blue eyes, dimples and is attractive - though hidden. My guess is that she is about five foot eight inches and weighs about 140 pounds. She seems solid. I identify myself.

"I'm Ezra Loew's son."

"I see the resemblance."

"How so?"

"In the color of your eyes and shape of your face."

I'm invited into the house and we sit in two chairs in the living room. I hurriedly glance around, but my mission of learning about my father assumes priority.

"My name is Dan Michelson, by the way."

"I'm Amelia."

"I'm told you don't talk much."

"That's right."

Her short answers throw off my usual calm. Damn it. My eagerness betrays my emotional state. I'm so eager to learn something about Loew that I'm almost feverish.

"I'm hoping you will talk with me because I am a son of an invisible father. I never saw him as a child and, as far as I know, he never saw me - even as a baby. I never met him. I didn't even know his name was Ezra Loew. My mother summed him up as 'a good man."

"He was."

I'm trying to not show my frustration with her short answers. "That's all I could get out of mom. He always paid child support, provided money for my college education, and came up with a major sum for my entrepreneurial adventure in architecture. How he knew I needed a beginning pile of cash for my business, I never found out. He's a mystery to me, a phantom. I filled my mother's words 'He's a good man' with all kind of fantasies. My imagination did not and does not fill the void."

"I can understand that."

Shit! I'm becoming almost desperate. I ramble on: "I've had an ache inside that I've been unable to fill with any alternatives - even pseudo dads I selected from admired academics and architects, older friends, and literary figures such as Goethe, Shakespeare, and Tolstoi. Freud. Thomas Jefferson. I've been an equal opportunity identity thief. My psychoanalyst has the hubris to think I'd ingest his personality and maybe I have got a few bits - not much really. My imaginary desired father had to be someone great, noble and famous. Nothing has worked to solve my need. Many people in my situation have gone for belief in God, particularly if they had a cruel dad, a mental incompetent, or, as in my case, a disappearing father. I've had too much science for that path. In order to know who I am, I have to know something about the man who provided half my genes. I'm hoping you will help."

"This is all new to me, also," she offers.

"I don't want to intrude in your life, Amelia. Maybe my fusillade of words is a wrong way for us to meet. I don't want to beg. I seem to be babbling which is unlike me. Maybe you need time to assimilate my father's death and my appearing on the scene."

"I do need time. I'm not against talking to you. A bit of time might be good. I'd like to think for awhile."

Good God! The girl is like a lead door. I'm getting nowhere. "If it is alright with you, I'd like to look around the house. All this is strange for us both. Since I did not know my father, I'm very curious."

"That's fine. I'll show you his room. He slept in a strange bed. It has a lever on the side which cranks it up close to the ceiling. Yesterday when he didn't show up for breakfast, I knocked on his door. No answer, I peeked in and the bed was up. His arm was hanging off. No movement even though I called loudly for him. I knew he was dead."

I'm relieved to have a little more information from her. I forge ahead: "Amelia, let's go see the room; the bed sounds strange. I can't imagine the mechanism that gears a bed so high. I also can't fathom why he'd want to do that. It's hotter, for one thing. He must have had a big bladder ... excuse me, but older men usually get up during the night."

"Here's his room. The police somehow pulled the lever and put the bed down. I changed the sheets."

My voice wavers. "Look, Amelia, you may think me odd, but for my own peace of mind I must get to know the guy ... my father. So, I'm going to lie on the bed, pull the crank and go up to see what the advantage is. Maybe nothing. Here I go.

"Why would he do this? It's stifling up here. In fact, it's miserable. You can't see anything out the window. You are definitely not more safe. There's nothing on the ceiling to look at. You are crammed into a corner right next to some crown molding. This is very peculiar. Okay, that's it. I'm having trouble breathing. I'm coming down."

"Now I want to examine each piece of furniture and the closet. Forgive me if I appear a wild man. It's just a son in search of a father. No coins in the chair. I'm going to put all the stuff in the oak chest on the bed. Socks in the top drawer and nothing else. Not many socks, really. Shorts in the second drawer. Nothing. Undershirts in the third drawer. It, too, has nothing else. Dress shirts in the bottom drawer. This all looks too neat for a man to do. You must have washed , folded, and put the clothes in the chest." (She nods.) Okay. I'll leave the stuff on the bed. There is nothing I want. If it's okay with you, we'll call Salvation Army tomorrow and get rid of it. Now I want to examine the closet. Where was the metal lockbox, anyway?"

"On the floor in the closet. I knew it was there because I also ironed his dress pants and cleaned and repaired his coats."

"Okay. I'll examine each coat, each pair of pants to see if I can find clues to his identity hidden somewhere. There must be something to show who he was. Did you know that he had a tattoo on his arm that looks like it was put there by the Nazi's?"

"No. The sheriff called and asked if he was a Holocaust survivor. I didn't know."

"Well, he probably was. I wrote down the tattoo number and my secretary will trace it on web sites carrying information about Nazi camps. I hope I can find out where he was and how he survived. He must have been young. My mother was thirty-eight when I was born. He must have been in his mid-forties, because he looked about eighty at the mortuary. No one knows how old. He didn't have many coats, did he? Or pants. God, he lived minimally. Almost raggedly."

"He never bought anything. His favorite coat was the black wool overcoat. You might examine it. He never left it out for me to mend or iron or anything. When he wore it, he looked hunkered down with the weight of human suffering."

"That's interesting. I'll save it for last and check it very carefully. Absolutely nothing in the linings of the other coats. The pants have no secret pockets. There's nothing else in the closet so it is time to examine the black overcoat. This is strange: he has a black opal the size of a marble, in one pocket and a horn-handled magnifying glass in the other. The collar seems to have an opening. Jesus Christ! This paper has information about me on it. Where I live. What I do. Where my office is. Buildings I designed. Christ! The man knew about me, but never communicated one damn word. That's hard to forgive. Then again, he somehow seemed to keep up with my life; that's something. Let's take this overcoat into the living room where there is better light and examine every inch of it. We'll get a razor knife, take out the lining and not miss a single thread in our search. I'm desperate. I must get to know this man.

In the living room I continue dismantling the black coat. "Amelia. Here's another important piece of information in the coat: a man's name in New York City. It's a German Jewish name: Shlomo Loew. His name, address, and phone number were tucked into a secure tiny pocket up in the shoulder area. This causes a flood of more questions in my mind. I'm scared to call the number and contact the man. Do I have a brother or some other mysterious relative? I'm too upset to call. Not now. All this is too much." The coat lay in shambles on the coffee table.

I pick up the large opal and study it. "I have a jeweler friend in Chicago. He knows Australian black opals. He said Shakespeare called them the 'queen of jewels.' Diamond merchants, fearing for their trade, immediately started rumors about them being unlucky. Ezra evidently didn't believe that. My guess is that this black opal has a story. I hope we can find out what it represents. I'll tell you one thing I learned from my jeweler friend. This stone is very valuable ... probably in the range of fifty to sixty thousand dollars. Opals with this red fire flashing and a black mark on the back aren't cheap."

Amelia looks surprised but says nothing. I think to myself: "The old man wasn't a beggar; that's for sure."

Snapping out of my reverie I say, "Amelia, I'm on sensory overload. I'm also hungry since I ate about 11 a.m.. I ate at Gluttonyville on the Interstate and had to leave when I noticed massive gobbling around me. Patrons wolf down macaroni and cheese by the bowl full. Is there something we could fix to eat, something nourishing that is not loaded with fats? I cannot stomach a fast food joint along the main drag. Even eggs and toast sound good."

"Yes. I propose green beans, mashed potatoes, and a breast of chicken."

"Please say baked, not fried. Okay?"

"Done. I'll fix it. You are free to see the house."

While she begins preparing the meal, I talk about my ordeal at the All You Can Eat Buffet along the Interstate. I describe how people were dressed and what they ate. I laughingly end with this: "Amelia, I was tempted to stand at the door when I was leaving and loudly get everyone's attention and yell "Charles Darwin's theory of evolution is correct!' Then, run out the door and have my tires burn rubber as I make my getaway!" Amelia nods without laughing. She stays silent.

Wandering the house for a few moments before dinner, I notice twelve foot ceilings like I assumed prior to entering. The wood floors are yellow poplar, a wood almost impervious to termites and rot. The steps on the stairs and banisters are oak. Ezra must have paid a decorator to fix the interior before moving in several years ago. The wallpaper and paint job look almost new. It's a very nicely done Victorian home.

We eat in silence, something that appears perfectly normal to Amelia. It still bugs me. I peripherally study her for the first time. She is rather good looking though her simple clothes hide her curves. She seems to know how to be invisible which also rather obscures her face. She probably learned anonymity from Ezra. Still, there's some kind of nobility in Amelia, a sort of self-assuredness though I sense that, back in time, she suffered an immense blow. Her fingers are long and adept. Her cooking style and the way she handles her fork and knife while eating, reveal culture. Somewhere in her background there is 'city' - not the plains, farm life, and chores.

As she moves around the kitchen, I notice a certain grace, a flow, a kind of dance. Nothing overt. Nothing planned. Just there. No jewelry. No eagerness in any way. No anxiety. No wasted motion. No uncertainty in terms of how to cook, set the table, or sit silently in her accustomed chair. I bet she's not L.A. or New York and definitely not Abilene. She does not seem to need anything or anyone. I find her very attractive. She's not the old dumpy housekeeper I expected. I'd best not pry, though.

Out of the side of my eye, I see Amelia occasionally glance at me. There is no search in her eyes, no need to ask questions, no sense of anything out of the ordinary. She seems to take death in stride and feels no need for meaningless social patter designed to provide superficial kindness. Her quietness, however, does not imply an empty void. It speaks of an identity forged out of intense moments. I won't interrogate her, but I have mountains of questions, not only about my father but about her take on him, her observations across the several years, her ... God, I hate to admit it ... just her. She seems unlike any woman I've ever been around. Another mystery. Dammit.

"I'm tempted to keep asking you more and more questions about my father."

"We'll get to them, Dan, but not tonight."

"Amelia, I saw a couch and, with your permission, will sleep on it. I can't bear sleeping in his room. If you want to know the truth, I don't know whether I hate him for abandoning me or appreciate him for his secret support across the years. Maybe both. Anyway, I want to sleep in the living room, if that is okay with you. I want to familiarize myself with the house, with its night and day sounds, with its ... I don't know how to say this ... with its secrets. Maybe I can glean something that soothes my soul. This has been a long road for me. Since childhood I've wondered where he was and who he is ... along with wondering who I am. Now, I'm in his house. I've got to feel what it was like to live here. Sense him, if you know what I mean. I have a bunch of questions for you about the man, but I'll spare you for now. I'll go on the front porch and just soak it all in."

Amelia said, " Sleeping on the couch is fine. Your father listened on his iPod when he was on the porch in the evenings. Here it is ... I guess it's yours now."

I take the iPod and look at her with appreciation. I head toward the porch

"Do you want the same breakfast he had in the morning?"

Intrigued by the ability to listen to the music Ezra heard, I simply answer "Yes,"

The wind is slight but significant as Autumn winds on the plains are. The swaying of a neighbor's willow tree is nice. Nearby kids are playing and making the free sounds of childhood. There are no noises from downtown or the strip, despite being only a half mile or so away. Some tall trees reach up into the sky obscuring homes nearby. There's a kind of country peace about everything. It's the perfect setting for someone wanting to be anonymous, who either had no need for human closeness or shunned it fearfully. Boxed hedges and tall flowers provide relative invisibility on the porch. The house and setting are places to have one's brain go to sleep.

Sitting there, I remember an article about people in a Death Camp. "The way to survive is to melt in and never stand out in any way - not too tall, not too short, not too fat, not too slim, not too aware, not too beaten down: just blend so you are not noticed. And never, ever look an officer in the eyes." Everything about the house fits that description. I guess this place metaphorically tells the story of Ezra Loew. The man may not have known how to be a father, but he knew how to survive.

Other thoughts come to mind. The tattoo. Now that's interesting. I wonder if he was searching for something at the Eisenhower Center. After the bank, that'll be my next step on this crazy quest for answers. This means staying for awhile in Abilene and, hopefully, learning more from the mysterious Amelia. I resent her for her silence.

Alone on the porch, I note the mournful sounds of a passing train, a train coming from the unknown and going to the unknown. That's like my father. A hooting owl with a throaty melancholy sound also provides a somber mood. Thumbing through the selections on the I-Pod, I note an array of classical composers: Beethoven, Mozart, Tchaikovsky, Strauss, Bach, Mendelssohn, Haydn, Mahler and Stravinsky. No Wagner. Nothing modern. The solid old standbys.

I feel both awkward and strange putting the ear pieces in my ears, knowing they were conveying music to my dad only several days ago. It actually feels good knowing that Ezra Loew had music as a staple in his life. I listen for an hour. Later, I remove the ear phones and begin to think again.

I'm mentally comparing Abilene to my beloved Chicago. Caustic sarcasm returns and I think how barren this country Kansas town is. The tempo is different. Chicago is hurried; Abilene hushed. Chicago is multi-active; Abilene seems to be almost motionless. I'm having difficulty slowing down to the mood of this small town. I well know that my busy rapid big city style is contra-indicated for Amelia. The pace of this place is like wading through a molasses swamp. I'd better not say that aloud to her tomorrow.

Almost despite myself, I begin thinking positively of Ezra, and how the quiet slow movement of the town might have been therapeutic for a man who probably experienced a different world as a young child only to have it catastrophically transformed by Hitler. With thoughts running along these lines I try to let the Abilene mood set in. It doesn't work. I yearn for the noise, bright lights and options Chicago provide. As the evening mulls on and hearing only crickets, I'm lulled by the quiet of the small town. Yawning comes for real.

Entering the house, I lie on the sofa and am asleep almost immediately.

****

Therapeutic Analysis

I find myself quite pleased with the overall response of Dan. He courageously pursues answers even though he is scared about what he will find. That is characteristic of the true pilgrim as is evidenced in all journey stories, be they Homer's Ulysses, John Bunyan's Pilgrim, or people in real life like Marco Polo. They plunge forward. As the Old Testament says of Abraham when he left Ur in Mesopotamia, "Abraham went out not knowing where he was to go." Some think courage a virtue only for soldiers in combat; far more difficult is the march of the soul through its own terrors on the way to real identity. Another key story in the Old Testament is that of Jacob's wrestling with an angel. He would not let go until he got a blessing. I see that kind of courage in Dan as he tussles with his main neurotic issue: the missing father.

In this regard of continuing to fight against the immense blows to the psyche caused by major traumas, I reflect back on clients, male and female, who struggled with systematic physical or sexual abuse during childhood. Their bodies writhed with the insult of it all, but they continued to struggle for personal freedom.

To repeat something said earlier, a person can fold and cease to grow due to such issues as PTSD. Or the choice can be made to fight on and join with those in history who refused to give up. Being 'on journey' is not just exercise; it is a test of will and soul.

Underneath all Dan's thoughts is an undercurrent of old sadness that is very appropriate to his life and the situation. Before someone goes off on a mis-diagnosis of 'Depression,' one must first be aware of the human journey with emotions. All of us feel sadness and, maybe, all of us have a small current of it simply because we have lost, due to the passage of time, parents and friends plus we miss things we loved during childhood. Sadness is about things we lose and miss. Dan's sadness is appropriate.

Going deeper, the death of Dan's mother didn't take, take in the sense that it provided a mortal blow to his Narcissism. It appears that the death of his father, Ezra Loew, shakes Dan to the foundation of his personality structure. This is clear in his blurted talk to Amelia, something totally uncharacteristic. In his Chicago personae, he is cool and detached, all the while making sure that those he encounter reveal their selves leaving him with the upper hand. As he enters the house his father lived in and meets the housekeeper, his desire for knowledge to re-build himself causes him to uncover a new layer free of old Defense Mechanisms. He is not as arrogant with Amelia.

It is therefore appropriate to unveil the three psychological mechanisms underlying Narcissism. First obliquely noted by Freud and later elaborated by Erich Fromm, they are Irresistibility, Omnipotence and Immortality (IOI). The first, Irresistibility, refers to personal beauty and attractiveness as in the Snow White story: "Mirror, mirror on the wall, who is the fairest of them all?" Dan is exceptionally handsome. Women desire him. The second mechanism, Omnipotence, refers to societal power so that a person basically gets his/her way. Dan has proven through his work and his presence on key Boards and photos in Chicago papers that he is popular and powerful in the right circles. In Abilene, he is helpless. That's good, therapeutically speaking. The Immortality delusion is one where the individual has no sense of personal death, feels muscular, strong and healthy and believes that will continue ad infinitum. Dan just saw death in Dry Ice: that leaves a startling mental image.

Quite weirdly, I discovered that boundless Narcissism can also be unleashed by a sense of Ugliness ("I'm the Beast"),

Helplessness ("Poor Me, I'm beyond hope"), and Death-obsession ("Since I'm going to die, nothing makes sense"). This is one of my contributions to psychological theory, by the way, which should qualify me for IOI.

Many decades ago one of my patients was the epitome of the IOI problem or stark Narcissism. Candy was an only child, inherited great wealth, was extremely beautiful in both face and body, and - due to the adulation she received from everyone - had no sense of ever having to die. She fought wrinkles and gray hair by all means possible. Her presence in therapy was due to thinking it the social thing to do. We got nowhere. She thought me blessed to be her therapist. Candy used her feminine wiles to seek to seduce me into also thinking her the ultimate prize so I'd not confront her delusions (thought issues) and illusions (wish fantasies.) I was not so inclined and finally told her we were failing in the therapy process. I recommended she go elsewhere to carry on meaningless conversations with another therapist. Just the whiff of abandonment startled her and she responded hatefully: "I can destroy you!" I responded "That may be, but my concern is how you are destroying yourself by your fantasies caused by personal beauty, money, and societal power. Psychotherapy isn't psychological cosmetology." That confrontation didn't work. Narcissism can be a deep obsession that leads to drowning - as the old Greek myth has it. She went elsewhere in her dilettante pursuit. I wasn't destroyed.

Dan is finally shaken by irretrievable death. Viewing his father's corpse and fantasizing himself in a casket shakes him to the core. Further, all his life questions now are up in the air. The encounter with Amelia, an unassuming beautiful woman in and of herself, also rattles his cage. She seems unimpressed by him.

***The Script Narrative**: Dan's need for information quells his normal role of being the cool sophisticate who can abandon - the Strong, but Hated Role of his father. He also does not fall into his Adapted role of being the carefree rake, the free spirit who* *does his thing oblivious of others. Interestingly, he skates close to the Weak and Helpless role played by his mother in the original story he developed as a child. All this is good. None of those three roles will work with Amelia. He'll be forced to create a new style.*

***Emotional Confrontation**: It is critical to point out exactly at this point how significant emotions are in the tool bag of the Analyst. Here's how it would happen in therapy.*

"Dan, what did you feel prior to going sarcastic on the Abilene trip?"

"Feel? I guess I was scared."

"What were you scared of when you drove into Abilene and met the sheriff?"

"I was scared of not appearing in charge. I was scared of looking like a fool who had never seen his father, some bastard who was rudely rejected by his own dad. I was scared of being weak and needy like my mom. I was scared of learning that my father was a bum. I was scared of not being as smart as the sheriff and the mortician. There are probably other scares, but that is all I can come up with right now."

"Thanks, Daniel. That's honest. When you started your rattling talk with Amelia, what were you feeling?"

"Scared again. I was scared that she'd not talk to me. I was scared upon entering the house where my father lived. Part of me was feeling like a little boy. I was scared she'd see that and lose respect for me. This was all new to me. I had no pattern for what to do or who to be. I was lost and scared shitless."

"And why, Daniel, didn't you just come forth with the truth both with the Sheriff and the housekeeper Amelia?"

"I already told you. I did not want them to know what was going on in my head."

"Then, Daniel, it's only fair to tell you that you get a flunking grade in terms of emotion in these two instances."

"Are you shitting me? Are you nuts, Doc? That kind of honesty would leave me as vulnerable as a child. I've only been in therapy for several years. Now you want me to be perfect."

"Not perfect. Real. That's our goal. I will compromise with you Dan on one point. Some people cannot handle realness and it may well be that the Sheriff is one of them. So I'll back off on being straightforward with emotions with him. I'll give you a C rather than an F."

My point is that the microsecond unconscious emotional trigger can stop real self-knowledge and identity strength while keeping us chained to childhood. The scare trigger has the power to thwart pure soul-partner intimacy. Thus, transparency of real emotions is the royal way for solid identity and fulfilling open partnership. Many never take that path. They hide who they are. That is very sad.

***The Script**: Note that my pushing about the initial emotion does not also include confrontation about the background Script. I think it too early to do that. Besides, awareness of emotions has its own value quite apart from Script. Emotions are like radar in that they identify what is real. They allow a person to keep body and soul in line with what is valuable. Thus, they have intrinsic worth. Without knowledge and expression of them, a person is likely to be a drone rather than a free human. As for the Script, I'm monitoring it. I'll confront as I think appropriate and as I think Dan's resistance is down sufficiently so he will take a large growth step.*

Finally, no matter the initial problems with emotions Dan revealed in this sample segment, there is great hope he might become a human being rather than a plastic, soul-dead, relationship-avoiding social butterfly. Dan is rather raw now; his social level bandages hiding his inner wound are slipping. Studying his entire contact with Amelia, he reveals part of himself to someone other than his therapist - a woman!

This chapter of his life book has him vulnerable like he has not been since infancy. It's scary. But he forges on. The only option left for him in his quest for answers is to be up front with emotions. It appears Amelia won't tolerate anything less. If he wants information, he must cease all forms of manipulation.

Chapter Five

Rapport with Amelia

Upon awaking, I smell coffee in the kitchen. I wander in and say "Good morning" to Amelia who is making scrambled eggs and toast. She asks if that is sufficient and I nod yes. On the breakfast table is homemade peach jam. We begin in silence. I tell her that the coffee is very good.

Glancing out the window, I view an incredible sight. The morning light is bouncing off dew on the grass, flowers, and hedges. The appearance is that of a backyard sprinkled with millions of diamonds. Sarah sees me noticing the jeweled morning and remarks, "That happens occasionally in the Spring and the Autumn. I love it."

"So, do I, Amelia. It is startling and makes it difficult to concentrate on other matters. Still, I will. I'm hoping you feel like talking today. I am so curious. I'm afraid I might be over-eager like yesterday and ask a thousand questions you may not want to answer."

"I'm hesitant. I thought you terribly sarcastic about people yesterday. If that is your style of listening about your father whom you seem to dislike, I prefer silence."

"Amelia, thank you. That is straight on. I apologize for my sarcasm; that is but a small part of me. It certainly does not enter into my deep desire to learn about Ezra Loew. Maybe you need to know more about me. I'm a successful architect in Chicago. My firm builds schools throughout the Midwest. Most people like me. I'm good to my employees. I serve on humanitarian boards. The next part hurts: I've had an ache in my heart for a father since I was a little boy. You are the only person I've encountered who can tell me about him. I don't want to beg. I don't want you to go against your conscience. I promise to not be sarcastic or hateful. If I can use psychological jargon, I was defending myself with arrogant talk. I just need to know who the man was. I hope you will help."

"I'll tell you one thing that may be genetic. You think like him. I noticed you on the porch last night with your head tilted a bit to the left and down - an exact copy of Ezra Loew. In a way, it gave me the creeps because you looked like him on the porch."

"That's interesting. I have a bad habit of self-talk. I run things through my head without speaking aloud. I guess that's what he was doing also. I appreciate your observation."

"Okay. I'll talk with you about Ezra and the way we lived. I actually decided to talk late last night. I wanted assurance that you'll curb your sarcasm and now I have it."

I interrupt. "I'm curious about your decision since you've had such a long period of silence."

"As I pondered about it, I decided to honor Ezra's kindness to me and what happened as a result of my living here. I figured it was time to share with his son. Furthermore, it's time I personally come out of my shell. It's been a very long time since I've held a conversation. No matter. Ask what you will and I'll fill in what I know."

"Well, if I ask too many questions or ply you to talk too much, just wave at me and I'll go out on the porch. You are probably not accustomed to talking."

"Hmm. I can talk. I just don't. As for your father, we had a quiet understanding that never involved any chit chat or conversation whatsoever. Talking now is like leaving a convent dedicated to silence. I've carried on conversations in my head, but not aloud. I'll try to help you fill in the blanks with your father........ Let's see. He was neat. Demanded nothing. I kept the house clean and made breakfast and dinner. He had the same thing every morning - eggs, toast and black coffee - like what we just had. I varied meals in the evening. He never complained. In fact, he never commented one way or another. I don't think he knew the difference between meat and soy burgers. In my first year here I learned to cook natural food. He seemed to enjoy it. And, you just heard more words than I have uttered aloud for eight years."

"What happened eight years ago?"

"I'm not willing to talk about that. Not now, anyway. Maybe later since I respected your father."

"How did you two meet?"

Amelia smiles at me. "You ask good questions. I was spending my last two dollars at a little café not too far from here. I chanced to catch your father looking at me. He seemed to study me - not in a sexual way - just a kind of penetrating psychological way. I was so devastated inside that his observation didn't bother me. I was cored out. Empty. But not raw empty. A kind of dry empty. He came over to where I was sitting, asked if he could join me, and I nodded yes. His words were both startling and arresting:

'You are at the end of the trail and don't know where to go from here, am I right?'

"I nodded and looked into his sad, but wise eyes. They were eyes I'd never before seen. The bony orbits surrounding the eyes themselves were covered with skin that had successive dark circles - as if a stone had been thrown into dark waters at midnight. I thought I knew suffering; I intuited this man had experienced more suffering than I had.

"Your father continued: 'My name is Ezra Loew. I need a housekeeper. You'll have a separate room. No responsibility other than cleaning the house and making breakfast and dinner. I'll totally leave you alone. Totally. Your time will be your time, your space your space. I'll pay, in addition to room and board, the going rate. I'll raise the pay as things work out. Are you interested?'

"I nodded. There was no push on his part to have me be verbal. I looked again into those arresting eyes. They appeared to have experienced the full range of human evil and suffering and had, somehow, overcome it with a measure of good - plus a fine layer of kindness. In a way, studying the pupils of his eyes was like looking down the corridor of the Twentieth Century. I knew immediately that I could trust him. I told him my name was Amelia and I'd take the job."

"Ezra added only the facts: 'Okay, then, after you finish your meal, I'll show you the house and your room.'

"That was it. We walked several blocks to this house. I liked my room looking out over several large blue spruce trees in a large backyard. In truth, I had no other options. I've been here since. Not much to tell, really. There has been several years of virtual silence. In very brief verbal exchanges he called me Amelia. I called him Ezra."

I study Amelia appreciatively and say, "That's amazing. The story tells me more than I've ever known about him. He was observant, intuitive, deeply aware of suffering, and kind. I'll let those facts soak into me over time. Now tell me about a typical day of my father, if you will."

"After breakfast, he left. I don't know where he went. He came home just before dinner. In the evening he listened to classical music on an iPod I programmed for him. He had seen me with one, inquired about it, and got one. He also provided a computer so I was able to access information. I learned from Ezra how to avoid conversations on the street or elsewhere. He appeared hunched over, always looked down and avoided people's eyes. If they chanced to speak, he mumbled one or two words and then moved on without stopping. Since I also wanted to avoid chit chat, I copied his style. It worked."

"How did he treat you, Amelia?"

"As I said, we lived in virtual silence. I took up gardening. Each morning after he left I'd either jog or run around this community. I went to theater to watch plays. I volunteered at a local senior center. He just did his thing and I did mine. He treated me well. The key thing was visceral acceptance of who I was and am. Other questions?"

"I'm pacing myself to not be too pushy, though I'm excited. I'm a bit scared that I am overloading you with questions, but please understand that the man has been a ghost to me since I was a little boy."

"That's okay. I made the decision to talk after my long layoff from verbal exchanges. It's like the dam burst. Words are spilling forth. Ask away."

"Well, since the two of you didn't ever talk, some of my questions are worthless. Part of me wishes he had said something about me or my mom."

"No. Nothing was said about family. I'm sorry."

"This is hard, Amelia. My questions are floundering. Did you know what he did with his time after breakfast and before dinner?'

"No. I didn't ask and he didn't tell. He also never asked about my day."

"I'll ask. What else did you do?"

"Other than jogging, I did gardening. Bought groceries. Exercised. I'd listen to music and read. Nothing really exciting. I was living the life of a nun in a cloister, in a way. Nothing religious. I lost that eight years ago also."

"I won't pry," I quickly say. "Did my father keep up with world events, read the newspaper, or listen to the radio?"

"Not to my knowledge. Not here in this house. My guess is that he was not interested in events of the day. He seemed kind of above time and this space of Abilene. But not in a mystical or rejecting way - more in the sense that his thoughts were historically and philosophically weighty. I really don't know. I do know that he was frequently lost in thought. I just don't know what he was thinking about."

"Amelia, do you know anything about the Dwight David Eisenhower Center?"

"Only that it is there. It's never interested me. I'm not political. I jogged over there a few times, but never entered a building. I only know that Eisenhower was President and that he was the Army commander in Europe when our forces invaded the continent and eventually beat the German Army. That's it."

"My guess," I comment "is that there is something there that brought my father to this town. I can't think of another reason. Wups. I just had a whiff of scare that might trigger you thinking me sarcastic. Please just put me down as an urban dweller. I build schools in small communities, but I've never lived in one."

My questions and our conversation begins to dribble down. She appears tired from her first major attempt at talking after eight years of silence and I'm not getting the depth of knowledge needed to fill my father void. I conclude, "Let's talk more later. I want to put on my walking shoes and see if I can get more information downtown." Upon leaving the house, I glimpse Amelia leaving for a run in a different direction.

Returning to the police station, I discover no one able to add anything about Ezra Loew. No one seems to know him at the several shops I go into. Evidently, he was not a consumer. They had seen him, but had never carried on a conversation. He was a mystery to them too. I'll wander down Buckeye to see if there is anyone who can add to my knowledge. At the Sonic Drive-in I eat a baked chicken burrito that is palatable. The milk shake is good. Walking back home, I'm unable to find any interesting person capable of providing more clues to solve the questions that plague me.

Returning to the porch, I'm pleased to see Amelia coming at the end of her run. Her sweat shirt is damp and clings to her a bit. Her face is peppered with perspiration. Her running stride impresses me because it is powerful and smooth. Her legs are beautiful and, like any man, I notice the attractive ripples in appropriate parts of her body as she takes each step. Catching her breath beside me while holding on to a porch pillar, she asks if I had learned anything. "No, he's still a mystery," I say.

"Don't forget. We still have the Eisenhower Center and Shlomo in New York. We'll solve this as we go along. I'm going to shower and rest some. Then I'll make dinner."

I sit there and dwell on the words 'We'll solve this.' The words strike deeply because I've never had anyone join me on my quest. This is different. So is Amelia. She's something else. I keep echoing the 'we' through my mind along with recent mental pictures of her jogging towards the porch. I like her. I like her a lot.

****

Therapeutic Analysis

***Emotions**. Stabbing through this account are several emotions. The veil of sadness continues in Dan, plus a new level of beginning excitement in two ways. As for excitement -that of sexual interest - it is obvious enough. When a vital man and a vital woman of approximately the same age sleep in the same house, hormones begin to activate. The second form of excitement is in Dan's gaining information about his father from Amelia. This is a first. Dan can hardly restrain his joy. All this is normal.*

An abnormal thing, given the earlier smooth Chicago personae of Dan with women, happens to be his urgency in regard to Amelia. His desire to gain information about his father causes him to become the man searching rather than the man pursued by women. The concept behind this revolves around the issue of abandonment, which is the top card in the human deck and Dan's most feared issue. Speaking generically, the long period of human dependency leads us to have a foundational fear of being abandoned. In our early days as babies that means death. Interestingly, that fear continues with us throughout our days - in some form or another such as being fired or being divorced. Dan has always had the upper hand with women because he had sufficient resources - plus his anxiety about commitment - so that he could end a relationship at any time. He kept the abandonment trump card, like his Script image of his father.

Now all this is changed. If Amelia refuses to talk or just disappears, it is Dan who'll be hurting. He needs her. This presents him with an altogether different situation. His first line of defense against a solid relationship does not exist. For the first time in his grownup years he's vulnerable. His sword of abandonment is sheathed, thus knocking off his cocky urban-

man-of-the-world-who-doesn't-need-you edge. The man is threatened at the point of Script. This is scary for him. Losing one's basic narrative is scary.

Cessation of using the tool of abandonment with others happens to be a mark of growth. Unless a person loses that and risks vulnerability, there can never be true or deep and lasting intimacy.

Therapeutically speaking, Dan uses the death of his father to make significant personal strides in terms of solving his basic psychological issues. He is aided in this by meeting a fascinating woman. If she had been a dumpy mindless housekeeper or a greedy gold-digger, everything would be different. He'd freeze and his therapy would last much longer. As it is, Dan's progress on himself is quite admirable. He is unaware of it, but his Defense Mechanisms are crumbling. His here and now emotions are becoming more real. Pretense has faded. Raw life is what he is encountering at the moment.

***Therapeutic problem**: It needs saying that, as an Analyst, I am at a disadvantage due to not being able to actually observe the couple. The reason is that print doesn't reveal the incongruities that shine forth like beacons for Freudian trained psychotherapists. That is very unfortunate because the voice, the bugle of neurosis, provides a great range of dissonance. Some people, for instance, talk out of the top of their throat, sound nasally, and recite rather than think. They listen, not in order to learn and then give thoughtful responses; rather, they immediately come forth with memorized rhetoric that supposedly shows superiority. The voice betrays the shallowness. Unheard, I must rely upon words and reactions of characters.*

Freud once considered using hypnosis in order to find out the unconscious level of his clients. He realized that incongruities were obvious in every angle of head, movement of eye, breathing patterns, voice sound, and body movements in arms, hands, legs, and feet. Freud learned that these incongruous movements signal erratic feelings and errant modules that escape conscious rationalizations of the client. In addition, once one is able to observe it, the different sides of the face (lateralization) provide enormous information. Both sides of the body also send unconscious signals.

Psychoanalytic therapists know that all these unconscious markers happen to be the main menu. They are the focus. No one can hide. If they were even to try to hide, their body betrays them and slips by conscious formulations and rationalizations. Therefore, one just as well be transparently honest with a therapist.

Thus, basing an analysis just on the basis of print, makes my work more difficult. I have to rely on adjectives, adverbs, sentence structure, and the reaction of the person spoken to in order to understand. With just those available, I'm intrigued by the transformations seen in both Dan and Amelia. True growth is percolating.

***Observation of Script**: Parents and grandparents have the advantage of seeing how a child adapts and how that adaptation sticks across the decades. They can see how a little four year old girl can manipulate her father by sweet cuteness, observe as the child grows and uses the same manipulative ploys with boys, and watch, helplessly, as they see the same mechanism ruin the grown woman's marriage. It is a quiet tragedy for the older generations who have a platform perspective. They simply do not know what to do.*

Understanding the dilemma of grandparents facilitates readers in grasping how therapists must go beyond content (the word formulations of clients who rationalize and show how they are the aggrieved party in relationships) and aim directly at the Script. Of course, there is resistance to hearing that. No client wants to learn that he or she is a dupe to their own childhood, contributed to an unhealthy marriage, or has some major changing to do. In their minds, they are innocent and their partner the cause of all the difficulties.

Psychological surgery takes time. This is why analysis is not brief therapy.

***PTSD and the Script**: Let's say that a person comes back from war traumatized by the viciousness of seeing a friend's head blown off, a bomb drop killing little children, or having shot an innocent. How does this relate to the old drama that a child developed, said drama with three primary roles: Hated but Strong, Adapted, and Weak? It may not immediately. At first, the therapist must concentrate upon matters at hand, matters like how the person is breathing and re-creating the tragic scene, how the person uses his mind to keep re-playing movies, or, say, dealing with nightmares. Down the line, the hook-up with unsolved issues from childhood emerge. Then, the therapist will note how the old Script blends in. It would be extremely rare if that old drama came forth rapidly with a soldier. First things first. The returning combat survivor must be allowed to talk about the specific problems arising from the war itself.*

It is to be remembered that psychological freedom is the goal. Therapists want clients to achieve spontaneity, awareness and intimacy. Therefore, everything is sifted carefully. The whole process is monitored by someone who deeply cares, but also someone who stays objective and looks for pain points. Then, the therapist figures out what to do about them.

***Script and Complexity**. Most people have long periods of daily time not re-playing old lost themes from the past. At work, during recreation, on vacations, with children and a host of other situations the person may be experiencing in the here and now. A few are stuck so solidly that they are always trapped in the caverns of childhood.*

Thus, if trying to understand someone, there will be many signals that will destroy your generalizations. When, for instance, Dan worked or architectural plans, managed his office, played squash, was with friends, or worked on a Board, he may well have not been touched by the narrative he developed as a child. This variation is why people get so confused in understanding the psychology of humans: people move in terms of their mental configurations. Since this book is about trauma, I focus on Dan's Script.

* * *

With a new client my tendency is to hold back on confrontations early on due to two factors. One is that confronting someone's ordinary procedure serves only to increase their resistance to change. The old standby comment is that "you must swim with the river," and not begin to fight upstream too early. The second reason is that I need to survey the entire landscape in order to get my bearings. It's like learning the music before starting to play.

There is one thing that I would confront because of its explosive negative effect for the client in terms of relationships. Narcissists frequently end their diatribes with others with a Passive-Aggressive chortle. This high-in-the-throat inauthentic laugh is intended to switch discomfort to the recipient of the sarcasm. In the high majority of the time, the person receiving the Passive-Aggressive laugh, is in a double-bind and does not know how to respond so he ingests the put-down and thinks himself mistaken and simply feels bad.

The double-bind goes this way: "I'll insult you and then laugh. The insult is hidden anger against your personhood. The laugh is to mute the insult so you, who normally go along with laughing humor, get confused. I can then walk away feeling superior while you feel like shit. I've avoided straight anger; you get angry at yourself."

The Passive Aggressive ploy must be confronted in therapy - even early on. Why and How? The Why is that it is a hallmark of rank Narcissism and ends up leaving the perpetrator relationship (ie. Loving relationship) free. It's destructive to one's identity. The key to gaining freedom from passive aggression is two-fold: one learning how to authentically feel emotions and, especially, de-fusing self-righteous anger that feeds the Narcissism.

The How is even more interesting. You interrupt the flow of the client and say: "I noticed a laugh. What were you feeling immediately before the laugh?" Inevitably, the client will say "nothing serious; just funny - that's all." That is not all. "I'm thinking you had a moment of scare that prompted the laugh.' The person will resist. "What do I have to be scared of?" You respond: "I'm not sure, but I will be analyzing it." Actually, the therapist is sure. Rapport and the avoidance of major resistance keeps utter confrontation in check. Rather, the idea is to lay the groundwork of further emotional clarification. This is the way I'd early on approach Dan's sarcasm.

It is to be remembered that testosterone and psychology go hand-in-glove. It is difficult to discern which comes first in many situations. My work entails following psychology rather than chemistry. Therefore, I have no staunch determinism about how testosterone automatically leads men to be competitive and, at the worst, go to war. Rather, I begin with human inadequacy and the necessity to prove one's manhood by being tough, sarcastic, or even violent - the next step of Narcissism.

Chapter Six

Letters from Hell

At breakfast the next morning, I'm hesitant. My Analyst would note that I'm scared. Still, I 'man up' and break the silence.

"Call me curious, but I'm thinking your real name is not Amelia Earhart. Don't be startled by me; I'm just preparing for the next step in this adventure. The will in the metal box in the closet says you get forty per cent of the assets of my father."

"I don't want anything. I've saved up over the last few years."

"As I was saying, you get forty per cent of his assets and we need a real name for the distribution - that is, when we figure the amount of money at stake. Please don't disappear on me either. It seems the man had some kind of integrity and both of us need to honor him at least that much. You can keep your anonymity for awhile; I'm just setting the terms for when we have to divide the estate."

"My real name is Sarah Bannock. My maiden name was Smith. That's all I want to say about my identity now."

I speak hurriedly. "Sarah, I have a confession. He knew your name and Social Security number. They were on the will: Sarah Anne Bannock. I guess he got it from your fingerprints and maybe this Shlomo guy in New York found out the information."

I talk rapidly to avoid her response. " I also note that the will was drawn up here in Abilene by a lawyer named Bolton. We need to contact him and have him go with us to the bank. We'll empty the deposit box. The key was in the metal lockbox. We'll probably have to show the will and fill out a lot of forms. Let's agree from the outset that if there is anything in there, you get forty per cent. And, of course, you get forty per cent of the house and the Black Opal. Whether you need it or not. That's respecting my dad's last wishes."

Sarah's face is red. "Slow down. So asking for my real name was deceitful. I don't do tricky. Right now I'm angry inside. Boiling. Since we met two days ago, you've called me Amelia when you knew better. Your behavior was phony. I don't like urban arrogant sarcasm and I despise gaminess. I hope this does not set a pattern. The future rule is: I'll be up-front, you be up-front or I'll be confronting you. You won't like my anger. Right now, though, I plan to keep quiet about what happened eight years ago, understood? Further, I need an apology."

"Sarah, If I can defend myself without being defensive, my thought was that I should get to know you on the terms you set with my father. There was no intent on my part to deceive. Rather, I wanted to establish rapport and get to know you a bit. Still, I sincerely apologize. From here on out I agree about being up-front. I have no major secrets, other than being screwed up in the head due to the absent father syndrome. What pisses me off is that you seem peaceful while I am stewing inside, loaded with a thousand questions. It seems I have a shattered identity that is being thoroughly mixed in a cheap dime store blender. All that after being in therapy for four years, so what do I know?"

"Dan, you just changed the subject to your mental state. I'm still hot inside. But, I'll go along with your switch. Peaceful? Me? I guess so. That's been a result of living here in the presence of a man who simply accepted me for who I am, mysteries and all. Maybe, for all its faults, the quietness of Abilene sunk in - the total absence of any major stress. Who knows? You are not the only one puzzled by this business. Somehow I have come to accept myself, though there are tragedies back there that left major scars."

"Great. You peaceful, me in a turmoil. My dad helps you; he craps out on me. Lovely!"

"Curb your sarcastic soaked cynicism. I meant it when I said that I have no tolerance for misery talk, particularly from an arrogant Chicago guy. If we are going to go through this together, I don't need you dragging us down, or, in fact, your sarcasm about Abilene. Sometimes you need an attitude adjustment. What is, is."

"You used the 'us' word again," I respond. "You are one step ahead of me. I guess we are partners since the will links us. I haven't thought of it that way. Does this mean you are in, not only for the financial split, but for solving the mysteries as well?"

Sarah studies me for a long searching minute before responding.

"In Abilene speak that is 'in for a penny, in for a pound.' I don't know what all this means, but (sigh) I suppose my days as an anonymous housekeeper are definitely over. We'll need to set some rules, first among them - I repeat - total transparency. Though I feel a bit hypocritical because that's not the way I've been living. You don't pull any more gamey stuff about already knowing my name but not telling me up-front. That still irks me. I repeat: I don't do gamesmanship. If we are going to be mystery sleuths, we share aloud. Agreed?"

"I'll shake on that. There is another question apart from your unmentionable past that intrigues me. You seem to be psychologically adept and I doubt seriously if you have been on the couch like I have. Are you a self-help freak or have you been in therapy?"

"Nope. Neither. Just silence and thinking. Gardening and nature. Living with your father who with no physicality whatsoever just accepted me for who I am. Silence worked for me. That's it in a nutshell. Maybe going through some craziness in my life and still staying sane also added its portion to my mental makeup. I haven't looked to others for help; I've examined myself."

"Like Socrates and Freud?"

"Like whoever. I read and study great literature and poetry. Stop this head stuff, will you? I'm ready to enter the next phase of our mystery trip. Let's contact the lawyer, go to the bank and get on with it. You're not the only one who is curious."

With a wry smile, I say. "Go easy with me Sarah: I'm accustomed to being in charge, not part of some equal thinking team."

I phone and set an appointment with both the bank and the attorney for 11 a.m. Things happen that fast in a small town. The lawyer and banker were old friends so at the appointed hour accessing the large security deposit box presents no difficulty. Sarah brought along a large purse in which we empty the contents of the security box.

Sarah and I return to the house. At the Fifth Street residence we go to the kitchen table, pour glasses of iced tea, and sit down feeling a bit queasy about the whole thing. Sarah pours the contents of the purse on the table.

After counting, I note: "About twenty grand in cash. We'll split it 60/40 which means ... which means ... 8 for you and 12 for me ...at least it's in hundreds ... still a lot of lettuce to carry around. What else is here? Shlomo Loew turns out to be Dad's brother in New York City according to this paper. That solves one mystery. I've got an uncle. There is also a small envelope addressed to Sarah Anne Bannock and a thicker envelope addressed to me." Neither of us are jumping up and down eager to read the letters from the dead Ezra. Silence reveals both of us avoiding the next step. We sip tea.

It's Sarah who breaks the silence "Since we are beginning this transparency thing, I see no reason the letters should be private. Agreed? I'll read mine aloud first, if that is alright with you."

I'm scared but nod assent.

Thoughtfully, she begins reading Ezra's note: 'Sarah, I owe you an apology. I have respected your privacy since we met, but there was no way I could prepare a legal will without your real name and Social Security number. My brother Shlomo found out who you are from fingerprints I sent him. Again, I apologize. Please understand that I went no further than your name and number. Your secrets are your secrets. For me, you will always be Amelia, a kind woman who must, with all your mysteries, have something in your past that approaches the pain of my personal history. I have treasured our silences. You accepted me and I accepted you. That was our rule, but more than rule, it was the grace in which we lived and shared a home. As I watched you heal across the years, your courage and advance as a human taught me ... how do I say this? ... from the heart. I occasionally looked at the music, the poetry, nature writings and literature you were reading and found my soul touched, though if you knew my past, you'd discover someone with deep permanent scars throughout his psyche. I never said it, but I loved your flowers, backyard vegetable garden and our shared meals. In our forged quietness there was an exchange that meant something beyond words. Therefore, I have put you in my will at the rate of forty per cent of all I have. Please accept it with my gratitude.   Ezra Loew.'

I lean back in my chair, take another sip of tea, and say thoughtfully "That letter takes a lot more reading than just once. He helped you, and it also appears you helped him. Out of the deep silences you two shared came a kind of mutual admiration society. I'm impressed. As my psychoanalyst would prompt me to be honest now, I admit to having a wave of envy for what you two forged together."

Sarah reaches across the table and softly touches my arm. "I may have been too forward in suggesting we both read the letters aloud. He was your father. Perhaps you would rather read yours privately."

Her thoughtful gesture moves me. "Thanks, Sarah, though it may even help me to have you beside me as I read this letter. Besides, I agreed to transparency. I have a huge lump in my throat as I unfold it because this is the first transmission, the first contact other than money from my mysterious father. But, lump or not, I'll read aloud."

'To Dan Michelson. Your mother's maiden name. She was wise to remove my name from your history. I'm sure you've had emotional turmoil from my disappearance. I'm convinced that you would have had a ton more of mental unrest if you had experienced me daily as a father.'

"Sarah, how the hell does he know that? I guess I'm supposed to forgive him. I don't. Childhood was painful."

"Dan, I think you should just read the letter now. We'll dissect it later and add your emotions if that's what you need to do."

Impressed by her measured reaction, I return to reading. 'I was totally ambivalent as I watched you grow in your mother's womb; not about you, but about my anguish as a human being. I was not fit to be a father. With the exception of your mother and my brother, everyone I touched seemed to die horribly. When I held you as a baby, I had to leave suddenly before something tragic happened. Your mother knew portions of my past and understood. She pledged to never tell you anything about my history.

'Shlomo will tell you about our original family. In this letter my intention is to say bluntly to you that your father was a murderer.

Not just once, but dozens of times - maybe as many as hundreds. Because of me an entire village was wiped out by the Nazi's.

'In 1933 our family moved to France from Germany due to Hitler. When Germany took over France in June of '42, the turncoat Vichy government joined in the persecution of the Jews. There was a large roundup in July of 1942 where many Jews were arrested. I hold myself responsible for all of us - Shlomo, me, my parents and my sister Madeline -being captured. I had seen the Nazis marching to our house in Paris, but I got there too late to warn everyone. The family, with the exception of Madeline, was jailed; she was sent to Gestapo Headquarters.

'The sadist Klaus Barbie, Gestapo Chief in Lyons, tore my sister's flesh apart in repeated torturing sessions which he approached like a sick religious ritual. He thought she had knowledge of where Jews were hidden. The information of Barbie's barbarism came to me in the underground. Barbie personally killed 4000 prisoners. He was a vicious sadist. For me, however, it was Madeline that scorched my soul. Madeline. My baby sister. I vowed to get revenge. It took a while before my chance came. Shlomo and I escaped and joined the French Resistance.

'I became a sniper. A Russian in the Resistance taught me how to conceal myself, patiently take aim, gently pull the trigger and shoot. I well learned his lessons. I got my Lee-Enfield sniper rifle fitted with a telescopic sight from a parachute drop of weapons by the British. It was accurate at nine hundred yards. I killed any German I could find. My resistance group was the Maquis, a French word meaning "bushes" because we hid in heavy undergrowth and took them out. While some guerillas destroyed train tracks and blew up trains, I was a loner - a stone cold assassin. I later read that snipers looked for the "pink mist" when a bullet went through a brain. I reveled in it. Every Nazi I killed was Klaus Barbie. I felt my beautiful sister in my mind as I began to tighten my finger on the trigger. I believed I was honoring her with each bullet fired.

'Dan, to understand me, you need to realize that my vengeance began to be pleasurable. I loved it (though I fantasize you will think me a monster similar to Barbie.) I was willing to wait silently in the woods with little food or water, until I got a bead on a German and dropped him - then, the head explosion and the telling pink mist.

'My parents were incinerated at Auschwitz. Each bit of news I heard of a Jew being annihilated fueled my rage. I'd seldom check in with the other resistance fighters. All I wanted was another pocket full of bullets, a bit of cheese and a little bread. Then I went off on my mission of death.

'A legend grew up among the Germans about a lone sniper. Then it happened. I shot several Germans and spotted a Nazi major from the Fuhrer brigade whom I captured and killed. It was near Limoges. The order came out from the High Command to show the sniper what his murdering German soldiers resulted in. The SS entered the village of Oradour-Sur-Glane, rounded up all 642 residents and mowed them down in the center of the town. They put up signs addressed to the sniper: me.

'When they left, I entered the town and viewed the corpses. Men, old and young. Women. Children. Babies. One little dead baby boy branded my brain. He was shot in the stomach and his little fingers had dug into the dirt as he died in terribly painful misery.

'That picture of that little boy flashed in my mind when I held you in my arms just after your birth. Your tiny fingers wound about my index finger and I saw the death diggings in the dirt by that innocent baby. At that moment I knew I could not be in your life. I was not just tainted; I was a bloody avenger, not a loving father. I knew how to kill. I didn't know how to be a parent.

Madeline was in my head. My parents at Auschwitz. The baby boy at Oradour. The 642 innocents torn to pieces by machine gun fire - lying in heaps in the village square. The host of pink mist pictures in my brain. The Nazi note on the wall written to me, the sniper. All those possessed my mind.

'What would I do if you, as a little boy, were to ask me about the French Resistance and my part in the war? What would I have done if you had found out as a child? More than those, how would you have daily learned to be a man from a father who was mentally vacant? I can only bear to tell you now about the atrocities because you are past your mid-thirties. I can't ask you to forgive me for my murdering during World War II, nor can I ask you to forgive me for my absence in your life. If you know what you'd have had as a damaged father, a walking survivor hating himself for three years of vengeance and another lifetime of being nothing more than a walking cadaver - not a caring human or a doting father - you would forgive. But I cannot ask that. I'm not sure I have forgiven myself.

'You may have a question about my relationship with your mother. With every shred of what I could manage in terms of love, I loved her. She knew I was damaged goods when we married. It is even true that we decided to have a baby in moments when I thought I could heal and be a resource for a child. The mind is a complex organism. At times I got in a mood or space where all the hatred, violence, and killing was not really me; I was the same happy boy with a loving mom, a brother and a sister, living in Germany and then France. I could talk myself into thinking that and almost feeling it.

'Then, Madeline's destruction appeared in my mind. My parents incinerated at Auschwitz. Klaus Barbie. Pink mist. Oradour and the innocent baby boy. I knew what Freud said about libido and mortido, the life instinct and the death instinct. Looking into your eyes and sensing the beautiful growth in your baby body there in my arms at your beginning, I saw Life Energy. In me, however, there remained an abundance of Death Energy. I had immersed myself in killing. I also could not understand why I survived and not my parents or beautiful Madeline. It was all so insane, so irrational, so sunk into my mind and being. I did not deserve you; I could not be in your life. The decision was made.

'Your wonderful mother understood. She knew I would never forsake her in terms of financial support. She kept her silence. I kept my bargain. Now you are a respectable grown man. I cannot ask you to understand. I want no pity. This is the true story.

Your father,
Ezra Loew.

P.S. Go to the Eisenhower Research Center and speak with the archivist. Later, visit my brother, Shlomo, in New York City. He will tell you more.'

I look up from my reading, my eyes brimming with tears. "Sarah, this letter leaves me mentally exhausted. I'm on the verge of sobbing. Now I'm the one who needs silence. I'll read the letter over and over until I get it - if, indeed, I ever will. I'm going on the porch to think. Tomorrow, I suggest we go to the Eisenhower place. As for now, I disappear. Please forgive me. My heart is overflowing. My pain is great."

I can tell Sarah definitely understands as she nods with a measure of compassion. No words. No touch. Just eyes that speak deep care for a fellow human being.

Adding the letter to the previous viewing of my dead father heighten my awareness on the porch. Buildings, cars, trees, grass and sky seem to vibrate with color. As darkness descends, I find myself appreciating the coolness of evening signaled by a softer breeze. Abilene seems nice. I watch the light cast different shadows on the blue spruce trees themselves. I'm especially aware of the smells of the flowers, bushes and trees - as if for the first time in my life. Quietly, Sarah gently places a blanket and a shawl around my shoulders and neck. I mumble a thanks. Neither of us speaks further.

Part of me, the cosmopolitan know-it-all from Chicago, is dazed as if hit by a cement truck. My inner little boy is writhing with grief, joined with an understanding and nascent love for a man I never met. Through tear-filled eyes I re-read the letter. I keep being struck that the letter shows absolute concern for both the Dan across the years and the grown-up Dan sitting on this porch. My father had a heart for me. What an incredible story of human suffering, more than all my shallow reading about the Holocaust, more than all the stories I've heard from survivors, more than anything my imagination can construct. My God, what the man went through in France! And the utter honesty of the letter is astounding. In a way, I don't know what to feel. I think even my psychoanalyst would be in a quandary.

As night wears on and I read again and again by the porch light, other questions pound away in my head. What did Ezra do prior to coming to Abilene? Did he really live in New York City, the origin of the checks? Why was he here? While it was now understandable that Ezra found himself incapable of being a father - I can certainly identify with that decision - was there anything more to it? Who is this Uncle Shlomo? What does he do for a living? Hopefully, he's still alive and will add more about the Loew family. What is the attraction of the Eisenhower Center? How can that have anything to do with some ancient quest of Ezra? Did he hope to find a measure of peace for his soul from a study of World War II documents? Mysteries. Now, for the first time in my life, I begin to have hope that some of the dilemmas are capable of being solved.

I know that, even in my dreams during the coming night's sleep, the letter and the ever tormenting questions will repeatedly run through my tortured brain. I don't know what to conclude about the man named Ezra Loew. One thing is sure: my father is no longer a ghost. There's definition, though not cosmetically pretty definition. My internal anxiety has quieted, only to be replaced with a form of grief I'm unable to quell.

Snuggling in the blanket and shawl, I dreamily watch the full moon over Abilene, I suddenly have a major, almost poetic realization: if one is unprepared for complexity, he best not study humanity. A lifetime of questions may have answers, but they are definitely not the easy ones I've previously fantasized. Everything seems both more clear and more muddy. There remain a vast array of mysteries. I have much to learn.

About my father.

About myself, for that matter.

And also about the intriguing Sarah Anne Bannock.

****

Therapeutic Analysis

***Script Revision**: There are occasions in our lives when time compresses as the past and present merge so quickly that everything changes as if in a cosmic time warp. Dan and Sarah experienced that compression as they absorb Ezra's letters, letters blood-soaked with history and wisdom. Neither of them will ever be the same again.*

Accompanying that cosmic time warp, a radical revision of their personal stories is occurring. As briefly mentioned earlier, humans have unconscious running narratives about life and one's own life in particular (The Script). The human brain needs software and the unspoken narrative provides a sense of what is valuable. The inner story also provides an understanding of what is worth doing, who to be with, what to work for, whether to be close or separate, and continues through other matters all the way to an understanding of death. The narrative is not conscious; it is super real, however.

During my therapeutic training I was cautioned to not suddenly disrupt a client's religious or philosophical belief system because it would totally disorient her or him. In the case of Dan and Sarah their personal non-religious philosophies went spinning out into space with the two letters. They were both shocked; Dan more so. His Script was gone. It would take immense effort and lying to himself to maintain it. Personal re-integration is now paramount. He has no other choice than go forward.

The construction of a new narrative happens to be a golden opportunity to re-construct all of life's values. Here I think of men and women who learn that their married partner has had an affair, said breach of trust leading to a divorce. While their new single status is shockingly painful, it often leads, after a period of time while the body empties out grief, to a new awakening. A growth spurt is not automatic. The reason is that the individual has a choice. There is no clear path to victory. Instead the person must make decisions, work for the future and begin to see life anew.

***Identification as method of redemption**. As Analyst, I note that this is the third time in the text that someone has mentioned the path of identification as a way to exit great trauma. Dan sought father figures, Sarah identified with Ezra's method of avoiding conversation, and now, Ezra admits that he learned from Sarah. The final point is rather remarkable.*

In real life, identification with a healthy model is a legitimate path for personal salvation. We all need heroines and heroes - possibly even in fiction - who have shown us the way to a better, more victorious form of life. Heroes, of course, also have failures.

***Therapeutic review**. It is obvious that both Dan and Sarah are stunned by recent occurrences, particularly the letters. Sarah is hit by the knowledge that she was not poor and had resources. She is also shocked by learning that her benefactor, Ezra, had received beneficial help from her very being. That's very good news. Dan is stunned by death, by being in a strange town, being in his father's house and receiving a letter from the grave that totally destroys all his previous father formulations.*

It may surprise the reader to know that I, as therapist, actually relish events in the world that shake a client to his or her toes. This is not morbid of me. Nor is it sadistic or immoral. Naturally, part of me is sad when something came along that is deeply problematic to a client. But, internally, I know that the occasion can well mean a re-awakening, a deep revision of old narratives, a newness that offers hope and new life.

Without the cataclysmic occasion, therapy takes more time, boring client repetitions more customary, occasions for breakthroughs less frequent. When tragedy occurs, the mental shake-up can be colossal. It opens new doors. A person listens more intently. He or she is ready to take a new step in order to relieve the mental suffering. If there is no pain from a tight shoe, why change? If life goes along swimmingly, why get out of the swamp? It is therefore good to be shaken to the foundations, though again I repeat, I, as therapist, have deep rapport and presence with the person undergoing suffering. It's my honor to be a companion during grief episodes and a rational Sancho Panza as Don Quixote continues to venture forth in discovery of new territory.

The above three paragraphs are not said lightly.

Finally, I return to a point made earlier, namely that, in order to free a person from a Narcissistic Personality Disorder, it is often necessary to have a blunt encounter with death. If Dan doesn't get it after these two letters, it is questionable if he ever will. If his meeting with a vibrant and vital woman unlike any female he has ever encountered doesn't shake his superior abandonment Script with women, he may well live a life of serial sexual affairs until he dies, thinking all the while, that life may be banal, but sufficient. Bland. But acceptable. Not fulfilling. But enough to make it through.

Death, disrupting tragedies, and startling love are the difference makers.

Therapy helps.

Chapter Seven

Sarah's Confession

Eggs. Toast. Black coffee. For some reason, perhaps embarrassment, I avoid Sarah's eyes. The letters have changed me. I'm no longer the cocky Chicagoan with the sarcastic remark a fraction of a second from my tongue. Missing is the easy anger I've maintained since childhood, anger at a seemingly irresponsible father who left me to my own wiles at home, on the playground, and in school. I'm thinking my eyes and physical carriage display a new openness, a kind of surrendered acceptable peace smoothing the worry lines in my face. I feel softer. Perhaps I've reached a point where I can listen to others with an inner ear. Sarah must sense my difference.

"Dan, your letter did not just transform you: it also affects me. The vastness of Ezra's suffering is mind-boggling. I'll even venture to say that he could not be an everyday father precisely because of his love for you - though you may dispute it. In the light of the letters we read yesterday, it's time to tell you my story - if you are willing to hear it. I've decided to trust you. When you invited me to open up and talk, you may have pulled the plug holding a huge lake behind the dam. I know you are on overload so if the time is not ripe, just shrug me off and we'll talk when it's appropriate."

"Sarah, my brain feels like it's been taken out of my skull, squeezed and re-configured. I am now curious about everything. It's like a re-birth has taken place in my body and soul. So, if you are willing to talk, I'm honored to listen."

"Your father's confessions hit me deeply. You'll be the first to hear my story. Back in 1992 at age 22, shortly after college, I married a wonderful man. I loved George as I understood love at that time. At my young age I was possessed by romanticized fantasies leftover from the dreams of a girl who wanted the perfect home, perfect husband, perfect children, perfect life. Things proceeded according to my illusion-filled plan for awhile. We had the desired boy and girl and lived in a nice suburban home. Things were going along as well as a little idealized girl dreamed. Four years into our marriage George began feeling badly. Medical tests revealed pancreatic cancer. Surgery followed and we held our breaths. Nothing worked. He died in 1997, our fifth year of marriage. At age 27 I was a single mom with two children.

"My kids, Lance and Laura, were beautiful. Pictures of them came to my mind when your father described the boy shot in the stomach at Oradour. They were everything a mother could want. In 2000 when Lance was seven and Laura was five, we were driving to their respective schools through hilly country in suburban Pittsburgh. This is hard. I'm sick as I tell this. I got distracted. I looked back at the kids, lost control of the car, and we rolled off the highway and overturned. Both kids' necks snapped. Their breathing stopped; I was trapped in the crushed car and helpless. The wreck was my fault. An ambulance showed up shortly. There was nothing the EMT's could do. I was physically unhurt. I was also mentally destroyed. My children were dead."

Sarah stops her story and sobs uncontrollably for a few moments. I don't know what to do, so I softly touch her shoulder. Sarah takes deep breaths and continues.

"The zombie days had begun. I began to sleepwalk through life. I walked through the funeral for my children like I, too, was dead. Many times I wish I was. It took a while, but I sold the home. All family business was settled over a one year walking nightmare. I was in a total daze, something like the Jewish survival community calls Night and Fog. When all the insanity of financial details were settled, I went to the bus station and traveled in whatever direction the first bus headed. I didn't care if it was Mexico, Canada, Seattle or Tampa Bay. It made no difference. There was no longer any reason to keep on living, but, somehow, I did. As the busses rolled along, I vacantly looked out the window at the passing landscapes of North America like a zoned drug addict. I was a lost human with no purpose whatsoever. When exhausted, I'd arrive at some anonymous place, get a room, sleep and rest for a few days and eat at some bland tasteless diner. Rested a bit, I'd go to the bus station, board a bus ... completely directionless. Hollow. Reamed out. There was no drinking to mindless oblivion, no desperate sex with strangers, no turning to drugs, no nothing. I just traveled. Aimlessly. Didn't care. Didn't care about others. Didn't care about myself. I was uninterested in people and sought to be invisible so no one could see my guilty face.

"One other thing. I carried the Collected Works of Shakespeare with me. Sometimes I couldn't read and held the book lifelessly in my lap. At other times, I'd read several pages of words but nothing registered. Every once and awhile, something sunk in. Now I have quotations of Shakespeare that run through my head. They help."

"I do that with Robert Browning's poetry," I tell her.

Sarah nods at me and continues. "Three years went by and I had spent all my money. I was down to a few dollars when your father spotted me here in Abilene.

"I've often thought since living here that I went through four stages, not stages of grief, but four stages of growing up. The first stage was a sense of utter abandonment. That came with the death of George and accelerated with the death of Lance and Laura. I felt like a young child forsaken by family - both my original family who had also died and the Bannock family we created - George, Laura, Lance, and me. Yes, there was even a sense that I lost 'me', the 'me' that was a suburban housewife mom, the 'me' of childhood. My identity was shot.

"After the stage of abandonment, I rode the busses and felt stage two: a searing desert-like loneliness. The adult 'me' re-emerged in part but, as I stared out the windows of the busses and sat in Greyhound Bus Stations, I felt vast loneliness - like a nomad lost in the Gobi Desert. Actually, I healed a bit as time went on in my travels. I moved to the third stage: aloneness. I was not pining for others to assuage my situation, I developed a kind of acceptance that I was alone and that was simply the situation, nothing more. Alone in life. Aloneness felt endurable.

"Then, Abilene and Ezra came along. Here in this house, under the kind watchful care of Ezra, the fourth and final stage arrived quite serendipitously: solitude. The realization came forth that I'm all right and even good in and of myself. I never intended evil. Nature is good. Life is good. I'll survive and, if no one ever enters my life again, there is a sense of peace within. I need no one. Further, I decided I will never ever live partially with someone just in order to have a man around. I always have me to come home to. Solitude happens to be very, very good. That's my story" she says looking me fully in the eyes.

I swallow, am somewhat stunned, and don't know what to say. "Sarah, the healing silences of you and Ezra now make full sense to me. I'm at a loss for words. I want you to know that your painful journey - it sounds trite to even label it like that - deeply touches me. I fear I may be utterly shallow in what I say now. I cannot imagine either your or Ezra's pain. I came to Abilene thinking myself mature and the original suffering victim; I'm discovering that my journey was easy - shallow even. I'm a neophyte in terms of human tragedy. At times as you talked, I wanted to reach out and hold your hand. If you are willing, I want to hug you and hold you for a few moments."

She doesn't draw away. My arms encircle her as long as it seems appropriate. In a way, the hug actually consoles both of us. I think there's a spiritual dimension in the embrace that neither of us understand, but both of us know to be real. There is forgiveness, acceptance and a newness that feels right - a kind of soul joining. It's like we both want to cry, but hold back and don't shed tears together.

After a few minutes of silence, I come out of my trance and say: "Sarah, my analytic scientific brain suddenly clicked in I realize there are parallels in all of this that exceed my ability to draw them. You and dad had survivor guilt, however that is defined - I'm no psychologist. You both had some sense of being empty which I can identify with because part of me has been there since a boy, though I want to quickly add that my suffering is minimal compared to Ezra and you. Somehow the healing nature of quietness has been good for all of us. Each of us has been scared to love again: me after my mother's death, you after your husband and children, my father after his original family. History's events sometimes grab us and we are helpless. I'm struggling here. I just know we three are alike in profound manners. To tell the truth, I'm overwhelmed with so much pounding in my brain that I need to stop, breathe, smell lilac bushes, pick daisies, and ... what? ... stand on my head, scream out the window. Who knows? This whirlwind of honesty and reality we're facing is both exhausting and exhilarating. One other thing: I'm thinking there is a soul connection in all this, but I don't understand it and am afraid to give it any definition. This will take time. I hope we will continue this journey together until we find some meaningful resolution."

Sarah closely studies me and seems to realize there is not a single shred of negative judgment in me whatsoever. Her story is accepted as a segment of irrational, unavoidable time. Events happen beyond our control. There is no way we rationally choose some of the utterly meaningless paths life provides. One can only wish for total control of our destinies, a world where wars, abandonment, and accidents never occur. That is not the real world.

"Maybe, Dan, we need to go for a long walk. I suggest we tour this neighborhood and I share with you what I saw and felt during these years here in Abilene. Walks can be quite healing."

I nod in agreement.

"On my morning jogs ... sometimes a run ... I'd confine myself to about a thirty square block area. If someone said something to me, I'd say a rapid 'Hi' and keep moving. Ezra and I never neighbored - to change a noun into a verb. Neither of us knew anyone. We kept it that way. My lack of knowledge about Ezra's life is astonishing. I didn't know he went to the Eisenhower Center. I was too sunk in my own pain to notice what he did. Enough of that, Dan. You get to choose the direction: East, West, North, or South?"

"North."

"Okay. I usually jog all the way to the Eisenhower Park. It is near the fairgrounds. The school playground occasionally has children swinging or sliding down slides. That has been painful to me in the past so I accelerate during that block as I head East. Notice Dan, the wrap-around porches on many of the old Victorian homes. People move to another side depending upon the sun, wind, or rain. In the summer they look for a breeze; in the late Autumn or early Spring they avoid cold wind. I like the porches."

"So do I Sarah. They all seem to have comfortable chairs like Ezra's home. The houses range from Georgian to Federal to Victorian to even middle income houses without porches. This is really a unique neighborhood."

"It reminds me of my home community," she responds. "I have a soft spot for large trees. I got a book from the library and can identify them all now. Also the flowers."

"Not flowers for now. I'm on overload. I can handle the trees," I tell her.

"That one is a walnut. There is an elm. I'll just point them out and say their names. Ash. Linden. Maple. Locust. Redbud. Golden Raintree. Red oak. Mimosa. Crab-apple. Now I turn South before I get to Buckeye Street; it's too busy for me."

"Sarah, please spare me Buckeye; I've encountered enough chaos."

"Okay. Over there is the largest church in this area. Methodist."

"I'm not into churches, Sarah."

"Neither am I, but I don't scorn the people. They are who they are, intend good, and, quite frequently help those who hurt. As for religion, I grew up in a family that didn't take it seriously; nor have I across the years. At times when I've seen everyone all dressed up on Sundays, I've thought: 'No one here can understand my pain.' That's arrogant of me. Methodists are part of the human condition and suffer also."

"No comment, Sarah."

"Okay. Continuing on, I like some of these houses. There are wonderful trees along here that have big limbs with protecting arms watching over this silent female jogger. Nature helps me. Now we are nearing the downtown brick buildings … the police station and the funeral home, as you know. There's the Natural Foods Store. They'll order anything I want. Over there is the library. They get me any book available in the State of Kansas, including universities and colleges. The Café where Ezra and I met was over there, but it's out of business. There's the Post Office. That shop does pedicures and manicures. There is the Art Council."

I look with new awareness. "There is a world here I didn't see before you and I took this walk. You are opening my eyes. There is a lot to this neighborhood, that is, as long as you are not into buying clothes and purchasing all manner of things."

"You're right, Dan. This is not a consumer-oriented neighborhood. I, personally, do not buy in order to replace what I bought last year. Ahead is the Union Pacific Railway tracks and the old train station. Those knick-knack stores and antique shops over there bring in tourists. We'll turn west now. There is the Senior Center where I volunteer occasionally. That abandoned limestone church houses a performing arts group that puts on interesting plays. They're pretty good. Anyway, they do their best and I respect that."

Finishing up our walk, I say, "Despite my urban Chicago self, I admit to being impressed. This is a world in and of itself. You have everything but a nice restaurant."

"Spoken too quickly, Daniel. Five blocks east of our home happens to be a restaurant called the Kirby House that you'll like. We'll go there this evening if you brought your credit card." I smile and nod.

"Sarah, I want to take a shower and change clothes before dinner at your fabled eatery. I phrased that wrongly. Before I take you to dinner at this fabulous Kirby House."

After each of us take a private shower and change clothes, we commence walking again. I'm skeptical. We pass the old brick buildings of downtown, are beside a railroad spur and walk straight towards an immense old flour mill with large storage silos. Then I see it. A pink Georgian building surrounded by beautiful flower arrangements. The sign is there: The Kirby House.

"Looks good, Sarah." The old doors and floors creak as we enter into a demure waiting area where a hostess asks if there are reservations. "No", Sarah responds. We are seated in a window well area at a table for two with a white table cloth. There are 16 ft. ceilings with gold painted crown molding, nice wallpapered walls and a beautiful crystal chandelier. On the table is a wine list. I see that this is no backwoods café. Despite my old Chicago cynical self, I'm entranced. The structure may be like a return to the early Twentieth Century, but it's an elegant return. I'm equally impressed by the food and service. At one point, I come close to asking Sarah to pinch me so I'll know I'm awake. She asks why I'm smiling. I tell her. She lightly pinches my arm.

Though neither of us is still hungry, we order and share a light dessert followed by coffee. Both are excellent. "Pinch me again, Sarah" I say with a coy smile. She laughs, and gives me another soft pinch. Sarah then takes me on a tour of the building, showing me a coffee bar that opens each weekday morning with various coffees, teas and homemade baked goods. "I buy unique coffees to take home" she said. "Since I'm buying, Sarah, I'd like to choose the coffee for the morning.". I choose what I think she'll like. Then, we climb several flights of old oak stairs to the tower which has a private table for two. "This is the room I want to reserve for our next dinner," I say gallantly.

As we walk home. I break the silence. "These have been the craziest several days of my life: a total Kansas tornado. I recall a picture from the Wizard of Oz where everyone is tossed and flying through the air. I now know the feeling. Am I coming or going? Worse: Am I me?" I say looking at Sarah with a quizzical smile.

"You are you, Dan. Both of us may be in Kansas, but we are on entirely new flights. It has been a relief to honestly tell my story and face no judgment. You are like your father in terms of having a deep quiet acceptance. I deeply appreciate that. My life is also in a swirl. Ezra's death. The end of a long silence. I'm like the nun in the Sound of Music; kicked out of the convent and walking down the road with mountains ahead to cross."

"Let's cross those mountains together, Sarah." I softly say. She looks at me and nods in agreement.

Upon arriving at the house I decide to sit alone on the porch like my father once did, just in order to hear the sounds of approaching night. I sit in Ezra's rocker and secure the blanket and shawl over my shoulders. For hours ... who knows the time? ... I sit listening to the children finishing their play and being called home. The same owl hoots not too far away. I watch the lights turn off in neighboring houses. A train rumbles by. I again think how trains are so intriguing. They come from mysterious places and click by going to still other mysterious places. I know the feeling. Entranced, I doze in the chair only to wake up hours later. I move to the couch in the living room and sleep soundly.

****

Therapeutic Analysis

***The Trauma**. There are no accurate measures for human suffering: nor can there ever be. Sarah's encounter with death and a meaningless period are no less tragic than any other story in this book. Her solution included enduring a long period of time: part silence, part literature, part nature, part exercise, and, significantly, part genuine acceptance by a caring, though silent, Ezra Loew.*

As alluded to in the Preface, one subtle Narcissistic ploy is to think one's pain worse than that of others. I've listened to many dying clients. Would you prefer dying of ulcerative colitis or prostate, breast or lung cancer? Can you imagine having cancer of the optic nerve that spreads to consume part of your face and eventually destroys your brain? What kind of Special Needs child would you prefer to raise? The reader's hesitation reveals the absurdity of thinking one's own specific trauma the worst of all possible ones. We are all one with historic humanity: we suffer. The loving presence of another greatly mitigates our individual situation. Utter loneliness can be hell. It should not be self-imposed. It is better to love and be loved.

Imagine Sarah coming to your office shortly after the death of her two children. If you, as therapist, were to introduce reason, she would toss it away like a broken dish. She thought herself guilty for the death of Lance and Laura - end of story. Any quickly stated optimistic remarks simply don't fit the situation. She would not be open to shallow understanding. In a way, she wanted to suffer as punishment for her car error.

What strategy works? My thinking is that it becomes necessary to analyze what she is doing in her mind. Namely, the internal Superego vs. Naturalness internal dialog needs to be made front and center. I'd have her sit in an opposite chair that is berating her, questioning her driving ability, accusing her of driving idiocy, telling her she is a failure as a mother, etc. When she empties out that bile, I'd have her switch back to the chair she normally uses in talking with me and ask her what she thinks about the diatribe.

Perhaps Sarah would dissolve in wracking sobs. It may seem strange to a reader, but I'd then have her switch back to the Accusation Chair and do it all over again. At the next session I'd repeat the same pattern. The idea is for her to grasp what she does in her mind. Down the line in the sessions, I'd ask her if she had purposely hurt her children. She'd look at me with fury. Then, I'd suggest "Then tell the Accusation Chair about your love for your children and add that you did absolutely nothing intentionally to hurt Lance and Laura." She'd do that, and, in the process, some light would begin to dawn.

A therapeutic tangent I add for the reader is in order. Not clear in the last two paragraphs is why I put the Superego Accusation Chair away from her usual seat. The reason is I want, by location, to separate the vituperation from her normal self. This paragraph may seem incidental. It happens to be critical.

Love happens to be central in healing from trauma. One can never tell where the nice healing breeze may arise. It can be from the natural response of a smiling child. It may come from a friend, a therapist, a partner, or even a stranger. In Sarah's case, the breeze came silently from a caring old man who was also a survivor of irrational events. Control is an illusion. Things happen beyond our power. That's simply the way it is.

***Script Analysis**. Though we must shake off the eventual pain the grownup Sarah eventually faced, it is of value to consider the Script she had in her marriage. She may have come out of childhood as the only spoiled child of a doting father and caring mother. With only a small amount of the story and knowing her* *attractiveness, we can surmise that she was able to manipulate her father with her utter cuteness. He'd be an easy mark. If she followed the Electra model, (the female equivalent of the Oedipal drama), she'd also have been in competition with her mother and see that she got more love from her dad than her mother did from her husband. That's a reasonable guess.*

Thus, Sarah's old Script would go like this: Avoid personally appearing like her designated 'weak' parent (her mom), getting her way with her husband George by using seductive ploys, and, when cuteness didn't work, switch to the stronger and harder role of her father, with subtle intimations of abandonment.

Now. I know this analysis appears hard, and at this point to be sure, it's a thesis built on only slim evidence. I must draw upon other cases similar to hers. Understand that my suppositions will be tentative until there is future confirmation.

It appears that the old Script was dissolved after the succession of tragedies (George, Laura, and Lance), and the years of 'wandering in the wilderness.' The old narrative didn't work against the reality of death. She was stunned into a multi-year re-analysis of her life. In this book, she lives in a post-Script world.

Interestingly, she continually chose and chooses life-filled options, options that add up in healing her soul.

If Sarah were in therapy with me, it would be my role to witness her growth. Since a confession is good for the soul, I'll give a confession of my own. I doubt that I would add any major thoughts save for around the edges. She only needs a witness to her journey. I'd be honored to watch and listen. And I'd be growing in the process also.

Chapter Eight

The Eisenhower Center

We are at our typical morning breakfast, sitting in a silence given birth by the stunning revelations of the last few days. Each of us occasionally sighs as pictures and words filter through our minds. We are certainly the very opposite of cheery tourists eating at the same time in fast food restaurants on Buckeye a few miles away near I 70. A seriousness beyond normal seriousness reigns as we both consider the life of Ezra Loew and the hideousness of the Holocaust, the tragedies Sarah experienced, and our newly developing personalities.

Silence is not unknown in that kitchen. This quiet is different because, in addition to our seriousness, there seems to be a measure of excitement in our bodies - certainly in mine. We are on to something - in more ways than one. Mysteries are being solved. Old delusions are being evaporated. New understandings are liberating our minds. Another minute current, down near the bottom of the river of experience, is running along due to an encounter with a most interesting companion, a fellow searcher, one that is different in terms of quality of soul than anyone previously encountered. Soul is not a gift of birth. Rather, it arrives as an unknown bonus by overcoming traumas in the hall of tragedy.

I break the silence. "Isn't it strange how the Eisenhower Center is rather invisible? It, too, is like so much of our lives: somewhat hidden. It houses private suffering as well as accomplishment by a President, and yet, it is relatively unknown."

"Are you starting the day being philosophical, Dan? I recall you seeing all manner of similarities yesterday in the journeys of one

Sarah Anne Bannock, Daniel Michelson, and Ezra Loew. You must have a philosopher hidden beneath your architectural layer."

"Now that's funny. Me? A philosopher? Anything but. After the last few days of revelations, I feel more like a putz, a clod, a dimwit. I've had delusions of my previous thinking falling like rain. If it were not for your steadying presence, I'd be questioning both my sanity and my very identity."

"Before we get that far, Dan, let's head over to the Eisenhower. Interestingly enough, I know virtually nothing about it. In my time here I've shopped for food, gone to the library and plays, jogged, and then returned to the sanctity of this home and my garden. I didn't even know Ezra went to the Center. My naiveté, birthed through my being sunk into my own suffering, left me rather oblivious. I caught myself sighing for the twentieth time of the morning as I mention the Center, but it's a trip we must take. Otherwise, we'll never understand Ezra and, also, never understand ourselves. The truth is that Ezra Loew materially informs both of our identities… is, in fact, a partial father to both of us."

Ignoring her words to leave the house and looking pensive, I respond humorously, "I don't think of you as my sister, Sarah. Let's cancel that thought. Anyway, I have an epiphany. This is tornado country. Maybe the swirl in our minds is due to our being blown away to Nebraska. We may not be in Kansas anymore, Dorothy."

"No, Tin Man, we are in the process of finding you a new heart. As for me, Dorothy, while I'm weary of the chaos, I, too, must re-affirm the real world and find a new - this sounds strange to my ears - measure of joy. The Yellow Brick Road to the Eisenhower Research Center is a strange way to find that, but I believe it necessary."

"Joy. That's a novel concept. Not sure I understand or have experienced that one. Furthermore, I'm the man without a heart or brain, and am just in search of normality - or at least what I've thought of as normality - a new normal will be okay also."

"I knew joy once, but it may have been encased in an illusory world. When with my kids, though, it was real. I want the experience back even if it is but for minutes. Actually, I've had moments in the garden here ... with butterflies and even tomatoes! My favorite line in poetry is by Wordsworth: 'surprised by joy, restless as the wind'."

I respond, "I'm the Tin Man and the Straw Man going through motions without the emotions. I haven't learned to skip yet like they did on the Yellow Brick Road."

"It's interesting that you left out the Cowardly Lion. And that's what both of us need today - courage to face the starkest reality in the history of mankind - the Holocaust. The only way to find our courage is to study the documents at the Eisenhower Center."

We silently walk, without skipping, the few blocks to our destination.

I see how the Dwight David Eisenhower Center is easily missed by travelers on I 70 who stop for a meal and a motel in Abilene. You must traverse the main drag for several miles, go through the old town, cross railroad tracks and venture South two blocks until you arrive at a fairly modern set of buildings - quite unlike the rest of the city. Only tourists and educators in search of historical material venture to the Eisenhower, plus a few old history buffs. No mere commuter on the Interstate bothers because Abilene is seven hours from Denver and another three from Kansas City. The small town is in the middle of the vastness of the American plains and travelers are not prone to become curious tourists. Paris it is not. Abilene represents a hot meal, an overnight at a motel, a quick breakfast, and driving on to one of the larger cities East or West.

I think the Center is worthy of heavy concentration, however. Researchers looking for old models that might help more modern situations go there and study. And, certainly, my father Ezra Lowe thought it worthy of seven years of his advanced life. Sure, Abilene is a good place to hide and forget, but no one who enters the Eisenhower Library is allowed the luxury of forgetting or hiding from the maelstrom of human insanity. Viewing the ugly horror of war does not encourage gabby tourist talk. Among other things the Eisenhower is a place to remember what it was like for the American army to encounter the vicious murdering and murderers of the Holocaust.

While walking to the Center, I have another sudden thought: "Maybe, Sarah, my father only planned to be here in Abilene several years. Then, you came along. What started as a compassionate act by having you become his housekeeper migrated into his amazement as you began to heal - something he'd been unable to accomplish. I get from his letter that he began to become partially alive as he watched you. You became his secret teacher in how to climb out of Hell. There is no need for you to comment."

I see Sarah reflecting on what I said and then she made a very telling comment: "It's fascinating to think that Dante took us into the receding levels of hell - I studied his book while living here - but we've had no equivalent book taking us out of the depths. Ezra and I knew the lower reaches, and, though your journey was not as sharply horrific, it, too, had its hell." She threw her insight out almost casually. I think it weighty.

Upon entering the Eisenhower, we identify ourselves as relations of a frequent visitor, Ezra Loew, who had just died. We obtain permission to enter the tightly restricted research area, receive explanations of rules of the room, and sign papers that allow us to study for the day. The archivist said she was not as familiar with the deceased as her predecessor who had just retired due to illness, but she knew that Ezra studied Holocaust material. We are ushered to an area dealing with Nazi phenomena and settle into oak chairs. Though the furniture is solid enough, we are about to be shaken by colossal material that makes any human's mind perilously close to absolute madness. We bravely divide the work before us. Sarah studies the origins of the Nazi period installed in Hitler's massive Mein Kampf (*My Struggle*) while I study pictures and accounts of Eisenhower's encounter with concentration and death camps. We sit beside each other at a three foot wide, four foot long Formica topped table.

We become absorbed in our tasks. Sarah finds herself distracted, however, by my rapid riffling through the gruesome pictures of dead and starving stick-like figures staring blankly and almost unbelievingly at Army cameras.

Sarah whispers: "Slow down, Dan. We need to let it all sink in, ghoulish though it is. We must understand the real journey of your father. There is no way we can do it if we do the rapid tourist trek through these materials. It goes against our very bodies and minds to absorb this, but we must. We can stand it. Neither of us have had such vast losses and enormous tragedy as did Ezra. He managed to cope; so, too, shall we. I suggest you use his magnifying glass and look as if searching for family members among the dead."

She startles me, but with a quiet library voice, I say "You're right on all counts. I am so shocked by it all that I had begun, unconsciously, to shut it all out with mere glances and an all too short attention span. My gut does not want to heed your advice; I know I have to. I'll slow down and let it sink in even though my mind is shrieking at the raw insanity and utter inhumanity of it all. I shall study as never before."

After a few minutes, I have a stirring revelation. I covertly whisper: "Sarah, I've been stung by a radical thought, a tangent of what I'm studying. As an architect, I've designed multiple school buildings that are all built on concrete slabs. None have basements. Is that a metaphor of my shallowness? I hope not. My normal successful Chicago image has left me oblivious to human suffering. I drive by ghetto buildings and never blink. My entire pathway through life has been one of relative luxury."

"Hush, Dan. Make no grand generalizations about yourself. Read. Study the photographs. We are both on unplanned journeys. We'll both have disturbing insights. Right now, neither of us should reject the material as our minds are prone to do. We must seek to absorb the horror as much as we are able, though, I have no doubt that we'll fail due to our own finitude and limited experience. This study is a way to honor your father and, as much as we can, grow to be deeper and more compassionate persons ourselves."

I study her and am again amazed - stunned by her wisdom, hard-won as it has been. I'm also shocked by the shattering of all my previous prejudiced views of women. Sarah is like no one I've ever met. I return to my study with a sigh that actually covers several experiences at the moment.

Though we're separated by only two feet of desk, I find myself leaning in her direction. It also seems she is leaning my way. Maybe it's for the sheer comfort and nurture of knowing a supporting soul is nearby. I'm beginning to suspect that, for me, it's something else.

Later, as we walk back the mile or so to home, Sarah refers to notes she made.

"Hitler had killing Jews in mind from the very beginning: that puts another shock on this unimaginable abysmal tragedy. I wrote down several quotes from chapter two of Mein Kampf which was dictated in prison in 1925 to Rudolf Hess, who, in the 1940's, became commander at Auschwitz . Hitler has been self-righteously analyzing the decay of Christian values in Vienna and said a moral poison was everywhere destroying the grand character of the German people. The source of all the decay was obvious to Hitler: international Jewry. He writes that his position on anti-Semitism had come slowly because he was first friendly to Jews, but 'cold reason' finally won out and he 'realized' that Jews showed no resemblance to 'real' Germans. 'Zionists' were ruining the state.

"The source of all the profligacy was clear to Hitler who said: 'If you cut even cautiously into such an abscess, you found, like a maggot in a rotting body, often dazzled by sudden light - a kike!' He calls Jewish activity 'a spiritual pestilence worse than the Black Death of olden times, and the people (Germans) are being infected by it.' Hitler continues: 'Nine-tenths of all literary filth, artistic trash, and theatrical idiocy can be set to the account of hardly one hundredth of the country.' Germany had become infested with 'foreign inhabitants.' "The conclusion of chapter two of Mein Kampf provides a grand politicizing self-righteousness that convinced the Lutheran and Catholic German people: 'Hence today I believe that I am acting in accordance with the will of the Almighty Creator: by defending myself against the Jew, I am fighting for the work of the Lord.'"

"Sarah, that is appalling. And it was dictated and released in 1925! Amazing. Years ago I read in a book by Erich Fromm that Hitler and the Nazi's portray what Fromm calls 'necrophilism'. By that he means they were intrigued by putrification and death. In what you quoted about abscess, maggots, rotting bodies, and pestilence, Fromm appears correct. It's beyond sickening. My tendency is to spare you what I learned today."

"Don't take care of me, Dan. I can stand it, though - to be truthful - I'm not sure anyone not actually there has or will ever be able to mentally grasp the violent sickness of what happened. Still, tell me what you learned."

"Eisenhower was no dummy. He knew that some future writers whom he called 'bastards' would seek to deny the reality of the Concentration and Death Camps. He told General George Marshall in a letter that he went into every space of the first camp (Ohrdruf) his army liberated in order to brand his brain with the horrific insanity of it all. Ike viewed corpses, saw a fire pit where the Germans had partially burned bodies with big burning logs, viewed open graves, and looked at the hollow staring eyes of the stick-like survivors. Furthermore, he had the entire populace of Gotha (Golgotha?), the nearby town, tour the camp so they 'd see the stacks of 4000 dead bodies machine-gunned by the SS before they fled. Ike made the citizens smell the stench, and see what their immoral silence had perpetuated. When the Gotha mayor and his wife returned home after the concentration camp tour, they hung themselves. The shame was too much. I found Eisenhower's treatment of the townsfolk, and having photographers take a number of pictures, very prescient and wise. In one fell swoop he obliterated the nonsense of later Holocaust deniers. I've never encountered this story before. He called for editors of British and American newspapers to come, make notes, and take graphic pictures.

"I also learned that at another camp Eisenhower had the dead bodies stacked on trucks and driven through that local town making the inhabitants view what their Nazi philosophy had wrought. Ike had no tolerance for lies. He wanted all to know what Hitler had done with the subtle permissive silence of the German people.

"The Holocaust collection at the Eisenhower Center also contained three incredible pictures of what Ike did with the citizens of Nuremberg. In shallow pine boxes with no lids and borne on thick broomsticks, women and men of the town were forced to carry these decaying bodies to a cemetery a mile and a half away. German women in elegant Sunday attire with stylish hats, nice coats and dresses, silk hose and black shoes grasped the wooden broomsticks and carried these open pine boxes with their faces only inches away from the corpses. Men carrying the caskets were dressed in Homberg hats, wore suits, and dress shoes. Frequently two women were at the front of a casket and two men held up the rear. Pictures taken by the 166th Signal Corps are dramatic. The cortege was a mile long. Deniers of the Holocaust seeing those photographs cannot avoid truth.

"Further, Eisenhower set up detention centers for captured German soldiers in which he punished them by refusing to give them the rights of the Geneva Conventions. He created a new term: 'Disarmed Enemy Forces'. He refused to call them Prisoners of War which granted certain privileges. It appears that several thousand of the interred 'enemy forces' died of starvation and exposure due to the conditions. The General specified that there would be no building of barracks to shelter them.

"I also read an account of a Death Camp Kommandant's wife who viewed tattoos on prisoners. If she saw a tattoo she liked, the prisoner was immediately killed, skinned, and the skin stretched for a lamp shade or a wall hanging for her. This story was verified by Eisenhower's army. Is that sick or not?

"Sarah, it's so mentally exhausting. No words can describe what went on. The word 'shock' is all too limiting as are words like 'mind-boggling' and 'soul wrenching'. No one can phrase the mass murders appropriately. I find myself emotionally depleted. I want to protect you from the horror."

"I want to protect both of us" was all Sarah can muster at the moment.

"Here's a new piece of information, Sarah. I found the name of a person I suggest we see tomorrow: Janet Hocking. She recently retired from the Eisenhower Center due to major illness. Janet was the archivist who supplied materials to Ezra. I'm told that she was familiar with his research. We'll call her and see if she will meet with us."

Upon reaching our home, neither of us were interested in food that evening. Silence is the only remedy. I'm back to my familiar chair on the porch, covering myself with the blanket and shawl, and stare into the distance. I listen to Mozart on Dad's iPod, Mozart, with his rational rhythms, brings sanity back to life. Sarah loses herself in her garden just in order to feel the substance of dirt and flowers. She pulls weeds with a vengeance, quite unaware of her actions. Our day together will never be forgotten.

****

Therapeutic Analysis

As was said above. there are no words that can spell out the horror of the Death Camps. Silence is all. Even walks through the Holocaust Museum in Washington D.C. - shockingly real though they are, cannot capture the experience of the Hitler years in Germany, the loss of one million Jewish children, five million Jewish adults, millions of Gypsies, physically and mentally handicapped individuals, Poles, Serbs, Russians and others: over 20 million in all. We should not be seduced by a number and mathematically pass over them too quickly: they are innocent humans killed by brutal Nazi overlords.

Man's inhumanity to man reached its ultimate depth in the Death Camps. Those living by the words "Never Again" and "Bear Witness" seek to convey to all people, especially those in power, that we must ever be on guard against another Hitler. Lord Acton was correct about power corrupting; he could have gone further and said "When an egomaniacal Narcissist gains absolute power, the world is in danger."

***Emotions**: The reactions of both Dan and Sarah appear exactly appropriate. There are times when sadness and anger merge and people are left paralyzed. What can be done in the face of such evil? Yes, the Nazi phenomenon is past; the question is how to use daily activities, small though they be, to thwart future Hitlers. Further, it is the greatest of all ironies that an encounter with the reality of death - for those dedicated to human betterment - actually sparks a greater drive to work for love. As was said earlier, knowing one will die makes the creative urge increase all the more.*

Our first duty as citizens is to be on the alert lest some new Hitler emerge, because, no matter what we may wish, egomaniacal Narcissists seek power in every country in the world. They should not be allowed to grace a high public office. Unfortunately, they do.

***Therapeutic option**: A minister once quoted the Bible's first sentence about God creating the world. The sermon continued that, if one wants to identify with the life of God, the thing to do is engage in creative pursuits. Dan had that in his architectural practice; Sarah was creative in terms of flowers, gardening and cooking. All those engaged in creative pursuits know, perhaps secretively, that when lost in pursuit of creating something new, all questions of meaning and meaninglessness flee. Creativity seems to be a redemptive option Ezra did not know. The rest of us common folk who want full lives need to especially mark the knowledge that creativity frees. The human spirit begins to die when the creative urge is quiescent. As therapist, I frequently recommend artistic pursuits.*

The final line is that the destructive force of Hitler's merciless bombers that almost eradicated a small Spanish town and its inhabitants was brilliantly countered by the creative thrust of Picasso's painting - Guernica. In other words, the death force of mortido must be countered by man's drive to create - the life force: libido. Thus, it is a matter of urgency that humans who have experienced the violent disruption of extreme trauma turn to some form of art. Art plus love are the only long term solutions to the destructive instinct. In addition, art solves boredom. Again, Art is the answer in Edvard Munch's painting The Scream - the raw encounter with human suffering.

Creativity involves both left and right brains, both structure and dynamic flow, both strict adherence to intelligible form and the full play of individual inclinations. I cannot emphasize enough, as a therapist, the value of creative involvement. If lost in the labyrinths of a mind stunned by major trauma, a prominent path to sunlight happens to be the sinking of one's hands and minds in Art.

Thus, those who desire soul freedom, learn to paint, shape clay into pots, twist metal into new shapes, write poetry, articles or books, carve wood, design floral arrangements, cook creatively, re-do landscaping, play with graphics or whatever. The idea is to splash color, twist hard material into new shapes, or even string beads into new arrangements.

Or, and I say this sarcastically, one can mute the creative spirit and take a load of pills like modern drug therapy has it or live on the edge of alcoholism.. More honestly, creativity is an avenue of choice for those seeking soul redemption. It should be uppermost in the quiver of therapeutic options.

As therapist, I'd have these reflections as I deal with either Sarah or Dan in sessions. After the quieting of feelings and thoughts of their encountering the horror of evil, I'd set the stage for the inevitable questions of what makes sense. Everything seems so small in the light of immense tragedies.

In other words, therapy is a journey. Sometimes the therapist just paces along and holds the hand. Sometimes you clarify. Sometimes you confront. Sometimes you ask emotion or value-laden questions. And sometimes you introduce a very redemptive options like turning to creativity. That one should never be minimized because it provides daily meaning. Hopefully, one's creative work will spark someone else to create, thereby showing a fellow sufferer a way out of despair.

Nevertheless, in order to have a full life, one must create. Must.

***Values.** Let there be no mistake about it: Auschwitz and the other Death Camps provide the scales by which all human values are measured. Values that are meaningful and soul-fulfilling are the very opposite of what occurred in the Nazi Camps. If one fails to 'get' Auschwitz, the reality is that he may fail to understand what is important and worth doing. Lives built around beauty, truth, justice, goodness and love are value* *oriented. None of those existed in the Death Camps. Knowing and learning about the Camps intensifies a person's commitment to what is finally redemptive to humanity.*

Surely, each of us had mini-Auschwitz moments across the years when we saw inhumanity to others. Racism. Sexism. Human cruelty. Verbal child abuse. Political corruption. Greed. I won't list the entire list of human evil that invites each of us to wake up. The point is that each occasion we witness such distressing events, we are invited to know what is meaningful and worth doing - working for justice, being kind, telling the truth and being honest, making the world more beautiful, and living a life of love. In other words, ordinary events of life propel us to ethics. That is, unless we are lost in some form of Narcissism.

So: Should we, like Dan and Sarah, have the courage to view the horrors of the forties? It takes courage.

The answer is that we should if viewing the apex of mortido (death principle) impels us to give our lives to libido (the Life Principle.)

Chapter Nine

The Archivist's Story

At the appropriate hour Sarah and I arrive at a small dignified single level house several blocks east of Buckeye. Answering the door is a woman bent with the ravages of advanced arthritis. Janet Hocking is barely able to walk. With slow movements of her arms, she invites us in to a well-kept home. We sit on a couch facing her. She sits in a rocking chair that allows her some movement. Her voice is strong and authoritative.

"I want you both to know that confidentiality has been the hallmark in all my years at libraries and the Eisenhower Library in particular. If there is no respect for the privacy of the reader, my belief is that the very foundation of freedom is destroyed. So agreeing to speak to you about the reading habits of Ezra Loew puts me on edge."

I answer her. "As a son who first saw his father lying in a plain wood coffin at the funeral home, I confess that all this - everything here in Abilene about his life - is absolutely new to me. I never knew Ezra, never saw him, never talked with him and never heard from him. My mother always said he was a good man, but she never went beyond that. Now I have his will, his home - in conjunction with Ms. Bannock here - and all I have left are questions. It's literally true that I'm desperate to know the truth about his life and interests."

"What did the other archivists tell you at the Eisenhower Center?"

"Only that he worked with you during his time here in Abilene. You supplied him with materials and taught him how to access computer data. They said he was the most faithful researcher ever in the history of the institution. They also said you might be able to explain what he studied more than they could and add details of which they were unaware."

"I can tell you far more than that, but I am being wracked by my conscience because nothing like this has ever arisen before. For my own integrity, I must do what is right."

Sarah spoke. "I'd ask for one further step, Ms. Hocking. Our search for the truth is out of utmost respect for Ezra Loew and, indeed, for his son. An absent father leaves a torrent of questions: 'Did he love me? What was he like? How can I know if he was a good man?' If you will read the letter Dan received just yesterday found in a security box at the bank vault, you'll understand why we are here requesting your help."

Janet Hocking put on her reading glasses, sat back in her rocking chair, and read quietly. She appeared moved, but with the characteristic reserve of a longtime librarian, muted her response. "I see he ends with the suggestion that you learn more from the archivist at the Center."

Sarah continues, "That's right, Ms. Hocking. Researchers there led us to you. Be assured that our quest is honorable. There is no way anything we will do will sully, in the slightest degree, the honor of either you or Dan's father, Ezra Loew. Your vow of confidentiality is honored by us. We simply need to know the truth - wherever it leads."

"The whole truth as I know it?"

"Yes, Ms. Hocking. Everything," I respond.

Janet Hocking studies us both long and hard. Her internal struggle appears over. “Then you shall get it, knowing up front, that there is a difference between hard facts and my subjectivity. I’ll tell the story and you can edit it in your minds later, as you will.”

“Agreed. We are grateful for whatever you will tell us.”

“Ezra Loew was the strangest researcher I ever encountered. All superlatives are appropriate: ‘most’ chief among them. He was the most sober, the most serious, the most intense, the most dedicated, the most ... I could go on and on. When he asked for materials, he was gracious but never friendly - if you grasp the difference. I provided him with Holocaust files and photographs of Eisenhower’s soldiers liberating several concentration camps. In addition, he studied material from the National Archives on the research room computer. Day after week after month after year. He even had me order materials from all over the world for his study of the Holocaust. He’d be there when we opened and stay until closing time. He sat in the same place in the same chair, spoke to no one, and did not even pause to get a drink of water from the fountain. He was totally self-contained and absorbed. Naturally I was curious, but it was not my place to ask questions. He offered no explanations, either. Ezra was like a piece of furniture: silent all day long, eyes focused on what he was reading, and so unmoving one might think him a wax figure.

“He did have one characteristic and I confess to you that I thought it almost masochistic. He poured over the gruesome pictures from places such as Auschwitz, Treblinka, Maeterlinck, Buchenwald and the rest. He stared at them through his magnifying glass as if he was looking for old lost friends, family, or, maybe, just so he could imprint his mind with the inhuman viciousness of Nazi atrocities. I imagined all manner of things as he studied, eye to a magnifying glass, week after month after year.

"Was he seeking to salve his conscience about hating them so? Had he participated in killings of his own? I knew that he also was fascinated by articles about the French Resistance. He had me search through our library for any pictures of the resistors. He read famous authors like Camus, Malraux and Sartre who participated in the secret fight against the Nazis. There were no explanations coming from Mr. Loew about what he was doing. My fantasies went all over the place ... though, you must know ... I, as an archivist, seldom engaged in anything but cataloging and supplying sheer data. Still, what was the man doing? How could he stand it? What was he getting out of looking at stacks of dead bodies, crematoria, emaciated prisoners, Nazi guards, German prisoners, barbed wire enclosures, and all the rest? It baffled me. Now, with your father's letter, I understand a bit more. It's all so tragic. No words reach the reality.

"While I am not a morbid person, I - at times - wondered if I'd led a life of pampered privilege. Did I have anything of the dimension of depth personified by Ezra Loew? My answer was an accusing 'No.' Was I seduced by the nice life of Abilene and unwilling to view the essence of evil portrayed in the photographs Ezra daily studied? Probably. How shallow was I? Had I not read Camus and the other French Resistors? I've read All Quiet on the Western Front, War and Peace, Night and Fog, The Nazi Doctors, and a host of concentration camp memoirs. Dostoevsky's Notes From the Underground was a personal favorite of mine in understanding dark times. I read every book of Primo Levi. Personally speaking, I'm no total neophyte in terms of human evil and human suffering.

"Still, I felt like a naïve child in his presence. His absorption in such gruesome material led me to question my own identity, my religion, my personal thoughts about what is valuable in life. He could stare into the abyss, unblinking and immovable, day after day. His intensity and silence went on interminably in my research department. His eyes spoke volumes: war, death, suffering, murder, insanity - and yet, he was sane! He could focus on the black hole of evil with those penetrating eyes and not even blink at the hideousness of it all. Though I tried, I could not ignore his presence. The man un-nerved me and, if you study me closely, you will see that nothing like that had ever happened before. I'd go home somewhat depleted.

"And yet, first thing the next morning, there sat Ezra Loew. His deep, dark eyes spoke more than all my books. His depth was beyond - infinitely beyond - all my reading and experiential knowledge. I don't know how he could keep all of the material in his mind. I'd have gone crazy. What gave him any hope whatsoever? Was there any love in the man's life providing a foundation I could not understand? What made him tick? I was lost in his presence, utterly baffled and aghast at his concentration. Nothing had prepared me for the man. And his haunted eyes were always there searching. I avoided them. They were too intense for me. I confess: his eyes scared me. Gave me chills.

"Years went by. One day not too long ago I noticed a very slight change. He seemed to awake from a coma. He heard the laughter of a child when someone raised a window. Next door to our research section there is a playground that draws children from blocks away. Ezra went to the window, observed them for awhile, and it was like a sudden inspiration captivated him. I might add that up to that point there was absolutely no muscle in his body suggesting he'd ever even been a child.

"He then added a new ritual just before I retired ... several months ago, in fact. He'd study for several hours, go down the steps to the lower floor, go out the door and stand near the playground. He was like a dark marble statue in a black coat standing there. Motionless. Well, not exactly motionless because he'd turn his head to watch children run and express themselves. I could not see his eyes, but I could see that his body, with an almost indefinable micro-shift, came partially alive. Maybe it was that he began to breathe more. The children themselves were mindlessly and joyously expressing themselves; running, sliding, twirling, swinging, playing ball and going up and down on the seesaws. They moved and breathed and made the sounds of unleashed freedom. They also paid no attention whatsoever to their silent observer.

"From my office on the second floor, I watched him where he could not see me. Just his standing by the playground, doing nothing other than observing, went on for weeks. Then there was another change that startled me - shakes me to this day. Tucked between two of our buildings is a covert area where yard men store their equipment. From another window in my corner office I could see the interior of the storage area which was about thirty feet by fifty feet. I might say that my window overlooking this yard was occluded from the storage area itself due to being covered by vines and leaves. It was the only window in any building allowing sights of the courtyard. One day I saw Ezra take out a huge nail from a hinge at the gate, go in and investigate the space.

"The next part of this story is ... even with you two I must underline it again ...confidential and beyond comprehension. Ezra would watch a particular child, go over to the equipment storage area, re-lock the gate behind him, and ... how do I say this? ... seek to imitate the child. Without making a sound where he might be heard or discovered, he'd bend and weave his body as if he were laughing. Or, on another day, this deadly serious man would seek to skip like a little girl he just viewed on the playground. The full extent of the expressions he watched the children perform, he sought to copy. Or he would act as if he was running to catch a ball. He was like an elderly arthritic (me!) seeking to move after years of being immobilized in a chair. When he tried to dance, I caught tears running down my face because it was so tragically beautiful or beautifully tragic. He held his arms out as if holding someone and stumbled through dance moves.

“I hurt in my chest and heart even as I tell you this. As I watched him, I - a cold-hearted, cold-blooded research archivist - a specialist in words, became utterly speechless and intrigued.

“At one level all the man’s attempts were absurd. At another level, incredibly funny. At still another pathetically sad. It was like watching a cocooned chrysalis struggle to become a butterfly. A fully grown man was seeking to become an expressive child again! He wanted spontaneity in his repertoire and sought to get it back. Using a different metaphor, it was like witnessing a man frozen in a large block of ice seeking to break his way out. If he saw two kids argue, he’d enter the enclosure and switch roles mouthing a noiseless ’No!’ He’d then switch to an equally expressive, but still unspoken, ’Yes.’ If he watched a child run, he’d seek to run. If a boy swung a baseball bat, Mr. Loew would clumsily swing an invisible bat ... all in his utterly secretive enclosure where he thought no one could see. I even found myself feeling guilty for observing him.

“Coming back into the research room, his demeanor returned to his researching mode. There was no sign indicating his seemingly therapeutic exploits in the storage area. He said nothing to me and I most assuredly said nothing to him. Besides, he did not know that I had intruded in his privacy by peeking through the small aperture at the window over the construction area. Ezra Loew returned to his research and I returned to my other duties as if nothing whatsoever had happened.”

I stare at her with tears rolling down my cheeks and finally find words to speak.

“That, Ms. Hocking, is the most amazing story I’ve ever heard in my life. And it was my father! In his old age he was seeking to come alive again. This was my father. He was trying. I’m so proud of him. He did not give in to cynicism and despair. He refused to let the insanity of Hitler dominate his life. He was not just a morbid old man. He was not simply an assassin or murderer as he thought of himself for so many decades. He was a man trapped in the quicksand of history who sought, by any means possible, to pull himself out of the muck.

I'm exultant. "I'm so appreciative to you, Ms. Hocking, for telling us this story. My heart is full. It is amazing to me. It is as redemptive to me as all the horror has been dismaying. It says something about the human spirit that cannot, will not, be quenched or silenced. I want to cry aloud. I also want to swing my arms, skip, shout for joy and be like a child on a playground. But then, my social conscience kicks in, and I fear I'm being too expressive. Forgive me."

Before Ms. Hocking spoke, Sarah interrupts: "You are being real, Dan. Just real. I, too, find that I want to both cry and dance because, not only was Ezra freeing himself, he was also freeing me right within his home in a way I never discerned. Janet's story calls to mind something I had forgotten. When I worked in the garden behind the house, I'd feel eyes on me. Several times I saw him at the window studying me ... particularly when I paused and sought to identify where the song of a bird was coming from, or, say, was entranced by the imaginative flight of a butterfly, or would softly shoo away a bee. At that moment, he'd forget to hide and I'd see him for just the fraction of a second. I also caught him studying me when I'd look thoughtfully at an apple, carefully cut a tomato or washed each lettuce leaf from the garden. Do you think he was re-orienting himself in some manner?"

"I don't know what to think right now: my mind is overwhelmed," I reply to Sarah. "It's all too much to assimilate right now. I need time to think this through. Absorb it. Feel it. Dance with it. Cry with it."

Janet Hocking looks at us intently and says: "Listen you two love birds, I've shared the story and it is time for me to take my nap. If you have further questions, call. We'll arrange a time."

We both profusely thank her, being careful to not squeeze her arthritic hands too tightly. We want to hug her, pick her up and swing her around, but know that such emotionality is not indicated due to Ms. Hocking's physical condition. Or, for that matter, her professional archivist image. We leave with waves of our hands hoping that our grateful eyes express what we both feel in our hearts.

Janet Hocking's phrase "love birds" echoes in our ears as we depart, though neither of us pick up on it. Before a hundred steps were taken, each of us seem to lose the melody of love, first heard, in the old archivist's words. As for me, I'm visualizing Ezra Loew seeking to break the armor locked in his musculature, armor that went back to his childhood encounter with the Nazi's. Combining all our knowledge together with that of Ms. Hocking is so shockingly stunning that silence embraces us both, as does the cool of the evening on our walk home. I'm aware of Sarah in a new way (my partner!), though I say nothing aloud. It's silence time again, but acceptable silence time. Thinking time. Absorbing time. Appreciative time. I want to hold her hand but I restrain myself.

****

Therapeutic Analysis

Before any analytic comments, it is necessary to pause and consider Death Camp experience lest any reader run by it too quickly. Let's use our imagination, paltry though it happens to be. Imagine that you are the one with the yellow star, captured and put in Auschwitz with your parents. The guards think of you and treat you as less than human and can kill you at a moment's whim. You witness your parents stripped and humiliated and then pushed into a line headed for live extermination in a crematorium. Hours later you smell the remains of your parents in heavy stinking smoke covering the camp.

You are put in a barracks and given a flea infested bunk. Hope has gone out of the eyes of emaciated prisoners around you. No escape seems possible. You are doomed. Nazi guards look for an occasion, at random, to kill. Snarling dogs walk along the perimeter of your encampment. You are powerless. Beatings occur randomly. Your projected end is a heinous meaningless death. Any show of identity means certain death. There is no music, no books, no Nature, no entertainment, no joy. Fish head soup provides your food. All around you is death and its rotting smells. As for smell, imagine a hundred pound slab of meat rotting in your living room for months and months. How does this affect your mentality for the remainder of your life?

A Philosophical Point: *I contend that the Holocaust provides a test of our awareness of human evil. Evil is and it will remain. Why is a test important? The reason is that a full encounter with evil and death compel us to squeeze the utmost out of life. Otherwise we may dream along and fritter away the years. And decades. And fourscore and ten. If ignored, the horrors of the Holocaust can lead to idle Narcissism. The Holocaust shouts out its irrationality of death and says: "Live! Live for us! Use your* *energy to help others to live!" Thus, there is an identity issue and a life mission issue. "Who am I?" needs to include "I am post-Holocaust." As for mission, "I am post-Holocaust and have a duty to mankind to see this never happens again."*

Despite the shouting immorality from the Death Camps for all of us to awaken, I must proceed with analytic considerations. So, I turn on my Analyst brain and add thoughts about personal psychology.

***Script Considerations**. Is it obvious how Ezra's Unconscious secretly programmed a major part of his adult life? His adaptations, given birth by the Nazi years programmed much of his later life. Play was outlawed. Bodily expression was limited. His survival in the camp made him non-expressive. Even with Amelia, Ezra managed to be objective and analytical. Silent and thoughtful. He did not, until his moments in the storage area, achieve moments of freedom of being. His Script was anchored like many others caught in the net of Nazi violence. This stark and beautiful lesson is one for us all. It shows what must be accomplished in order to re-gain the spontaneity of a child.*

I'm hesitant to deal with Ezra's psychological issues. The reason is that I honor survivors who make the steps they do to accomplish whatever freedom they gain. I mean no negative judgment by being analytical. Survivors were not heirs to the information I share here, information developed by my sifting through a century's psychoanalysis. My task in this book is to explain matters that will aid the next generation of those who experience severe trauma. Using Ezra's story is therefore justified.

***Major Lesson**: Liberal members of every religion born of Father Abraham (Judaism, Christianity, and the Muslim Faith) have long since ceased belief in life after death, some wondrous respite in a heaven above with golden streets, bowls of ambrosia and everlasting bliss. Followers do not, however, discard the entire* *mythology, if, by that, one means helpful human stories and primary metaphors. The greatest ancient idea of them all is that individuals can be redeemed, re-born, resurrected. Humans can leave miserable failing lives and still have the opportunity to turn to vital meaning. Those lost in alcoholism, drug addiction, hatred, violence, criminality, emotional failure, and utter depravity of any sort still have a chance to become an authentic member of the human race - meaning the living of a life dedicated to beauty, truth, justice, goodness and love. If this were not true, therapy itself would be a cruel hoax, a farce perpetuated to gain income, a way to give shallow comfort.*

Sages say the awakened life is possible, but none say anything about it being easy. No priest, imam, pastor or rabbi phrases the hope of personal resurrection in a glib, careless, or saccharine manner. There are stations of the cross to be encountered. Other religions talk about the remodeling of the self copied along lines of noble forebears who awakened. There are mountains to climb, deserts to cross, oceans to traverse. Thus, the grand declaration from religious history is that hope is possible. Radical personal transformation is available. But any shallow tourist thinking the way simple needs to visualize Ezra in the storage area seeking to unlock the chains surrounding his body. He contorted, struggled with locked muscles, and sought to become as free and spontaneous as a child. What matters is not the level of his attainment; what matters is his devoted attempt to liberate himself.

***Dan's Therapy**: As for our hero Dan Michelson, the Ezra letters and Ms. Hocking's revelations have done their work. Dan now knows that his previous mental childhood formulations are shallow to the extreme. Reality unbound by fantasy has shaken him to the core. All his Poor Me thoughts across the years have crashed to the pavement and dissolved to pathetic nothingness. Changing the metaphor, his old armor was not only rusty and didn't suit him; it's blown away in the winds of history.*

***Emotions**: As mentioned before in terms of the guiding narrative, humans need mental software about what is valuable in order to have a story that guides their emotional and rational lives. The problem is when the Script is prompted by a second of scare. It is obvious now that Dan's old story about father abandonment was based on inaccurate information. The new story obtained in Abilene propels him to an altogether new emotional life. Ms. Hocking also provided one of the last blows to his urban hubris. She was not the local dumb belle of the generalizing sarcasm he possessed of all country women when he drove into Abilene. She was a person of great depth. All his Chicago superiority prejudices folded. He is ready to start feeling for real. And appreciating others for real. He is ready to listen. He is ready to re-learn people and life.*

***Script**: Long term psychotherapy is basically a re-writing of the pre-conscious narrative. I say "pre-conscious" because the person is only slightly aware of it. The Script narrative, however, is huge. It controls not only historical remembrances, but actually predetermines how one's life will advance to the future. The narrative is doused with values as to what is worth living for and dying for, whether and how much to risk love, how to raise or avoid kids, and even such seemingly arcane matters as one's health. Script informs other sensory matters such as touch (who and whom and how tenderly), sight (what is noted and considered worthy of attention), smell (food aromas or flowers, locker sweat or perfume), taste (hamburger or soy, cookie or fruit) and hearing (classical or modern music). The narrative covers everything from clothes to exercise. It is life-embracing and, when destroyed by reality, a cataclysmic re-ordering of effects are equally profound.*

At this point in the novel, both Dan and Sarah are hurriedly re-writing their stories in their minds. Mental computation is whizzing like a massive computer. This is real change at its greatest depth.

Finally, like Dylan Thomas' poem asking his dying father to not "go gentle into that good night" but "rage, rage against the dying of the light," Ezra had done just that. He raged against the glued viscera of his very body. The man of the Holocaust had tried to dance! This fact provides a key element of a new narrative that will last until Dan's last day and last breath. Like father, like son: he will "rage against the dying of the light." This is still another main ingredient in the narrative re-write: the last chapter.

Ezra Loew provides a model that will never be forgotten. When Dan comes to his end, he will still be seeking, in his own way, to affirm life.

What better example can any son want more than that?

Chapter Ten

Re-gaining Equilibrium

Eggs. Toast. Coffee. At first there's a continuation of the silence that has gripped and graced this home for many years. I'm feeling a new unspoken element, however, a kind of electricity moves in both Sarah and I. We seem afraid to look at each other, accidentally touch, or inadvertently have a sound in our voices that might imply what's going on in each of our brains, hearts and bodies. The unspoken reality is that I'm feeling a certain magnetism exceeding sexual attraction which, in and of itself - I guess - is but natural for any two vital individuals living in separate rooms in the same house. This particular magnetism, however, seems to be something more. My repressed feelings are not the unspoken emotions mid-life stirrings - the equivalent of a college graduate's senior panic. Though I am a highly sexual man, I am no vibrating teenager who simply wants a fling. Something larger is at work. I feel it. Again I say it: it's magnetic. And I think Sarah feels it also. Why else is she avoiding my eyes?

In just a few days colossal transformations have taken place for us both. I've been in a blender of awareness leaving me groggy, but more deeply at peace with myself than ever before in my life. I do not understand all that has transpired because it's simply too much to mentally process in such a short period of time. Certainly, the old patient deliberative one hour sessions of psychoanalysis provide me with no pattern that can unravel or explain the emotional blizzard engulfing me in just a few days in Abilene. How can I mentally process seeing my dead father, reading a transformative confessional letter that rips my heart out, visit the Eisenhower Center and view chaotic horror beyond any human's mind to understand, and then, of all things, hearing of my father's attempt to resurrect himself from the swamp of despair? And, on top of that, I've met the most amazing woman of my entire life. She has authentic soul ... in addition to other interesting features. I obliquely study her more closely. Smooth skin. Perfect shape.

I'm thinking that Sarah's many years of silence came to a sudden, almost threatening, closure. Her previous understandings of living with a kind old gentleman escalated to the point of appreciation of a Holocaust survivor who is miles beyond, in terms of soul, any human she's ever admired - in books or in person. I mind-read that she is still wondering if I'm in any way judgmental about her driving error and the death of her two beautiful children. If my thinking is correct, she'll never see negativity because I have none. I've taken it in with all the other tornado-like disclosures and placed it away from consciousness. I understand as a fellow human. Shit happens. Like my father, I have no sense of being a judge - now or ever . Events occur beyond our control and against all rules of logic; I know that all too well from my own life. Further, it's interesting that we have been thrown into the role of partners through a mutual inheritance. I must admit I hope she feels a magnetic attachment to me. God knows I do to her.

"Who will speak first?, " I'm wondering.

Facing the open refrigerator as she places the egg carton back on the shelf, Sarah casually asks: "So what is your suggestion as to how we spend the day or, for that matter, the next few days?"

Without looking up, I reply, "I feel the need to return to the Eisenhower Center. I want to review his entire trajectory through historical documents. I want to see what he ordered, from where, and the extent of his research. I wonder if he was looking for his relatives with the magnifying glass as he analyzed dead bodies. I want to visit Janet Hocking's office and view the playground from her vantage point as well as see the storage area from her covert peek hole. I also want to go outside and watch children play. You may think me crazy, but I hope I have the courage to copy them and not care what anyone thinks."

"That's not crazy, Dan. I think it's a beautiful idea. In fact. I'll join you if the occasion arises. We will not repress what is real: that's one of our new rules. Instead, we will express it. As to the study, I want to have the courage of you yesterday, and your father through time, in looking carefully and studiously at the concentration camp photos so bring the magnifying glass. I've never thought of myself as a courageous person. But to understand you, Ezra, and even myself, I think it a matter of duty for me to patiently and slowly analyze and absorb what evil in its raw form really is. If I am going to grow up and rid myself of remaining innocence, I simply have to do this."

"Sarah, these several days have hit me like an avalanche. I both don't know who I am anymore and also feel like, for the first time, I really know myself." Smilingly I add "It's like my Superego lacunae - my father brain hole - just got filled up! My head may be in a muddle, but at least my soul isn't empty now. As for any sense of forgiving Ezra for not being around in my life, that whole bitterly repeated scenario I rehearsed across the years seems centuries ago. The old narrative does not make any sense whatsoever anymore. The brash sarcastic cosmopolitan fop who arrived in Abilene has been buried here. You said I needed an attitude adjustment; at least part of that has occurred." Looking Sarah square in the face, I add, "I'm seeing everything and especially you in a new manner. Before meeting you, I thought you might be a gold digger. I now see ... I now see ... Whew.... Hey! The Library is open. Let's get on our way."

At the Eisenhower Center we immediately ask permission to see Ms. Janet Hocking's old office. That proves to be no difficulty. Each of us look out the larger window facing the playground and the small aperture overlooking the maintenance area. Curiosity sated, we return to the study table and settle into a half day's study of the gruesome, yet glaringly real, Holocaust material. Every human would desire to avoid the results of the Hitler philosophy; no honest and aware person can. We study. No sound escapes our mouths, but our bodies betray the tension of being confronted with the virtual insanity of what unveils before our eyes. "Sarah is my partner," I say to myself and really feel great in that knowledge.

We both look up when we hear, outside the reading room, the sounds of children laughing and playing. Without speaking a word, books and photos are closed and returned to the archivist. We walk down the staircase and proceed to the park.

Imitating our new model - my father and Sarah's benefactor - for a long period of time we stand erect and silently watch the children noisily flow around us. The kids exhibit joy released. Boys and girls mark our presence with only a slight flicker of attention and then they spontaneously burst in all directions. They run, squeal, skip, swing, slide, play ball, roll in the grass, taunt each other, shout encouragement in the games, jump rope ... and, with the utter lack of caring what others might think ... wildly dance. It's all so lovely - the total opposite of the dread documents in the archives next door. The children don't know of the utter madness of human cruelty and I'm very glad for that. The aggressive insane violence of Hitler has never been part of their lives and, if we all stay vigilant, never will be. The children have what they have and do what they do: freely play with utter abandon, doing what children of the world need to be allowed to do, "Oh how I wish my father had experienced what these kids experience" I say aloud to Sarah.

Sarah began to sway her body. I suddenly realize that she, too, must have stiffened herself when Lance and Laura died. The truth is that she, too, probably has some major un-freezing to do. Eight years ago she froze her childlike joy. She can run and jog through the Abilene neighborhood, but she isn't able to play freely like a child. In the light of what she's told me, I bet this is the first time she's looked at children for any length of time since the wreck a seeming lifetime ago.

While I perceive her movements, it's impossible to know the depth of her inner struggle. I suddenly take off skipping, though any objective witness would know that this thirty-eight year old man needs Olympic training and a trainer for that kid-like sport. Sarah spontaneously acts like an outfielder in a softball game, going about catching an imaginary fly ball. I see her and laugh, a free sound I've never heard from my own throat. My god. I'm changing. I feel more free.

I run in a jagged, twisting way in Sarah's direction. She responds by acting startled and runs away like a scared little girl. I catch her, throw my arms around her and am shocked as she looked up at me and says "May I have this dance?" We both giggle, twirl a few times and then fall to the ground. Suddenly, we're aware that the children are looking at us as if we are full blown loony. It doesn't matter. We roll around on the lawn until both of us became aware something is happening in the middle of our bodies. We are not actual children after all.

Helping each other up, I start to brush the grass and dust off my clothes, but Sarah says preemptively: "Leave it. We have some more child-learning to do." I look at her and don't say what was on my mind at that moment. Instead, we walk to the maintenance area, take the nail out of the hinge, and enter the storage area. We look up at the vine-covered window, wondered if anyone is looking, decide it doesn't matter, and kiss - languorously, fully, meaningfully. We hurry home for other matters to unfold.

We almost run to Sarah's room, hastily undress and embrace in a way only loving adults know. Moments later we make noises the old Victorian house is not accustomed to. To be sure, I certainly have genital attraction, but there is a deeper union born of leaving old dead narratives and being on the cusp of creating entirely new lives. I'm feeling tenderness waves never before experienced. Our afternoon lovemaking in her room encompasses the whole gamut: genital excitement, enormous respect for the other's journey (attitude and mental presence), plus a boundless sense of nurturing care for each suffering chapter of the other's painful past. This is soul closeness - mental union in addition to physical fulfillment. Lying back and looking at the ceiling, both of us appear to be in shock. We lock eyes knowing something miraculous has just occurred.

I chuckle aloud. "Sarah, that was so dynamic that electricity ran down my legs so powerfully I thought my toes would explode." Sarah joins me in laugher. "Next time we'll electrify your arms and hands."

"I can't wait. Sarah, on my first night here, I came close to offering the same private arrangement of physical distance my father made with you. If I had made that pledge, I'd be a miserable liar now, a man going back on a deal. I'm glad I kept my mouth shut. Now I not only want to avoid any stupid pledge about separate rooms, I want to give the couch to the Salvation Army. I guess we shouldn't act like newly weds on an Abilene honeymoon, but I no longer want to sleep in separate rooms."

Sarah said, "Shall I be coy? I'll forego that because sharing my room with you seems logical, correct, and fun. I know passions of the moment need to be measured over a long period of time lest emotion destroys wisdom. What we are feeling, however, needs to be followed to its ... conclusion. Beds are one thing; our longer journeys are something else again. Where do you think our spiritual quest goes from here?"

"We live in a different world from my father, different in the sense that we do not need to physically be here in Abilene near the Eisenhower Center in order to access data. We can get a host of documents on the Internet if that is where our focus lies. As to what we do, I have several recommendations. One, that we go to my home in Chicago, visit my old haunts and take a bit of a respite while getting some bearings. Our gyroscopes are out of whack. My brain and your brain need rest. Please notice that I mentioned 'brains' and not 'bodies' that also need resurrection. I have no idea how long a mental rest will take and don't really care."

I continue, "We need to see each other in different contexts and talk ourselves silly. There's a lot of your history I don't know and a lot of mine you don't know. I want to show you how I live, where I work, what I do for a living, and a city I love with all my heart. Second, I think that, after we recuperate a bit, we need to go to New York and meet with my Uncle Shlomo. I hope he can answer many of our questions. We must not forget that you are entitled to forty per cent of whatever assets Ezra left, most of which we have no idea as to what it is - maybe nothing. Who knows? Still, we must follow the journey as far as we can take it."

"Dan, I do not want to sell this Abilene house immediately, no matter what becomes of us or what we discover in Chicago and New York. The place means something to me. I found peace and acceptance here. I found a foundation of self I thought long gone. I'd hate to treat it just like an old house and sell it like antique junk. Further, I want you to know that I have no particular connection to Abilene, though I do not want you or myself to scorn it. People act according to the circumstances of their lives. It's not like they had adjoining columns with science on one side and religion on the other and they chose faith statements. They live by the information and values taught to them. Sheer rhetoric may become their reality. They should be opposed only when their systems are destructive to others. Besides, if I cannot accept these people for who they are, how can I ever expect others to accept me for my history and who I am?"

"Sarah, you may find it strange coming from a supposedly sophisticated Chicago modern architect, but I find something solidly pleasant and good about this home and this particular community also. It carries the aroma - is that the right word? - of my father and you. I have no shred of magical thinking about me, but his 'ghost' is here. I feel it. Or him. I like the porch and his chair, and I like sitting where he sat in the evening. As for the people of Abilene, it may take some time for me to eradicate the superiority stance I've had. So let's keep the place until I learn. Furthermore, I've become accustomed to eggs, toast, and coffee for breakfast. I also like your bed," I chuckle.

Looking me square in my eyes, Sarah says, "So we are in agreement about the house for now. As for Chicago, I want you to know that you are under no obligation to me, short term or long term. You can go by yourself if you wish; I can meet you in New York to listen to the additions of the story according to your uncle. I'm open to all options. I want to assure you that you are free as am I. No chains. No new compulsory rules. No niceness out of etiquette or some compulsory need to please me. You are free. I am free. It's choices and decisions from here on out."

"Whew. You are tough. Will you go to Chicago with me, stay at my home, and tour the various avenues of my life in a together, shared manner?"

"I will. Make the arrangements and we are on our way. Packing is unnecessary. I'm thinking that Abilene attire won't fit in too well in the big city. I'll need to buy appropriate clothing to walk down Michigan Avenue and in order to meet your friends and business associates. I'll also need to have my hair done when we arrive. Ask your secretary to make an appointment for me, will you?"

I text message Jill and have a reply a few minutes later. "You're on for Macy's on Michigan Avenue at 10:30. We can make it on time. I'll go to the office while you are getting your 'do' and we can arrange to meet afterwards so you can buy some clothes. As for right now I'm feeling relieved, happy, and excited - my shrink would be proud of me in this moment. I'm so glad we are going to Chicago together."

At my insistence we call and make arrangements to eat in the small tower room at the Kirby House. Part of me wants to see if I've been fooled by thinking that the food is excellent and the décor outstanding. Despite the utter romance of having a small well-appointed room all to ourselves … besides being entranced by Sarah … I find that I really love the excellently prepared food. This place is a novelty. It's also excellence in the middle of Kansas. I do look forward to our trip, however.

****

Therapeutic Analysis

Cascading down the waterfall of historical documents dealing with love, the torrent acknowledges sibling regard, motherly care, fatherly protection, neighborly concern, family devotion, erotic fascination and a host of other depictions. None ever reach the dynamism of true love and, certainly, neither shall these few words. This time around, the love experiment for Dan and Sarah appears quite different, though it does involve eroticism. They were beginning at the point of soul union though neither of them are capable of explaining the difference in flowing language. Each knows the other has a sense of justice and believes in supporting the good against the onslaught of evil. Each knows and respects the other's journey. For now, that is enough and, further, their wide knowledge contributes to their almost wild and free lovemaking.

***Therapeutic questions**: Viewing the attraction of Dan and Sarah I'll consider its long term chances. I'd want to know if they daily seek to live good lives given their information at the moment. Is there an abiding interest in matters of beauty: flowers, birds, driving clouds, laughing children, art, theater, music, sculpture, dance and all the rest? The main question is whether an attitude braced by appreciation is lodged in their minds. Do Dan and Sarah both have a sense of truth ranging from basic honesty to integrity in business and matters of science? Further, is the other capable and willing to be utterly trustworthy in terms of a bonding type relationship? Neither of them is like a teenager falling in love for the first time. A deep relationship needs examination.*

To tell the truth, matters of the heart and mind such as the above are probably on the periphery of Dan and Sarah's minds at the moment. They each know that the bottom line reality is that, post-Holocaust, if you don't think of deep soul in a partner, you haven't caught the lesson. Is Dan capable of that? Is Sarah? Soul partners are hard to find. As therapist, I ask dozens of questions.

***Sarah's personality**. I've not concentrated upon Sarah's psychology in these post-chapter additions as I have that of Dan. She has done remarkable work on herself in the last eight years, years since her Script crashed to earth with rather colossal tragedies. Though there were no therapy sessions, she availed herself of solid redemptive options like good literature, nature, awareness of her environment, and learning from a quiet, but caring, mentor.*

In the light of the silence between Ezra and Sarah, readers may ask if I had silent sessions. Yes. In fact silent phases happened quite frequently. In a few cases I saw people who came to a session and nothing was said. In one case that lasted ten straight times. It is important to know that this was not some kind of passive aggressive standoff. Rather, I sensed that the person was internally working and putting things together. My presence and the safety of the private setting - somehow - facilitated that. There were other occasions when, though no words were spoken on the surface, I had the sense that the client and I were having a sincere deeply real conversation. Sometimes it was like a secret chess match. I don't understand it, but I know my brain was tired at the end of the hour.

Silent phases were especially true when visiting dying patients in hospitals. It has never been my practice to chatter or make small talk in the face of death. Sometimes I sat there, held a person's hand, and said very little. I believe that was frequently the right thing to do. As said by poets, some matters are too deep for words.

In a sense, that is what Ezra did with Sarah. Though there was no touch, he psychologically held her hand for several years.

Therefore, I have no sense of thinking her trajectory of healing any less than that of Dan's appointments with his psychoanalyst. Different. No less effective. The criteria is in the outcome, not the method.

In this chapter of the novel Sarah melts some of the solidified repressions of the eight years of denying her childlike feelings stabilized in frozen musculature. Clients with similar traumas as that of Sarah often told me they thought their expression of happiness, was a betrayal of the departed. My guess is that Sarah felt she should not celebrate when her children were refused the wonderful years of childhood. I rejoice that she is getting free because she encountered someone (Ezra) whose suffering exceeded that of her own. Dan also helps with his lack of negative judgment.

It is notable to again remark that, after over a half century, Ezra refused to give up. He sought to dance. That is a miracle. The model of the former Holocaust survivor granted superb permission for Sarah to completely come back to full vital life. As was said at the end of the last chapter, Dan can never return to his old narrative. He now has a model. To ignore this new father input, input that he always wanted, would be to betray his father's suffering. Dan is too much of a human to do that. Sarah also has a new model to emulate.

Like other important matters of personal growth, major transformation takes time. No reader should think that one imitative session at a playground will unleash Dan and Sarah's bodies from old repressions. They'll have to play and dance until their muscles re-learn what kids do naturally.

As partners, now, there is a sense that they will accomplish what they set out to do. 'Hope springs eternal' as Matthew Arnold began his famous saying, but in Sarah and Dan's case, the end of the sentence is "we will be blessed because we are willing to work on it as much as it takes." What more can any therapist want in clients?

Chapter Eleven

City of Broad Shoulders

I watch Kansas become Missouri become Illinois as Sarah peers out the window of the plane. She must be thinking of her years traversing the same routes by Greyhound Bus and how different the perspective is from up among the clouds. As the southern Chicago suburbs came in view, she breaks the silence.

"I have a confession to make, Dan. Full disclosure. I'm not the little corn-pone girl from Abilene you may think. I'm familiar with Chicago, at least the Chicago of fifteen to twenty years ago. I was born in Evanston and grew up for eighteen years in the first suburb north of the city. Downtown was one of my playgrounds as a teenager."

"Now you tell me. I was just assuming my cosmopolitan personae and was ready to instruct you about the Big City as if you were a backwoods barefoot girl who grew up in a shack! Thanks for destroying my pumped-up masculine image. I'm thinking we have so much to learn about the other that this will not be over in a fortnight. Not that I want it to be. I'm eager for you to experience how I live in Chicago and the Near North."

"Well, I'm relieved to know that I get to see your home. I was ready to spend some cash in my purse for a room downtown. Who knows? I was wondering if I'd have to get a room at the Park Hyatt on Michigan Avenue on this trip."

"Not if I have anything to do with it, you won't."

The private plane coasted to a stop at Midway Airport. My secretary had a black Mercedes waiting. It's not, Sarah mused aloud, like catching the orange commuter line for downtown and disembarking in the loop. "To tell the truth, Dan, I'm both impressed by the efficiency and unimpressed by the car. My years of traveling on a bus squeezed the last ounce of the oil of materialism from my makeup. I know smells - sweat smells from a drunken bum on the seat in front of me in Mobile, fresh coffee in a cup from my seat-mate in Seattle, and old powder makeup from an elderly woman on the way to visit her son in Indianapolis. The fresh smell of a Mercedes is nice but does not impress me. I told you I'd be transparent; you just as well know what I'm thinking. I'm immune to all signs of bourgeois life and will never again be seduced by things - that, too, died in a suburb of Pittsburgh, Pennsylvania. Rich paraphernalia mean nothing to me. If they mean something central to you, Dan, you'll drop in my estimation. First in my value spectrum happens to be soul. If you don't have depth after the encounters of the last few days, you're hopeless. I know this sounds tough; I've got to be me. I've been in a tomb of my own making for a long time and must be authentic this time around."

"I return to Chicago not as I left, Sarah. There's a different me sitting beside you. What I'd point out to impress you weeks ago is not what captivates me now. I simply want to see Chicago through your five senses and not put any of my interpretations off on you. Does that make sense? I'm not an effete snob anymore; certainly Dad's letters, you and Janet Hocking cured me of my urban superiority mode."

"Which part makes sense - the new you or my fresh interpretations of Chicago? If you say both, the answer is 'yes.' By the way, I believe the snob you has evaporated."

"You're tough. Okay, I'll immediately break my rule. This is my city. I love it to its raw Sandburg's 'city of broad shoulders' bones. I'm on the board of that library over there and, in several blocks, I'll probably brag and tell you that I am on the board of the Chicago Art Institute. None of the tall buildings were designed by me; they are out of my league. My firm builds schools; that's all. I'll show you my office later. I'm rattling because I'm so happy to be showing you my perspective on this place I love."

"Hold back, Mr. Cosmopolitan! I know this area. Many a time I've walked Michigan Avenue, know Old Town, State and Rush Streets, have visited the Art Institute a dozen times at least, and am familiar with several super restaurants around here - if they are still operative. I used to go to Second City theater. I'm not the Kansas dummy your debonair attitude is tempted to assume."

"That means I can't call you 'Hayseed', a name I'm considering as a pet nickname. I won't assume your country ignorance, though I had moments of that thought prior to meeting you back in Abilene. That notion has gone with the wind.

"Here we are at Macy's. I'll drop you off and meet you right in front here at 2:00 pm. You can grab a bite and I'll get one also. See you at 2:00."

I'm there waiting at 1:45. Good lord. I almost don't recognize her when she comes out of the Macy salon. Her hair is feathered and slightly touching her shoulders. This is a stunning lady. I say aloud, "Uh oh. I'm impressed. You are now approaching beautiful." She smiles and shakes her head so the feathered hair swirls around. I feel my heart flutter. "It's time now" she says, "to spend some of my hundreds on clothes. Stand out of the way. I'm going to go nuts and buy some new duds. Don't peek. I'm on a spending spree. Further, I'll decide on my clothes without input from you. I repeat: there is no need for you to sit in some Rambo chair near the cash register commenting on whether my choices are appropriate, pretty, or fit. I can manage; I'm a big girl."

"And independent as hell. Maybe I can go shopping for eggs, toast and coffee while you are making all those momentous, once-in-a-lifetime decisions - designed just to impress me, I'm sure." She just shakes her feathered hair even more at me. And smiles. That wonderful smile melts me to my toes.

During the shopping trip, I accept the role of baggage carrier. As soon as Sarah picks a store on the Magnificent Mile, I sit near the door and am careful to not look back and view her trying on clothes. I people-watch - always a delight in this part of Chicago. She buys so much that I look like a hotel baggage carrier hauling stuff down Michigan Avenue. In my car we head twenty or so blocks north to my home.

After a few minutes, I announce, "Here's Eugenie Street, the location of a gay young bachelor architect. I hope we can find parking." Sarah stares at my house and I find myself guessing what she thinks about it. All homes are not created equal. Each bears the stamp of the owner or owners' taste - and the variety is as unique as the house address. My home is efficiently modern - about as different from the Kansas place as two houses and interiors can be. The building has skylights, an entry spanning two floors, aluminum handrails on the open oak stairs, and exotic rugs on the floors swirling with color. There are chrome chairs with orange leather for backs and seats, glass tables, a mirrored bar, marble topped counters in the kitchen, modern chromed appliances in nooks, and wildly modern paintings spattered with paint like something by Jackson Pollock. There is also an immense flat screen TV on a wall. I try to see everything anew as Sarah views it. I'm unprepared for her first comment.

"Dan, do you have a bed that escalates up to the ceiling?"

"Escalations in my bed will depend upon you, love."

"Good comeback."

I carry the boxes of clothes to the upper bedroom. She says, "I need a shower and will dress in some new clothes before you fix my elegant dinner." I respond, "How does Thai food sound? I can order it in." Sarah eyes me scornfully. "Stop it. I'm a debonair woman now. I expect the best." She heads to the shower.

I hear oohs and aahhs which must indicate that the flow of water over her beautiful body has both the temperature and pressure to heal her from the day's travels. I shower on the lower floor and wash the dust of mid-Kansas out of my hair and off my skin. I decide to wear sweat pants and a long sleeved jersey with CUBS printed on the front. If she wants to go out rather than order-in, I can change quickly. I hope she does not come out in formal dress. I'm partially relieved when she appears in sweats and a baggy shirt, despite it saying WHITE SOX in huge letters.

"Do you have to dress down, Sarah? You have ruined the ambiance of my humble dwelling with one swift stroke of a South Side bat. What will my friends say? I'm hoping my squash partner doesn't drop by. Will you not go near a window?"

Sarah walks firmly to the front door, throws it open, and loudly yells "Go Sox!"

"My reputation just got shot down in one swift irrational moment. I'll never be able to show my face again in this neighborhood. The house goes up for sale tomorrow. This is no way to begin a significant friendship, nevertheless serious relationship."

We laugh, hug, and order Sarah's preference … Chinese.

After munching through Moo Shoo Pork and General Tao Chicken (both not available in Abilene, according to Sarah), our mood mellows. We begin to talk more seriously about what has been learned and the questions still remaining in our minds.

"I need to know how my father got the tattoo, the huge burn scar on his back and the bullet holes on his side and arm. How did he survive all that madness, nevertheless his years as a sniper for the French Resistance? What significance is the black opal? Or the high bed? I still don't know why he went to Abilene. How did he have the wisdom to pierce through your facial mask when he first saw you at the diner? How did he escape once he got the tattoo? What business was he in with Shlomo? Who is my uncle anyway, some old recluse hidden in a dark tenement? What will we discover in New York? A huge part of me is still overwhelmed and laden with mountains of unanswered questions."

"Dan, you need to develop the pace Ezra and I developed over the years I spent in the home in Kansas. You get in too big of a hurry. It's like you want everything solved so you can get back to your normal Chicago architectural life. We're not writing an overnight term paper for a college course on Life. Neither of us can return to rituals of yesterday, anyway. If we change as much after we meet Shlomo as we did in the last week, we might become ski bums in Aspen. Ezra obliquely taught me peace. With his training locked in my body rhythms, I think I need to teach you that."

"I love it when you talk dirty."

"You know what I mean, Bwana. Maybe that will be my nickname for you. Hayseed and Bwana, the Abilene twins in the Big City. Let's get back to our quest. We might discover that our inheritance in the Big Apple is so vast that each of us will bid farewell to the other and disappear in a cloud of Maserati smoke. Wups. I went off line again with little girl fantasies. More seriously, your questions for your uncle are mine also. I also wonder how the brothers kept such close tabs on you and your life. Does Shlomo know my full story? How soon did Ezra know my real name because he never said one word? It's nuts but I canned some tomatoes, green beans, and peaches one year and noticed that about a dozen jars were missing. Did Ezra mail my garden work to his brother in New York?"

"Great. That'll be our first question: 'How were the peaches?' You're something else, Sarah. 'And did you make marinara sauce with the tomatoes?' Unbelievable."

"Don't be snide. I know how to survive with stuff from a garden. Oh, I wish I hadn't used 'survive' in such a casual manner. Which brings us back to the ultimate seriousness of our search for answers. Knowing what we know, it is doubtful that we'll ever look upon another person with superiority for their story may be more suffering-laden than that of our own. It's like we've had brain transplants. The old logical brain is still perking along per usual but the non-dominant hemisphere has been re-configured and enlarged."

"The most amazing thing to me is that my father was seeking to re-birth himself. I don't think he had that in mind when he went to Abilene. Ms. Hocking believes he had the moment of inspiration when he heard the sounds of children on the playground. That makes sense to me. To think that he sat immobile in that library for years and had not heard them. He was sensory dead. His Right Brain must have shriveled to the size of a peanut. Then, the breakthrough came: redemption through identification with children! Just think of it. It's a new thought I've never encountered. 'Bearing witness' also means that joyous kids bear witness. 'Never forgetting' also means returning to what had been forgotten: bodily spontaneity. This is a beyond. It stuns me. Dad had his moment of awareness. And I had a lightning strike in my brain when Janet Hocking told what she saw in the maintenance yard. I'm so grateful to her. Ezra tried to dance! My God, what I would give to have seen that!"

"You already see it in your mind Dan. With your artistic architectural ability you have constructed an image that is permanent. With my simple drawing ability I can outline a picture of Ezra at play. You have a picture of his face. I have mental pictures of his entire mode of being. I suggest that, when we get all this settled and gather our little packages of money, we employ a good artist to paint a portrait of a dancing Ezra wearing his black overcoat."

"My God, Sarah: I love you with all my heart. What an amazing idea! With my art contacts from the Art Institute and with feedback from both of us, we can almost perfectly image my wished-for father. He will no longer be a ghost. He will be right over the mantle as an inspiration to me forever. Thank you so much for your beautiful thinking. I'll never forget this moment either."

"Was it not Robert Frost who said 'I have promises to keep and miles to go before I sleep, and miles to go before I sleep?' We still have many miles to traverse, Daniel. I don't know about you, but I know about me, I'm tired: it's time to sleep."

"There you go wanting to go to bed again. You convince me. To bed we go. I need to electrify my arms." She looks at me coyly and says "It's not all about you, my Chicago friend."

****

Therapeutic Analysis

For any observer knowledgeable of Dan and Sarah's encounter with human tragedy in the last few days, their verbal exchanges may appear strange. My contention is that their banter is not artificial in the least. It is not mere categorization to avoid the heaviness of the past. It's more like the shrill noise of maddened humanity has been built into their personal symphonies so that harmony and disharmony are more like a Schoenberg than a Mozart. To say it differently, a dimension of reality streaking through their souls does not impede their ability to have a tender conversation, studded with the seductive exchange of male and female. Their conversation is both a blend of their past and a new mix that adds depth way beyond the normal.

Again, can a loving dialog happen so quickly after the traumatic knowledge of the last several days in Abilene? Poor psychologists may think our couple in the denial phase of grief. Wiser Analysts know that it is none of the above. The ability of the mind to assimilate when two grown adults are nearing forty years of age is nothing short of miraculous. Neither Sarah nor Dan were virgins to human suffering prior to the events in Kansas. They had already swum through ocean detritus and harsh currents. Though of recent years Sarah hid from the world, her Pennsylvania life had placed her right in the path of visceral encounter with evil - if the word 'evil' includes cancer and the death of two beloved children. Dan slogged through a childhood without a father and, across the years, created a number of father figures to identify with simply because he ached inside. Sarah and Dan are mature adults who have the capacity to assimilate vast amounts of information, painful as it may arrive. Besides that, with Ezra's playground awakening, they have a model to laugh and play despite extreme tragedy.

Thus, their banter is a return to what is vital in life, the only real return of the emotional tide that makes sense of death and vicious irrationality such as war. Each day a growing individual must make multiple decisions to choose life. Why? Because some invitation to regression, some beckoning call to deteriorate, some physical summons to let go and forget health, some business reason to chuck it and escape to a beach, some downer from a friend … all of these are bugle calls to fall in line and march, zombie-like, to a cemetery of the soul. Bad news, irrational news, and mindless media all offer calls for us to be, as the poet says, "quarry slaves at night scourged to our dungeons." No human walks a straight line and chooses vitality every moment. Restful moments help.

At times in his life Dan has felt like a victim, feeling sorry for himself or according to the Script, the reverse: playing the role of carefree rake. There were times in Dan's adult years that Freud's Death Instinct had grabbed him in its clutches as he thought and acted like a narcissistic prick. Salesmanship for his architectural business had prompted him, in part, to assume the role of citizen for the arts as he served on boards. True enough, he was also searching for sales. A good deal of his service was done vacantly. Sarah's several year bus odyssey was a trip into the blackness of the grave where she saw no good, heard no good, spoke no good and felt utterly worthless. They both know the trough of despair. While it is not of the magnitude of Ezra's war experiences, their pain was sizable and real.

Many live in simplistic black/white worlds where a given individual is either a child of light or darkness, is consistently Christian or a worthless pagan. Those who delude themselves with such drastic polarities are not reality bound. Life mixes all the colors on the palate and some of them are smeared. Analyzed closely, matters prove to be quite complex. Analysis leads to forgiveness, not self-righteousness.

The passage of time plus an honest biographer reveal the truth of life: we've all had good moments and bad moments. Growing people fight fiercely against the regressive forces and keep equilibrium by choosing in crystal moments to be 'I-Thou, Here-Now'. That includes Nature and people and even the way one treats one's self.

And that is where we leave our couple: I-Thou, Here-Now.
In bed in sacred union. Life is an accumulation of moments.

Dan and Sarah are learning how to both embrace and create moments.

Further thoughts. *It may appear that my recommendation to create moments is simple. Actually, I have in mind the notion that this becomes a total matter. It begins in the morning with a delightful sharing of night dreams and ends only with the last kiss and touch at night. In other words, each partner is continually looking for an occasion to create a loving moment.*

This means surrendering the last shred of leftover childhood passivity. You don't wait for the other to initiate: You initiate. In this sense, then, maturity means taking charge of every transaction in the closest relationship life offers: partnership.

Yes, it's ironic. At first glance, the emphasis upon 'moments' seems like a matter of seconds. It turns out that creating moments becomes a minute-by-minute matter. Ironic? Yes. Does it work? Absolutely. (Caveat. This presupposes that both are working for deep love and one is not a passive receiver.)

If a person wants full intimacy, creating moments is the only way to go.

A warning against passivity must be phrased to those who have experienced great tragedy. It is quite natural to initially assume that others must bring healing to you. Over time, however, that kind of passivity results in despair. When you gain the insight that it is up to you to create moments both for yourself and others, you take a huge stride away from having tragedy control you. And, while gaining insight as to just what 'moments' mean, go to a playground and see how children continually create them. Waiting is for those who choose sulking and never learn how to initiate life-providing alternatives.

***Marriage and the Script**. It is clear that Dan and Sarah are warming up to each other. It's trite to say it, but shortly after marriage ceremonies something frequently happens that mutes the intensity of the romantic honeymoon. Men frequently say that the wives cease being as sexual or adventurous. Women frequently say that they want to be cherished and not used. Neither of these explanations really explain the problem.*

The real issue is that one (usually both) turn(s) on a latent unconscious Script. The spouse experiences a radical shift. At issue here is that each transfers a negative role on their new spouse. The husband may become the harsh father she hated as a little girl. The wife becomes the nagging mother he avoided as a young boy. The real problem is when the transference becomes set. Instead of "you act like my mother sometimes," the husband concludes "Oh my god: I married my mother!" The wife does the reverse: "I married my father!" Understand that there is complexity here. A person can transfer mother, father or even a controlling sibling. The issue is whom the person considered the biggest pain in their childhood: the spouse becomes that. Unfortunately. Script happens.

The transference problem advances as each relates to the other in the old form: he avoids his wife; she argues with him exactly the way she argued with her father. The subtlety of the interchanges can only be deciphered by the analytically trained. That means confrontation in therapy. "You keep avoiding her and treating her like a bitch and that's the way she'll become." "Watch out or you'll create your nightmare."

I do not see how anyone can do marital therapy without understanding transference - one of Freud's original observations. Some therapists have not done their homework. There are simplistic couple counseling sessions done by amateur therapists who put cute prescriptive bandages on major issues. They may attempt to install a few verbal solutions so there is more niceness in the relationship. This may work if both are very religious, do not learn basic emotions, and avoid being real.

It does not, however, heal the issue at a depth level.

As for Dan and Sarah, we can be sure that neither will settle for a Script Marriage where one or the other becomes the fall person. Dan is too analytically adept for that and Sarah is too wise. They either be real or will be alone.

Chapter Twelve

Urban Recuperation

Eggs. Toast. Coffee. Same breakfast. Different city.

"You know we could be having Eggs Benedict and French pastries at the Drake Hotel right now. They have a scrumptious brunch."

"Not for me, Dan. Plain scrambled eggs is good enough for this brainwashed Kansanian."

"I think you should put sass in the middle of that word - Kan-sass-ian - because you are certainly not some shrinking violet homespun frontier girl, if, indeed, such a person exists. You'll note that my superior attitude to residents of Abilene has diminished. Forevermore, Ms. Hocking will stand at the door of my old sarcasm and spank my tongue - like a good librarian should. Dear Ms. Hocking. What a fine human being. She was wracked with pain as she sat in that rocking chair and presented the most startling news of my entire life. When I think of her, tears appear in my eyes. Her observation of my father in the research department was instructive in and of itself. Then she added her watching him seeking to melt. That destroyed my old understandings of Ezra and - let's face it - is transformative to my own journey. I'll never forget Ms. Hocking. In fact, I'm going to text my secretary and have her send a flower arrangement with our gratitude."

As I type on my Blackberry, with peripheral vision I see Sarah look around at my home: it's Crate and Barrel all the way. I follow her eyes. She must be noting that the furniture is upscale and modern. The dishes on the table are colorful and look like they just arrived from the downtown Chicago store. Everything fits. And the 'everything' is at least a century later than the decorations in the house in Abilene. I hope she sees that both places have synchronicity and fit their locations.

"What do you want to do today, Daniel? Do you have to go to work? If so, I'll lounge around and watch images flit across that monster screen of yours. Then, in this Cinderella fantasy I'm creating, you will come home with two dozen roses and chocolates from Marshall Field's, There'll be caterers with a French dinner, said caterers bearing silver candelabras with golden candles and eventually pouring exquisite wine - while waiting on me in the manner to which I'm accustomed."

I smile. "No. I don't have to work today. With the miracles of the electronic revolution, I have already checked in. If something comes to me in the course of the day, I'll Blackberry back and forth with any necessary brilliant ideas. For instance, I've already arranged to have material sent to Uncle Shlomo - a copy of the Ezra letters and the will. I suggest we fly to New York later this week. As for my fantasy for today, it'd be okay with me if we stayed in, but I might have a different agenda than mere watching television or renting a movie. As for your food for the evening, I'm thinking burgers from Wendy's."

"You're such a romantic. Let's shake both fantasies out of our minds. Hold on to your britches. I really want to re-acquaint myself with this wonderful town. And, before I get ahead of myself, I want to go about this recuperation slowly. No bus tours going thirty miles an hour all over town, no tourist boats on the Chicago River pointing out architecture while going under rusty bridges, no sampling of major restaurants on a food binge - none of that. I need to re-acquaint myself with Chicago at my own pace. I'm thinking of sitting on a lakefront bench tossing popcorn to pigeons. That's my speed today. Maybe we can go to a White Sox game for a few innings."

"I was with you three-quarters of what you said until you turned profane. You are in Cubby land, the home of true American heroes. Even your cursing aloud the W S words sullies these walls of my abode. Please watch your language in the future."

"Do you want me to go to the door again and wake up the neighbors with the bellowing call of Comiskey Park?"

"It's not called that anymore. You've been incommunicado in the Kansas wilderness. I don't know its new name, but I'll buy your lunch if you don't ruin my reputation in the neighborhood anymore by nasty South Side hollering."

"Can we agree, then, on pigeons and popcorn in the park?"

I nod affirmatively.

Sarah continues: "As for lunch, there is, if I remember correctly, a corned beef and pastrami sandwich at a deli near the Art Institute that is scrumptious. I don't know how many years it has been since I've had cabbage, thin sliced pastrami and corned beef slathered with hot mustard and folded on fresh baked rye bread."

"Done. I know the place. I'll buy out of my vast sixty per cent inheritance because I don't want you to blow your money in one day. And can we just buy one sandwich and share it? There is no way you'll be able to consume such a meal. I have it on good authority that pigeons don't like pastrami. Out of my generous heart, I'll even graciously pay for bottled water. We can gather our sandwich and sit and eat by the bronze lions on the Art Institute porch. Is that a deal?"

"The bronze lions. How I've missed them. You've got a deal on buying my lunch. One problem, though. The weather is good. I have decided to wear my sneakers, sweat pants, and my slogan shirt … name of which I won't say aloud."

"My heart just sunk. Do you want to ruin my downtown reputation on the very first day? Is there no mercy in your heart? If some Art board member comes out and sees me with you, I'll never live it down. Maybe you can sit by the lion on the South Side of the entrance and I will sit by the North lion - the prouder of the pair, by the way. That nobility fits my image. We'll occasionally wave unless I recognize someone. Then I, in my loyal shirt for the good guys, will look as if I 'm wiping mustard off my hand."

"Good plan. But where will we get the popcorn?"

"There are vendors in the park. If we cannot find one, I'll catch a cab, make a quick trip to Wrigley Field, the home of the true and the brave, and bring back two sacks of perfectly cooked popcorn … the kind all true Chicago pigeons love."

"Ah. My pet name for you at last: Pigeon."

In response to her, I blink my eyes like a good pigeon.

"You know, Dan, this patter is healing to me. I need a break. I can only delve into the utter depravity of mankind so long before I need oxygen. Blue sky. The Lakefront. Even though this is our first full day back in the city, I want to turn my back on the hustle and bustle and watch sailboats aimlessly meander across the waves of the everlasting Lake Michigan. My Lake. Our Lake. Chicago's Lake."

I nod in agreement. "I feel the healing too and it's good for my soul. Feeling talk about the curative powers of Nature reminds me that I need to contact my shrink. I'll tell him it will be a few more days before a session since you and I have to run to New York. In fact, I think it will be good if you go with me to the next appointment when we return. It will not be confessional time. Neither of us will lie on a couch and babble. I've sent him copies of our letters, the will, and my memory of our interview with Janet Hocking. I'll Blackberry Dr. Rabinowitz now if you agree." She nods okay.

"Another thing, Dan. I'm not up on all the electronic gadgets that are popular now. I don't know a Blackberry from a raspberry. Multi-purposed cell phones are beyond me. I don't want to become an extension of the entertainment and communication industries. I would like to know how they work and what all the commotion is about. So far I've gotten along quite well without them. Of course, I was in Abilene during the latest electronic revolution and did not need to contact anyone with a gadget."

"Okay, Hayseed. The Master will become your private instructor. Let's go on our downtown safari. I'll pack all the necessary implements in my cargo backpack."

"Thanks, Pigeon. Cover your Cubs shirt in the process, will you?"

By eleven a.m. a cab drops us off in downtown Chicago. We window shop at stores for awhile and wander over to State street so Sarah can re-familiarize herself with it all. I watch as she touches the bronze filigrees on the Carson Pirie Scott corner. I've never thought to do that. She wants to walk underneath the loop tracks and have a train rumble over us before garnering our massive sandwich at the deli around the corner. She intrigues me, makes me inwardly smile in point of fact, but I say nothing. In truth, I'm re-experiencing Chicago through her eyes and seeing it like I've never seen it before. I've never been so relaxed downtown. Nor have I ever worn sweats and a Cubs shirt in the loop, or on the porch of the Art Institute for that matter. Everything seems new with Sarah at my side. I also mark a popcorn shop on our short walk which will only involve a short dip back west before going east to the Lakefront.

At the Deli, Sarah's eyes grow larger as she watches the piling of corned beef, pastrami, golden-green cabbage and yellow mustard put on slices of rye bread. "I'm salivating" she says. I ask the chef to cut the sandwich two-thirds to one-third. Sarah pinches my elbow. I hastily change the order and said "Exactly in half, please." "That's better, Pigeon: you're learning. And have them half the pickle. Plus two bottles of water." I obediently nod my head like a pigeon and follow orders. The counter man looks at me and shakes his head as if to say "What a wimp!"

As for lunch on the Art Center porch, it's a pagan feast. Mustard leaks down our mouths, said mouths stretched in order to take large bites of the best sandwich on earth. We both seem not only exquisitely happy - viewers must see us as very much in love. Just the experience of eating on the porch by the lions happens to be incredibly romantic. With backs to the wealth of the fabulous art in the Institute behind us, Sarah and I are quite content to people watch, listen to the honking, observe the busses and cars, note the new flower kiosks in the middle of Michigan Avenue, view the incredible architecture and soak it all in. Is one sandwich enough? It's more than enough because we are also filled with the mystery of love permeating our bodies. It must be a new experience for Sarah to see people with iPods in their ears, talking on phones and even text messaging as they walk along. In just the few years since she's enjoyed downtown Chicago, the world - this world - has changed.

I run and get fresh popcorn as Sarah finishes her half of the perfect sandwich. We then head toward the Lake, cross Lake Shore Drive, and find a private bench facing the Lake. The bench seems made for two lovers … friends … soul partners. Traffic roars behind us; we do not notice. Pigeons, never timid, swarm around our feet pecking away at the white kernels. Neither of us speak. Talking is inappropriate for the moments we are sharing. The harbor with its huge luxury yachts, the lake reflecting the marvelous blue of the sky, the white sailboats dancing around like ice skaters: everything is beautiful. The scene is magically entrancing. We hold hands, lean in order to touch heads and say together: "Our Lake." The afternoon glides by all too quickly. We are in no hurry whatsoever. The time might as well be eternal. We are lost in the beauty of it all.

I think it ironic that - in the sophisticated modern world - Nature is still the best medicine. Various forms of entertainment all have their place. And yet, blue dancing waters like those waves of Lake Michigan heal like nothing else. The unconscious benefit of moving water is why so many people must live by a river, a lake, or an ocean. Sarah and I both know that the lake in front of us had been doing its ebb and flowing dance for eons. It hasn't changed since Indians lived where the Chicago River and Lake join only a mile or so away.

Sarah seems to be fully at home in her accustomed appreciation of silence, said silence that has new meaning for me also.

Hours go by. Sarah breaks the silence. "Do you have any of your massive sixty per cent cash left? If so, my half of a sandwich is wearing thin. I'm thinking we need to get home so we'll be there when the French caterers arrive with the candles, wine, and crepes."

I look at her mistily and think: "Where the hell has she been all my life?" My next private thought is "I wasn't ready for her until we broke through our delusions of the past week." Aloud I say, "I charged the French dinner to Sarah Anne Bannock since you still have hundreds upon hundreds stashed in your purse. Anyway, I want to switch plans. Since you've humiliated me in front of one of my temples of service with your gross sweatshirt, I think you should pay me back by taking me to dinner. I want Italian and I know just the place."

Sarah looks hurt, "There went a beautiful imaginative dinner. How can you think of lasagna after our beautiful sandwich? Let's walk awhile and make food decisions later."

We walk holding hands in the direction of the Drake Hotel - me with a proud CUBS shirt and Sarah with a disgraceful WHITE SOX emblazoned on her shirt. No one notices, really. Chicago is that way. Who you are is who you are and that's that. On an impulse, I let go of her hand and start skipping. I look at Sarah proudly. She shakes her head in fake disdain and says, "I hate to break it to you Pigeon, but you need skip training. If we ever venture to the Lincoln Park Zoo, I'll employ a six year old to give you lessons."

Sarah adds: "I almost forgot. When we were on our bench by the Lake, I saw you thinking just like your father did - as I told you once before. Your head and shoulders and body were an exact replica ... must be genetic. What were you thinking?"

"Actually, I meant to tell you that I made a kind of mental breakthrough. I'm thinking my next growth step is to become the kind of father to kids I always wished for. That means I'll say to them what I wish I had heard, words like 'you are lovable and capable.' Will you keep an eye on me, Sarah, and give me coaching as I learn how to do this?"

"Tell me more."

"Well, I've spent all my life wanting to have a father. My new idea is that, instead of waiting for some ideal man to come along and father me, I'll become like a kind father to any kid I encounter - park, playground, along the street, wherever. Is that clear?"

"Clear enough. Actually, I think it brilliant, a huge mental shift. I'm proud of you. We'll figure out how to do it as we go along."

"I'll savor that comment, Sarah. You think I'm brilliant! Talking about savor, I'm getting hungry. Another thought: I forgot to teach my hillbilly girlfriend the ins and outs of the Electronic Revolution. Will you forgive me?"

"If you had brought that junk out while we sat by either the lions or on our special park bench, I'd have crowned you. I'll learn later. There's no hurry. I'm not one who wants to cancel out the world and send text messages as I move along. Look where we are! As you well know, we're nearing where Michigan Avenue crosses the river: this is the Place of the Stinking Weeds (the meaning of the word 'Chicago'). And there! Look at the whiteness of the Wrigley Building. It always seems new. There stands two corncobs, the Marina Towers. The thought of being plugged in with an iPod or text messaging and not seeing all this architectural glory is an abomination to me. I never tire of the Magnificent Mile - particularly when in love."

I love her excitement and especially revel in her last phrase. "in love." God, I love this woman. Continuing walking, I suggest we go into Crate and Barrel and just ogle at all the beautiful glass and colored dishes. For a few enchanted minutes we do just that until I feel my stomach growl. "I'm feeling like a hungry pigeon" I tell her. "I wonder if management will allow us to eat at the Park Hyatt beside the Water Tower. After all, you look like a bum with your White Sox shirt on."

No voice is raised in protest at the restaurant. We eat appetizers and a salad, seldom talking, as the parade of humanity wanders down the street by the Water Tower and along the Magnificent Mile. Everything and everyone seems glittering. That's life in my downtown, I proudly think as if I own the place.

As darkness begins to set in, we hail a cab. We are exhausted when we return to home on Eugenie street. This day's chapter in our new book was and is perfect. We never turn on the television that evening. There's some kind of silent agreement to just quietly be together. Despite a small wave of fear, I suggest that the next day we follow my agenda; I bravely state that Sarah is to follow, one step behind. She gives into my chauvinism with a coy nod and says “then I get my agenda on the following day.“

We fall asleep on the couch in each other’s arms.

****

Therapeutic Analysis

An intimate relationship frequently depends more on little items that usually escape notice from onlookers or from readers of fiction. Those small non-verbal clues, however, are central to the Analyst. Unfortunately, as said previously, those micro-moment exchanges are not available in cold print. An example is the tone of voice. Tonality can communicate care, cherishing and respect or, conversely, condescending disrespect, manipulation for selfish ends, or lack of concern about the person's welfare. If a partner picks up one of the last three negative options, the confronted person can always change the tone and repeat, quite objectively, only the words that were said. As in, "Why are you getting upset? All I said was 'Where did you put the salt?" That sounds innocent enough, doesn't it? The problem is that the accusatory tone of the salt reference was originally said quite hatefully.

I knew a blind psychotherapist who was able to hear all background innuendoes. He was a master of picking up latent emotions. Mixing my metaphors, he said that the voice is the 'barometer'. Since content exchange in couple therapy is not where the action really is, I'd find myself - across the years - occasionally imitating my blind friend. I'd close my eyes and listen to the river flow rather than the dueling boats on the surface.

In the same way, demeanor signals the underground reality. As do eye glances, glimpses, and glares. Touch also has an enormous range. Just the mere act of holding hands can signal soft love or controlling direction. The vital reality is easy to miss if one only concentrates upon words. Focusing on content is the bailiwick of poor therapists who notice what is said rather than how it is said.

And so, in this chapter focusing on the blossoming of love, we must forego some of the armamentarium of the Analyst and note other very important matters. Six things stand out, one of which must be left to conjecture.

1. Knowing what you want. *Sarah initiated the agenda of the day. She wanted to heal by Lake Michigan, feed pigeons with popcorn, absorb nature's beauty, avoid the chaos of the Chicago downtown, touch the filigree on the Carson Pirie Scott building, walk, wear sweats, kid around and eat a meaty sandwich. Those items of knowing what you want may seem minor. The fact is that any solid relationship is based on both partners getting their needs and wants met. To accomplish that, they must first know what they want.*

2. A metaphor*. Halving the Deli sandwich and pickle may seem like a small insignificant matter. Actually, it is a Warning Sign to Dan that Sarah will make her own decisions and will not accept some 'little woman' lower place. She thinks. She knows what she wants. She decides about her food. She speaks out. He will not get away with subtle macho ploys, unconscious though they be.*

3. Awareness*. Both Dan and Sarah are hyper aware of the architecture of downtown Chicago and the beauty of the lake. If you ever people watch in a major city you'll be amazed at how many walking drones there are, just maneuvering along. Like zombies, they are oblivious to their surroundings. Not Dan and Sarah. They are aware.*

4. Humor*. Running through the account of the couple's verbal exchanges is a solid and good seam of playfulness. Let's say Dan simply returned to his former inner self-talk and was 'bodily there' with her, but not openly there. Vitality would dry up. Getting the other to smile and laugh through gentle kidding is central to real intimacy.*

5. Pet names*. The common male-to-male advice is to call all women 'honey' because you might mess up and call your companion the name of an old girl friend. In the case of our couple, Dan, so far, uses the kidding appellation 'Hayseed.' Sarah has chosen 'Pigeon.' These may change. The idea is to create private love names.*

6. Lovemaking*. Men during their twenties and thirties tend to think that love is sex and getting along. Women (given the task of child-rearing) tend to think that love is nurture and getting along. In the late thirties, the ages of Dan and Sarah, new understandings release the deeper realities of cherishing intercourse. Not only body meets body; soul meets soul. My thinking is that such intimacy is not a matter of public discourse. It is private and rather sacred. And, I'm sad to say, rather rare.*

Post-Script*. This chapter is a perfect example of living beyond the childhood clutches of Script. While it is true that some keep playing and re-playing the same old tune until death, some overcome the past - horribly traumatic as it may have been. In this chapter there is little of the ancient roles in either Sarah or Dan (save for the sandwich). Sarah did not use a cutesy flirtation adaptation in order to get her way; she's straight. Dan did not go into the Smart Alec know-it-all Adaptation, or keep his trigger finger on the issue of Abandonment like his father, nor did he go helpless like his mom. Both were straight with emotions, needs and wants.*

Just as true religion of any stripe emphasizes the primacy of appreciation, so, too, does Post-Script life. The couple in this chapter appreciate rye bread, popcorn, bronze lions, pigeons, blue sky, the touch of the other's hand, lake ripples, a sweat shirt, etc. When senses are re-channeled, colors are more vibrant, sounds more musical, tastes more intense. The old mournful dirges of previous tragedies, fade away.

Post-Script, then, the ordinary becomes extraordinary, the normal more luminescent. One experiences a new surge of freedom. Thankfulness for the sheer act of breathing and living becomes all. Privately, I add that I am skeptical about the number of people who live beyond the clutches of Script. I believe they are rather rare.

Caveat: *This does not mean that all flaws and flashes of the past will disappear. Script may raise its ugly head for moments here and there. I frequently told my clients who had kissed the past goodbye that they may experience ten minutes a week back in the old shit. I followed that with the comment "That's a victory. You were once sitting in it full time." I add this paragraph to head off any naïve optimistic celebrations of pure idealism. Past tragedies have weight. You can, however, live skinny with only an occasional splurge of a sugar high. Usually you'll catch yourself when the sweet becomes sour. It may be time to take a walk and renew who you really are.*

Chapter Thirteen

Dan's Testosterone Day

By contract with Sarah Anne Bannock, this day's agenda belongs to me - Daniel Michelson. Her day is tomorrow. I have the entire day mapped out in my mind. I want her to follow my masculine lead, moment by moment as I so direct. This gives me the testosterone kick that part of me has been screaming for since we met in the center of Kansas. It's time to teach her about my world in a manly manner. So there!

Not knowing what her clothes purchases were along the Magnificent Mile, I hope against hope that she won't wear that infernal White Sox sweat suit among my friends and employees. Still, respecting her choices, I force myself to be silent as Sarah dresses. Imagine my pleasure when she comes out of the bedroom dressed in beautifully creased black pants, a stunning cream blouse, a black jacket with cream and white trim, and black shoes figured with tiny holes and one inch heels. She also wears small black pearl earrings. My heart leaps. I'm impressed because she looks stunning.

Working myself back to my sophisticated lead dog control set, I announce "The first item of the day is my squash game at the club. I want you to meet my partner, Ned. Then I ask that you watch how masterfully I play. A glassed-in enclosure allows adoring patrons - such as yourself - to watch us debonair animals reveal our competitive natures. I ask that you do not smoke cigars, spit, or curse at the players like is typical of fans for a crude baseball team on the South Side."

The court play goes well. Sarah smiles as I glance up at her after a good shot just above the metal kickboard. She politely waves as one would expect from an adoring fan. After the game I introduce her to Ned, my squash partner who happens to be a good guy. She winks at him: “Thank you for going easy on Dan, today, Ned. He’s fragile and I’m glad you did not bruise his ego in front of his girl friend.”

“That’s perfectly alright, Sarah. I perceived his anxiety in the locker room before we played and knew it was a time to be generous - because in the past when I’ve skunked him, he’s sulked.”

“It’s good meeting you Ned, and, remember, when and if I’m around , be kind and let him appear manly.” They shake hands and the final thing Ned smilingly says is “You go, girl.”

“Item two on my agenda, fair maiden, is reporting in to my office so you can see how nobly I’m treated. You need a lesson in urban power scenes and I’m just the person to teach you. It’s within walking distance, if those cute black shoes and country feet can handle it.”

Sarah puts on a feigning female voice: “Oh, Master Pigeon, I’m sure if I get a blister, you’ll carry this poor damsel in distress.”

Internally, I think how I never am in control in our conversations - the way I always manage around other women. She just does not fit the mold. That doesn’t keep me from trying. “Okay, then, I’ll lead the way and you stay a half step behind,” I say with a slight grin as I gracefully take her arm.

The Michelson Architectural Firm is elegant; I‘m proud of it. It’s open and airy, the kind of place where my prospective customers are duly impressed. Before meeting the staff, Sarah wandered over to a window and peeked out at the view of Michigan Avenue and a slice of the Chicago River. “Nice,“ she remarks. I introduce her to my secretary and staff. Privately

Sarah whispers that she thinks they appear professional and the makings of an excellent team.

For about an hour, I preview several proposed school buildings planned for towns in downstate Illinois, Iowa, and southern Wisconsin. As Sarah looks on, she appears pleased. I point out to her that each design shows something unique and particular for the local area. "I make the work fit the needs of the given situation" I add.

I then lead her to my walnut paneled private office and say: "I keep thinking of Uncle Shlomo. I'm sure he will have many questions for us as we do for him. Right now I'm not concerned about any inheritance; my focus is upon solving the mysteries. Is there anything else you can think of that we need to convey to him?" Sarah says. "I can't think of anything else he needs to know at this time. I hope he is more verbal than Ezra. I'm really curious to meet him and place our information alongside his. Have you heard from him?" "We just received an e-mail welcoming us to visit. It also gave his address which is in a condo overlooking Central Park. So, unless he's the caretaker, he's doing well."

Completing office business and setting a plan in place with my employees for the next two weeks, I give Sarah my power look. "I'm famished; A fast squash game does that to me. This afternoon I have a board meeting at the Art Institute so we'll eat at the Cliffhangers, a private club straight across the street from the Institute." Sarah clasps her hands together like a monk at prayer, bends her body in obeisance, and smartly brings her heels together. I smile, take her by the arm, and lead her out of the office as if taking her down the aisle of a church. Near the elevator, we chance to overhear the employees cheer "Hurrah for the boss." "I think you passed the test, Sarah," I smilingly say.

We catch a southbound cab for the six or so blocks down Michigan Avenue and enter a plain door next to Symphony Hall. "I've never noticed that door," Sarah remarks. The entry is so completely lacking in any ostentation that only the most acute wanderer along the street would notice it. We mount well worn stairs and push through glass doors into a huge dining room with a thirty foot ceiling, crystal chandeliers, and a host of white clothed tables. "Surprise" I tell her. Leaders of Chicago lean over tables and exchange private thoughts. Several of the power figures nod at me and I see them discretely look at Sarah moments longer than ordinary. There is an unspoken code that, unless you come in with someone or have an appointment and join an existing table, you are not to rudely interrupt a meal or engage in idle conversation. Cliffhangers is a private business and eating establishment: no frivolity, pastimes, or noisy sales allowed. The order of the day is privacy and confidentiality over lunch.

No ordering of food is part of the procedure. Rather, patrons help themselves at well-appointed tables scattered covertly around the room, tables laden with decorated hams, quail, lobster, salmon, prime rib and an array of vegetables, salad and fresh cooked bread. Sarah is impressed for she never dreamed such a power-oriented gathering place existed right near some of her previously beloved areas of the downtown. She whispers to me that she really likes Cliffhangers. "It seems to be above the entrance of Symphony Hall and is right across the street from the Art Institute. Everything is impressive." Waiters quietly provide us with a simple check to be signed. I love the place; it is serenely and quietly graceful. Without looking up, Sarah remarks, as straight faced as possible, "I'm disappointed that they have no macaroni and cheese." I cough into my napkin and shake my head with feigned disapproval.

My board meeting is from three to five so I join Sarah touring several of the halls in the early afternoon. Still following my lead, I take her to the French Impressionists gallery, one of my favorites. I suppress an unearned pride of ownership. Sarah, un-self-consciously, takes off her shoes, puts them under her arm and walks with me to the gallery in stocking feet. Part of me wants to explain the Monets, Pizzarros (my personal favorites}, and, of course, the Van Goghs. I control my superiority urges and find myself pleased at the way Sarah looks at art.

There is no hurry to her. She seems to notice not only the balance of the work but the techniques of the artist. She studies and absorbs it. Despite my macho self, I discover that I'm learning more than teaching. "I've always been impressed," Sarah remarks, "at how such magnificent art worth multi-millions can hang right out in public so that anyone can get within a foot of the paintings and study them." I say nothing because, to tell the truth, I've never thought of it before. We continue on, gallery by gallery, until it's time for my meeting. I leave Sarah, quite entranced and scarcely noting my departure, as she continues on greatly admiring the glory of human achievement - men and women who produced such incredibly beautiful work.

She's in the main lobby near the gift area when I come down after my meeting, accompanied with some other board members. I note that she has her shoes on.

"Sarah, I'd like to introduce you to several members of the board." I hope she notes my pride in her, something that may be nice after so many years of being anonymous. She takes the hand of each person, looks in their eyes in a way that seems as if she's checking his or her quality of soul, and expresses her pleasure in meeting them. After the introductions, I proudly take her arm and steer her out between the lions to the street where I hail a cab. Part of me really enjoys being in charge.

"This has been a most interesting day, Daniel. You've been a super tour guide."

"It's not over. Now we have a drink at the Sybarus lounge atop the John Hancock building and view the entire range of the city and the Lake as twilight settles over my town. We'll watch the evening lights twinkle on in all the buildings."

"That sounds almost poetic, my white knight."

"For me it is rather magical - like Christmas in fairyland. I hope you develop the same love for downtown living (if, indeed, you do not already have it) that this Knight of the Woeful Countenance possesses."

"Ahh, Cervantes, one of my favorite writers. As the first novelist, he knew the insanity of life, the absolute craziness of our private journeys, and somehow managed to keep his wit about him. Miguel Cervantes taught the world to laugh at absurdity while keeping humorous perspective - something we both must continually learn."

"That was almost a speech, Sarah, but one I learned from."

"I wasn't just peeling potatoes, cooking, cleaning, and tending to the garden in Abilene. As I told you before, the library accessed any volume I desired."

An hour and a half go by as we sip cocktails watching the dark creep over the city. "It's time for the next event, fair lady, and I know just the place."

We descend from the heights of the Hancock Building in an incredibly fast elevator, and get a cab for a Rush Street establishment that provides a quiet booth, a fireplace, and excellent fare.

"Dan, I've already eaten my share of calories today. You go ahead if you are wanting a huge steak; as for me it is a small plate of appetizers."

"But your beloved Pigeon wants to show off his culinary wisdom! I know the chef. He'll be incensed."

Sarah tosses her head and her hair shimmers in the light. "You men have such delicate egos. Have him come over here. I'll give him my most seductive eye-blinking look and will tell him how he can please me ... with a small plate of appetizers ... which I will let him choose in order to salve his masculine ego. God! I miss my kitchen in Abilene. Men!"

I, too, eat sparingly, but not because I'm matching Sarah's food style. My appetite is not as ravenous as normal due to some other feeling in my chest. For the first time in my life, I confess quietly to myself, I'm feeling the kind of love that fills me. I need a poet, someone able to express the flutters in my heart. I find myself looking at her with a kind of art fascination, similar to what I saw in her eyes at the Art Institute.

Out of a clear blue sky, an unrelated thought pops into my mind: "Sarah, what do you think we should do with the black opal? We can't divide it sixty/forty unless we sell it. I don't want to do that unless you insist. I've been carrying it in my pocket, but that is not safe enough."

"That's a good question, Daniel. Though it's beautiful, I had forgotten about it. Is there some way we might have a jeweler make it into a necklace that I wear it forty per cent of the time and you wear it sixty per cent of the time?"

"Now that's a good one. Can you imagine me showing up for squash with a black opal necklace around my neck? Here I am thirty eight and unmarried. Rumors will begin that I finally found my man. Be serious. What can we do with the single opal?"

"Serious again. Okay. I suggest that we do absolutely nothing until we meet with Shlomo. Maybe he'll explain its meaning. If it is as significant as we both think, maybe we can sell it to him for some astronomical number. Until then, we'll alternate: you carry it six hours and I carry it for the next four."

"Was that your serious? My-o-my. What am I in for if we actually make it as a couple? Wups. Did I say that?"

"You did. Do you want to change it?"

"I want to swallow down an appetizer and have a drink of water before I answer that."

"Well..."

Coughing, I continue: "Well, this couple business **is** on my mind, but, as you have said, let's be patient. As for the black opal, I once again accept your wisdom. We both will carefully hang on to it until we meet with my uncle. Now please let me eat my appetizers before I put my foot in my mouth again."

Later, feeling more composure, I again attempt to take charge, I suggest - with full masculine authority - that we rent a movie, go home, put on something casual (not team sweat shirts), lounge on the couch and watch a Hollywood kid flick.

"Hmm", Sarah remarked, "and I thought you were going to say 'John Wayne,' or one of the violent Tarentino films. Don't they have Tarzan films at the rental place? You hairy-chested guys need models. As for me, I might be in the mood for one of the golden oldies like 'The Sound of Music', 'Oklahoma', or 'The Music Man'."

"Remember," I speak sternly, "today I'm in charge. You'll get your chance tomorrow. What I say goes today. I just might choose 'Rambo' or "The Deer Hunters.' I'm the boss for the day so there's no need for you to riffle through the options."

“Whatever you choose is okay with this dependent woman, my leader for a day.”

I mentally review the events of this day: Sarah at the squash game, Sarah at my office, Sarah at Cliffhangers, Sarah barefoot at the Art Institute, Sarah at the Sybarus Lounge, Sarah at my favorite restaurant ... Sarah. She’s like no one I’ve ever been around or even heard of before. The only person comparable to her is Natasha in Tolstoi’s War and Peace. And Natasha is completely fictional. Sarah Ann Bannock is definitely not fictional. She’s gone through the fire of mental suffering and is now refined gold. I’m even afraid to look her in the eyes because I might get lost swimming in them and surrender whatever separateness I still clung to.

At the film rental, I restore my tough guy image somewhat as I thumb through the stacks of films. Bravely, I decide upon a musical, but not one she mentioned (I have some pride!). I select Man of La Mancha thinking that it’s theme of quest and dreaming the impossible dream hit’s the center of the target. Besides, I swallow and think to myself, she said Cervantes was one of her favorite authors.

At home, some of the soaring songs fit our mood as we stare at what she calls “the monster screen.” More than any other person, male or female, who has been in my home, I discover myself noting every reaction she has to the movie, reactions which always seem appropriate. Sarah is strangely in tune with her feelings like what my psychoanalyst has bugged me about for years. “Damn,” I think, “I even find myself admiring her stocking feet.”

Studying her obliquely, I have a thought on how to end the evening that had nothing to do with watching dumb movies.

And, what the hell? I’m in charge.

****

Therapeutic Analysis

Dan's testosterone power day reminds me of a host of therapy sessions I had with couples in their twenties and early thirties. One pattern was constant. The man's agenda for his wife can be described as 'muscular.' His vision of marriage is that his wife is to be a buddy, a kind of male-female who's to accompany him to the bar, drink beer with his friends, laugh at sex jokes, and talk tough. She s to accompany him on sport jaunts and hunting trips. His wife's task is to cook and clean even though she may also work full-time. While he and his friends watch football and basketball games on TV, she is to haul in pizza and beer followed by home made cookies. The husband's masculinity is to be acknowledged at all times. The 'little woman' is to look at him with adulation. AND, she must never, ever do anything that might embarrass him in front of his buddies. He's the studly king.

The woman's agenda for her husband can be described as 'taming the beast.' Her view of marriage is that her husband will 'understand,' desire nice delicate things, and join with her in creating a wonderfully attractive, well-decorated home. He's to do everything equally with her: clean, cook, raise the children, and do all things in a sharing, kind way. She understands that he'll have his moments with the 'boys,' but doesn't particularly want to be a part of his 'male cave man regression.' Her husband is to realize that she likes time with her women friends. If he encounters her friends, he is to be nice and show that she is totally cherished by him.

With these two separate and un-yielding agendas, it is clear that young couples coming to therapy are tough. The man expects me, as a man, to scold her and set her straight. The woman, looking with a bit of suspicion at me but believing I'll be fair, anticipates that I will tell her husband that it is time to take off his adolescent Neanderthal costume.

What to do? What to do? Well, if they think therapy some kind of advice session with quick prescriptions, anything I do will be wrong. With a clue from a book by one of my mentors, Bruno Bettelheim, I surprise the couple by saying my conviction; namely, that marriage is for moments and that my model is that of Identity-in-Relationship. In other words, both partners must quit the fantasy of "two becoming one." I tell the man that his wife will not become a 'buddy' who accompanies him on all his testosterone trips. Then, I turn to the woman and say that it is highly unlikely that she will be able to remove his male aggressiveness, nor would that be desirable.

In other words, the problem is their understanding of marriage. Both of them are wrong. The key word neither of them knows happens to be "compromise." It's likely that he will leave his socks on the floor and occasionally burst out with some salty oaths. It is likely that she will not be interested in being his dutiful sidekick in front of his friends. It's likely that he will not be interested in nice house decorations.

I then look at one after the other and say: "If either of you think that you made a mistake and can find a partner who'll fit your imagination, the answer is 'Yes, you may,' but after awhile you won't like the situation. Why? Because your new partner will have no identity. He or she will be dominated to the point that, eventually, you'll encounter subtle rebellion which psychologists call 'passive-aggressive maneuvers."

Does the man want a dominated woman who has no identity? Does the woman want a weak wimp without any of his own genetically determined male aggression?

More particularly in terms of this book, there is no way that Sarah is going to Dan's squash games three times a week and clap gleefully every time he hit's a kill shot. She is not going to wear four inch heels and take a mentally invisible supportive role at his office. Nor is Sarah going to wander the Art Institute while her man does the power thing on a board. He'll not be ordering her food, nor will he push a button causing her to whip off her clothes and make love on his command. Again, if she were to become his female puppet, it would not be long before he tired of her. It's much better if she remains a mystery and surprises him daily with her own uniqueness.

Luckily, Dan is in his late thirties and has already been around women who sought to please him. He still has lessons to learn and, if his first encounters with Sarah prove to be typical, the lessons will be arriving daily. She has an identity and Dan must make still another growth step. Or, there will be a well-deserved separation. On the other hand, if Sarah became the woman-behind-the-man, he'd figure out some way to end the relationship.

Understand, this does not mean either will have to surrender what is considered fun and meaningful. It means that each will live rather separate lives and have wonderful moments that will expand as time goes by - if both are wise and keep creating them.

A legitimate question arises: What does this male vs. female addendum have to do with trauma and redemption - the main theme of this entire book?

The answer is threefold.

First, understanding mistakes of individuals in their twenties and early thirties removes an error frequently believed in society and, concomitantly, by trauma victims of the same age. I'm stating with no reservation, that each person is responsible for her/his own attitude, involvement in life-providing pursuits, and private joy. There is no one to blame - especially one's partner.

Colloquially: if you are unhappy, it's your own damn fault so do something to change your mental framework. Go to therapy. Or, if your partner won't grow up, get a divorce. Have the courage to take charge of your life. Only you are responsible. Long term blame can only be assigned to yourself.

Second. Understanding the husband-wife polarity battle allows the one blamed to turn responsibility right back on the blamer. This needs to be done gracefully sometimes. "I love you and will assist you in your journey, but you are the leader in terms of your own choices for happiness. I don't make you feel. What you feel is your choice." Trauma victims may also need that confrontation. No one makes you feel. You choose.

Third. One of the main sources of spousal abuse (physical, sexual, verbal or even passivity) happens to live right here with the macho vs. Cinderella symbiotic views of marriage. Men may want to slap "the little woman" around in order to get her to live according to his model. A woman with less muscle and afraid to speak up, may turn to passivity - meaning by that she may act lifeless in terms of the relationship. Passive aggression means someone hides anger and turns into a blob of nothingness in order to switch anger to the other. It's not a winning strategy or a decent tactic if love is the goal. These three principles also apply to the next chapter on Sarah's Day.

***One little Analyst note**: If you study the novel carefully, you'll be aware that Dan is tempted to fall back into his Script at several moments during his day. He's stopped due to two reasons: one, he is really in love for the first time in his life and two, Sarah won't put up with macho ploys: she'll be out of there if he seeks total control.*

In a mature relationship, both partners must have the card of abandonment to play if one acts irresponsible. It is fascinating to me that the greatest fear of children - abandonment (that can lead to a baby's death) - happens to be the cue card for vital grownup relationships. The cue reads like this: "Grow up, be real and let's have a mature love or I'm gone." Without the reality of abandonment, supposed love dribbles away into irresponsibility.

Chapter Fourteen

Sarah's Day of Tests

Sarah is dressed in a light blue outfit that matches the color of her blue eyes, an outfit that is extremely becoming as she arrives for breakfast ready to take charge of her day. "We'll need to use your car for part of our time this morning, Daniel. I want to show you my haunts as a child in Evanston, Illinois. Do you know the town?"

"Sarah, I was feeling so good from my Tarzan twenty-four hours yesterday, and you've already deflated me. I confess I've been such a city boy that I have never gone past fifty blocks_north along the lake. Must you continually punch holes in my ego?"

Looking indulgent Sarah parentally tilts her head and says, "How pitiful. You've been so sheltered. I bet you were a mommy's boy who didn't get out from under her arm until you went to school. Poor baby. I'm feeling sorry for you."

"Hold on. I was the man of the house. I grew up West of here in Oak Park. I played competitive sports most of my childhood. I only came home to eat and sleep. Mom let me roam. I developed my own friendship network. One of the things I've never told you was that she was a wonderful woman and mother. I miss her wise counsel."

"I'm glad to hear you say that. There have been glimmers of you being a freaky misogynist. I need reassurance that - early on, at least - you had a good woman around. Let me remind you: today is my 24 hours. When you finish your eggs, toast and coffee we'll be on our way. Because I'm charitable, I'll let you drive."

Having gone past fifty blocks north on Lake Shore Drive, Sarah becomes a tour guide. "Plan on a sharp curving left up ahead and then we will take an immediate right and head up through Rogers Park until we reach the boundary of the heavenly Evanston Illinois, home of one of the best high schools in the United States. First, however, we must drive through this canyon of high rise buildings for several miles.

"Unfortunately, Evanston begins with a cemetery we must circle around. Turn right. Now we go straight toward the campus of Northwestern University which is a bit snobbish and altogether too religious for my blood, but all in all a good place. To add to your architectural knowledge, Northwestern was the last place to gain permission to do fill work in Lake Michigan in order to expand the campus. Turn right by that chapel and then we'll drive a few blocks past the campus. Turn left on Lincoln, the street with the most elegant homes in the town. When Lincoln Street ends, pull over and I'll point out my home on Lincolnwood. My heart is a little heavy. See that elegant house over there? That's the birthplace of the present woman in your life."

I study it's architecture. "I'm impressed. How many kids grew up in that home?"

"Just one. A princess. Everyone loved her. She had an ideal childhood. The sad news is that her parents are now deceased. There are no relatives alive either. The princess is alone. She did have a beautiful childhood in this neighborhood. Turn right before I get too maudlin."

"Dan, see that nice park over there? I played there every week of childhood. Central Avenue was a friendly gathering place. People who lived here in Northwest Evanston thought this area the center of the earth. This community had everything one could want: an excellent small grocery store, the perfect old hardware store, antique shops, a candy shop ... everything. That world has gone, now, but it was truly wonderful. Pull over for a few minutes and let's look at the park. Interestingly, I've changed since we first met. Now I like to see children play. This was a lovable place to grow up." she said with a long sigh.

"Sarah, you said once that the community in Abilene reminded you of home. I see the resemblance. Interestingly, Oak Park has the same ambiance: large homes, tree lined streets, big trees, and amenities nearby. Nice. Very nice. Where do we go from here?"

"I want to show you my old high school. Evanston was one of the first integrated small cities in the North. Everyone got along. Of course, African-Americans had to have their own hospital in early days due to prejudice, but, when you compare this town to others, it was a place of dignity and freedom. After the high school, I'll show you Evanston Hospital where my mother was a nurse."

"What did your dad do?"

"He commuted to the loop everyday on the Northwestern train. He had a job in a downtown bank. I have to confess I don't know too much about his work because he died when I was in college. My mother moved to an apartment on Central Avenue and she died shortly after I was married. In a way, there are mysteries about my own family that I've never investigated. Too much on my mind, I guess. There's the hospital."

"Now, where?"

"I'm ready to get something to eat in downtown Evanston, the place, for your information, that invented the ice cream cone. There used to be a nice Old Ladies Restaurant on Hinman near a couple of retirement hotels. We can get some rabbit food there that will hold you until I take you out to a special dinner this evening."

We dine surrounded by gentleness. The establishment is like an English parlor throwback of the 1920's. Gray-haired women surround us, women who live nearby in the retirement towers, some with daughters visiting from afar, others sitting alone seemingly reminiscing about their lives. I find the place nice, not elegant but pleasant. Servings are small, but sufficient. I leave without my usual filling luncheon meal, but I've had enough. Sarah obtained a takeout container for the remainder of the bread lest I get panicky.

Sarah then takes my hand and leads us on a walk east to a little park along Lake Michigan. Massive oak trees give a grace to the park. Sarah points my attention to a huge old Ginkgo tree and informs me that Chinese missionaries brought back a number of Ginkgo seeds that were first planted in the United States here in Evanston. Overall, I find the town quaint, beautiful, and devoid of the unruly chaos of the city. It's comfortable, but I privately admit to myself that it's a good place to sleep and even stay for awhile, but I definitely don't want to live here.

Sarah senses my thoughts: "It is old to me, too, Dan. I loved it once, but now it seems too 'yesterday.' That's funny for me to say given that I've been dwelling in Abilene which has the same mood that is here in my old neighborhood. Now that I've been mentally liberated by Ezra and the revelations, I find myself open to exploring the world and not getting attached to one single location. Don't get me wrong. I'm still not willing to sell the place in Abilene. Yet. Maybe at some time in the future. Just not now. I like the idea of exploring with a fallback option when the world becomes too much with me."

She takes a few long sigh-filled breaths as if to shake off memories of the past. Perhaps feeling that she's seen Evanston for one of the last times, Sarah looks around and climbs into our chariot to head south to home in Chicago. She confesses an ache as we leave, but knows it is the right thing to do. She studies the houses as we depart.

I'm directed to go to downtown Chicago and park in a lot near the Picasso at the State of Illinois building. Though curious, I say nothing - after all, she's in charge today. After parking Sarah powerfully says "Follow me" and we walk- of all strange places - into the Greyhound Bus Terminal.

Sarah explains: "During my vacant years I ended up here several times because it is a kind of hub for the top of America. I'd switch busses here. During those dark nights of the soul, I didn't return to any of the old areas I'd lived in like Evanston where I was happy as a child. A bus would come along, I'd board it, and head east, west, north, south: I didn't care. I just wanted to get rolling. Tell me, Dan, what do you see?"

"It's an interesting building, actually. And what a location! They have one of the prize pieces of real estate in the entire city. It must be worth millions. More particularly, I see an array of benches, ticket booths, a place to get coffee and donuts ... maybe some other basic food ... signs for bathrooms... that's about all."

"Start over again. What do you see?"

"Well, there are a lot of people here. They are mostly Latinos and African-Americans. Over there are poor whites. Some people are sleeping on the benches."

"What else?"

"Okay. I see people I've never seen before in downtown Chicago. I don't know where they come from. Looking at each grouping one by one, I see a Mexican family in that direction who looks like they are on the edge of poverty. That man over there must be an alcoholic who came in here to rest. The black couple appears like they just got here from Mississippi and are lost. That woman looks desperately in need of help."

"Wait here a moment, Dan." Sarah approaches each of the persons I pointed out, and says something which I can't hear. Repeatedly the individuals involved stare at her and smile. The Mexican mother, the black woman and the_woman traveling alone immediately stand up and hug Sarah as she hands them a hundred dollar bill, part of her inheritance from Ezra.

"What did you say?"

"I told them I've been in real hard places myself and hope they will see better times and, to help them on their way, here's some money."

"You didn't give the alcoholic money."

"No, I told him how to find food and shelter. Now we can go. You are beginning to see with the eyes of your father and how he picked out a lost woman in a café in Abilene, Kansas. It was important to me that you be able to see this side of humanity."

"Was this a test, Sarah?"

"You're damn right it was." I remain silent to that direct, almost harsh, response. I tell myself that the girl has some kind of value boundaries I'd best not cross.

Sarah then directs me to take us home so we can relax a little and change clothes for dinner. I get no more instructions other than to be ready at five for we'll be walking to dinner. I mentally review each of the nice restaurants nearby: Thai, Mexican, Italian, Korean, Mongolian, Swiss, and even American. I dress nicely, in a manner that will fit any of my fantasized options. I put on a comfortable pair of shoes for walking because I have no idea what Sarah has in mind. The lettuce of the Old Ladies restaurant in Evanston is wearing thin. I'm getting hungry.

When she comes forth from the bedroom in her sweats - with WHITE SOX on her jersey - I take it in stride, say nothing, and march along where she instructs. At each turn I am a bit confused and shorten my mental list of the food options. Noting my puzzlement, Sarah says "I phoned ahead for reservations." I ask no questions and she offers no hints as to our destination. As we come closer to Chicago's Lincoln Avenue, I narrow it down to a nice Mexican place or an American sandwich shop that is fairly decent. I'm astounded when she turns, abruptly, into a walkway of the St. Paul's United Church of Christ. I start to ask "Are you sure?" but know that it would be wasted breath on this strong-willed woman. I'm smart enough to know when to shut up and follow.

We enter a cavernous gymnasium with old beaten-up collapsible tables scattered around, folding chairs tucked underneath them, and - I can't help but notice it - a Christian cross on the wall at the end of the room. She sees me look at the cross and says: "It stands for inhumanity to man," I do not respond. I can see that interpretation.

Sarah determines where the kitchen is and heads in that direction. She finds the pastor.

"Hi. I called earlier. I'm Sarah Bannock. This is Dan, my assistant. We are ready to work. Someone suggested that we ladle out the food."

After shaking hands with the pastor, I study the food to be served: baked chicken legs, a vinegar-like spinach concoction, macaroni and cheese, bread donated from the local Treasure Island store, and canned peaches for dessert. My stomach tightens. We're given instructions on how to ladle out the food on the trays the homeless bring by. Sarah says brightly "He'd like to pass out the macaroni and cheese." Bravely, I remain silent. No grimace appears on my face. I assume my place in the chow line and, to the best of my ability, avoid looking straight down at the dish I'm serving. I also avoid memories of the I 70 eatery.

Sarah notes my demeanor and says cheerily: "It's okay to be friendly to the people as they come through, Daniel. Say something like 'Good evening' or 'Hello' in a nice way. It won't kill you. I know all this is new because you are fresh help, but with your grand experience in life, you'll manage." Sarah's laughing smile spreads all over her face and I think to myself "By God, I'm going to show her that I am not some snobby pin head unaccustomed to giving. I can do this." I ladle all the harder and am pleasant to everyone.

I get into it. I pass out macaroni and cheese as well as anyone. Before I know it, time passes. There's no longer anyone in line. "It's time for us to eat now, Dan. And, by the way, I observed you giving out huge portions so there'd be little left over and you'd avoid eating macaroni and cheese with the rest of us. What do you want on your plate?"

Noting that no one could hear, I said: "Sarah, if it is alright with you, I think I want a peach sandwich - if you get my drift." I look at her with a smirk slightly showing on my face. She understands my covert sexual reference. Looking away though, she grabs several slices of bread and puts a soggy half peach right in the middle, places it on a plate and hands it to me. She takes some of the other food - sans Mac and Cheese. We sit with the other patrons, some of whom are homeless, and ask general but not intrusive questions. We have some interesting conversations. Suffering is universal.

On the way home I slyly ask, "Another examination, huh? Are you testing how flexible I am? Is your view of me that I am a Silver Spoon baby, a Trust Fund booby who's been given everything in life?"

"No," Sarah seriously responds. "In a way, I'm checking how deep your soul is. For several years I've lived with a man - your father - who had soul from head to toe. He was pure egalitarian: no person was better, no person worse to him. What matters is whether a person chooses to fight evil and live for the good. Your dad cared nothing for power, prestige, wealth, physical attractiveness, or aggrandized history. His eyes searched for soul. And, by the way, I think he saw some of that in Janet Hocking. So, yes it was a test. I'll never quit testing, either, to be honest. I'll never settle down around anyone who cannot live from the heart. Mark it well: I'd rather be alone."

"Sarah, I don't know how many times I've already said it, but you are tough in a way I totally respect. Only months ago I thought I had it altogether other than a Superego lacunae and you are checking me out from head to toe in terms of soul. It scares me a bit. More than the scare though, it thrills me. Since I've have been living with so many delusions about my father I'm ready to check my assumptions about life and people, I welcome your examinations. I hope I pass today and in the future. I wouldn't have gotten into psychoanalysis if I'd not wanted to grow. Now I have a therapist in my own home."

"Dan, I'm certainly no psychotherapist. I simply know what I want and whom I'm willing to be around. It is either silence and the garden for me - even working at a Greyhound Bus Station - or an authentic soul partner. Nothing less. And if we are doing more than just investigating old memories, garnering some kind of inheritance and having an affair, I want to keep clarifying my own mind and my position in life."

"I'm honored. In more ways than one. Sarah. Your day and my day could not have been more different. It leaves me wondering if you have no use for my world."

"Not at all, Dan. One can never tell by external circumstances who is a giver and who a taker. A banker at Cliffhangers may be thoroughly committed to helping those in need. A poor woman at the Greyhound Bus Station may be deluded by Narcissism. We are both growing Dan. As your father observed me in the garden, I, too, observed him in the evenings on the front porch. He had a curious mind. It was like all forms of life held mysteries he was trying to fathom. The man did not sit there like a lump blindly staring at nothingness; he was learning. For instance, he'd listen to the crickets quite carefully. I saw him pick various flowers and examine them closely with his magnifying glass."

"So you are saying, and what I believe, is that one of the main tasks of life is to fight off the delusions that entrap us. The job - our job - is to concentrate upon what matters in this global fight against evil while still maintaining the curiosity of a child."

Sarah nods affirmatively: "That's a good summary of what I believe, also."

"Okay, Sarah but I keep one major prejudice: Cubs rule and the White Sox suck."

"That's not a prejudice. That's a major delusion," she says with a chuckle.

"It's funny Sarah. In the old days I thought I was the superior hunter. Now I discover that a more wily huntress is nearby. Foregoing the hunting image, I think I am falling deeply in love."

"Patience, my son. We have miles to go before we sleep. Miles to go. I will say that I am wondering if your father did not have some ulterior motive in hooking us together. He may have been far wiser than either of us have given him credit. He read through my condition once in a café in Abilene and now I'm thinking he knew both of us in a way neither of us have ever conceived. Enough talk. Let's go home and go to bed."

And we do. Happily so.

****

Therapeutic Analysis

Interestingly, Sarah does not do the traditional female-tame-the-beast thing with Dan. It may well be true that she tried that in her first marriage where she was younger and dominated by a mind-set seeking to establish a doll house marriage. In this chapter, Sarah reveals a different agenda. She wants soul and she wants a companion who believes in compassion. If neither occurs, Sarah's ready to head to Abilene.

If that last sentence sounds harsh, remember that Sarah has mastered solitude. Achieving solitude means that she is not vulnerable to a another's manipulations. She can live alone quite happily. She doesn't need a partner; she is free to choose one. This removes all scare out of the mix. I'm hesitant to say it, but my experience is that absence of scare in a relationship is rather rare. Frequently, one or the other has a measure of fear of abandonment or is lost in old Script junk.

She has also learned from enormously painful tragedy that the only thing left that makes any sense is caring for others. Sarah heard her own two children breathe their last breaths. She was helpless then. She hated her helplessness. It still weighs heavily on her. In her new freedom she's intent on being the helper from here on out in her life. Years ago she went through the slough of despair and was directionless. That exists no longer. From now on, she'll use her stubborn ounces of power to help those who hurt. Nothing else makes sense to her.

A male still using testosterone for hair tonic, may find Sarah entirely too pushy on her day. In therapy terms, it's knowing what you want and what you will put up with in a relationship. Analytic type therapists like me encourage this. We can predict what happens when one partner dominates the other. We can predict what will happen if one person gives up a legitimate dream. Neither of these outcomes are desirable.

It's almost funny that Dan is confused repeatedly by this different kind of woman he's encountering. He is unable to gain control. Sarah is unpredictable to him. He is forced to leave his standard Script assumptions and process, in each moment, what the hell is happening. With his revolution in terms of father knowledge and urban-rural knowledge, Dan is undergoing a massive revision in terms of his understanding of women. Every therapist who has encountered the male/female testicle-ovary battle would cheer.

So, the hope is that the model of Identity-in-Relationship is emerging. Dan may well continue to play squash on alternative days while she does whatever-the-hell she wants to do. She has needs; he has needs. She has wants; he has wants. It is her responsibility to pursue what is meaningful to her and it's his responsibility to pursue what is meaningful to him. Neither will merge their identity into that of the other.

Most importantly, each is responsible for his/her attitude and drive to life-filled options. Neither can blame the other for unhappiness, poor mental health, or lack of adventure. "I do my thing; you do your thing and, if we meet, it's wonderful. If not, it can't be helped." was the abrupt formula of the psychotherapist Dr. Fritz Perls. It makes sense. Though, as said earlier, we must watch passivity and learn to create moments.

Empirical Validation for my Script Theory.

Off and on throughout the analytic notes I make mention of Script's three major roles that are designed by a script-writing child. It is totally fair to question my thesis and ask for evidence. To answer that I propose a number of avenues for verification.

***A.** A home for the elderly. Ask a resident to tell you about her childhood. My contention is that, in short order, you'll hear the three roles: Adaptation, the Strong but Hated Role, and the ascribed Feared and Weak Role. Let's say the person tells you that she was very nice and always pleasing as a child. Then inquire if she followed that during adulthood (ie. Check out the Adaptation). Sometimes the person may have maintained the sweetness and never went into the Hated role. Ask if someone in their marriage ever came on like the disliked person in their original trauma drama. Carefully, you might check if one of her children happened to play the Weak role. I say "carefully" because it is often the case that this role is passed down (transferred unwittingly) to a child. Sadly, this happens too often.*

***B.** Listen to confessions on a TV channel interviewing a prisoner. He will unwittingly tell his Script writing childhood and how, unconsciously and unknowingly to him, he repeated the drama in his adulthood. You will also note his significant rationalizations as if he was justified in criminal acts.*

***C.** Interview a person dying in a hospital. Inquire about their childhood per ' A' above. Ask: "And how did those old scenes affect you during the course of your life?" In listening to a dying patient, you are likely to experience one of the most beautiful moments in your life.*

***D.** Become a psychotherapist (or bartender) and listen closely to the Script as it unveils during the first session and how it keeps being repeated in subsequent scenes the person reports in therapy (or at the bar). You'll find it startling. It is also challenging to figure out how to get the person to go beyond the chains of childhood.*

***E.** Talk with a grandparent who has observed the life of a grandchild over the course of thirty years. The 'Grand' will be able to tell you the pattern of the child and how he or she keeps* *returning to the same issue. (Objective parents can also be questioned.)*

F. *Talk to someone who has physically abused someone. The person will tell how the pattern began in his childhood, how he switched to the Hated abuser role, and how others in his adult family plays the Adapted and Weak roles. Understand that his Adaptation as a child was being mute, hurting, and suspicious.*

G. *Talk to an aware sibling who has viewed, say, a brother who has played the Adapted role since childhood. Maybe the Adaptation is a Pretend Parent older brother, a baby brother who keeps expecting others to take care of him, or a rebel brother who is always quarrelsome.*

H. *And, of course, check out how both men and women change after the marriage ceremony. If you talk to certain women, they'll relate how their husband was so nice and pleasing prior to marriage and how he became rather hateful as soon as the ceremony was over. The rap of men will be equally instructive although they will think that the switch has to do with sexuality when, in fact, it has to do with taking an old Script role and transferring to the partner another old Script role. One question that works for the spouse is "Who am I like?"*

* * *

The idea is to check the original trauma and how it is repeated across the years. Some of this is dismaying when you see how people have been robotic and not free. You will also understand what Freud was learning when he first began his hours of listening. He heard repetition and human lives ruled by the unconscious. You'll hear the same thing in your listening jaunts. I find this challenging. Personal freedom and the ability to deeply love are the goals. It takes skill to accomplish those with others, but it is well worth doing. And, lest anyone get the idea it can be done rapidly, I counsel patience.

Chapter Fifteen

Uncle Shlomo

New York, New York. In the cab Sarah and I review the dozens of questions we want to ask my uncle but decide that, first of all, we'll seek to get him to talk - if, indeed, he's not as ensconced in silence as his brother Ezra. The building where Shlomo lives is excellent architecture. It overlooks Central Park. We enter a lovely apartment and are greeted by my uncle who warmly shakes Sarah and my hands. It feels strange. My eyes and his eyes match. My uncle is dressed in a gray suit, buttoned down collar white shirt, dark tie and worn dress shoes. He wears wire- rimmed glasses. We sit in comfortable leather chairs. He begins talking which relieves our fear that he'd be non-communicative.

"So we finally meet. I've known of you since your birth and have watched your development over the years ... 38 years ... it seems both a long and short span."

"Uncle Shlomo, Part of me is tempted to express bitter thanks for your 'knowing of me' but never contacting me across my lifetime. I needed father figures and had none."

My uncle calmly responds. "If you want to be angry, Daniel, it gets even worse. My brother Ezra knew how to be invisible, an old survival tactic from the 1930's and 40's. There were times when you were a boy that he visited your school playground and watched you express yourself. He was at your graduations from high school and college. Once, he watched from a gallery and saw you play squash. After you started your business, he'd blend in a crowd and see you on Michigan Avenue. He never told either you or your mother: still, he watched and in his own unique way guarded over you."

"This all hurts, Uncle Shlomo. I feel like crying. All the bitterness ends at this moment. What was, was. Dad's letter explained so much. We're interested in the personal history of my father and you. We have so many questions. I don't know the family whatsoever. And we desperately want to understand Ezra. Please talk freely."

"Our family is from Berlin, Germany where our name was spelled L o e w i. In the late twenties and early thirties, my parents owned a firm dedicated to buying jewels and pearls from around the world and selling them to private individuals and jewelers. They had three children: me, Ezra and Madeline." There's a painful pause. "Your grandparents were killed at Auschwitz as you already know." Sarah and I nod with respect of those who were so viciously murdered by the madman Hitler.

I gaze at Uncle Shlomo and say "I ... we, again ... have so many questions. Will you expand on the history so we can understand more?"

"By the early 1920's the family had become assimilated. The fact of being German meant more to us than any religious heritage even though we were well aware of seams of anti-Semitism in Europe. We were educated, cultured, and enjoying the life of fairly wealthy people. Dad's business supplied jewels all over Europe. He had mastered the supply lines, knew dealers around the world, and, though his small office was covert and not huge, patrons made appointments and came in to analyze and buy diamonds, pearls, rubies and other precious stones. Dad and mom kept up with political matters because our Jewish history has never afforded the luxury of blissful ignorance on issues of state. Demonizing Jews went back at least eight centuries in Europe.

Our parents read Hitler's Mein Kampf as soon as it was published in 1925. They knew trouble was on the horizon. By the way, I know some of this from Ezra because I was the youngest and not born until 1931. When I was two, the family left for France. Hitler had become German Chancellor in January of '33 and on April 1st a decree was sent to boycott Jewish stores. We left for Paris shortly after in order to re-locate and be safe."

"Before I continue this narrative, I'll switch and add pertinent facts about Ezra that will explain more to you about his emotional state. He was four in 1933 when the family left Berlin. In the process of packing a truck, Ezra was given the task of watching after his grandmother. He was to make sure she was on the back of the covered truck before they departed. According to him, he got to playing, was told it was time to leave, and completely forgot about getting her on the truck. When they stopped hundred of miles down the road, father discovered that Ezra had failed in his mission. He raised his voice in anger at his oldest son. It was too dangerous to go back. The unfortunate truth is that our grandmother was killed at Ravensbruck where the Nazis took women prisoners."

Sarah speaks up abruptly. "That was not fair of your parents. They were responsible, not Ezra. That must be the first great scar on his psyche ... being blamed for the death of his grandmother."

"And scar him it did. As I grew up and watched my older brother… imitated him, admired him … it was clear to me that he was always serious. I never saw him smile or play. Ezra did not have a normal childhood. He assumed responsibility for everything that arose. In France, our father continued his jewel business and all appeared well, that is, until the Nazi's took over France in 1940. It happened so suddenly - a virtual blitzkrieg - that our family did not have time to flee. On November 17, 1941 all Jewish assets were frozen in banks.

While Ezra was still a young boy by age, he dedicated himself to saving the family. According to him, he failed. I never blamed him for what happened; he blamed himself. On July 16 and 17 of 1942, 12,884 Jews were rounded up. It is true that an additional 10,000 escaped because they received advanced warning. Ezra acted like he should have known; I never thought any of the evil that occurred was his fault.

"We had a beautiful sister. Madeline. Late in 1942 she became a sadistic subject for Klaus Barbie, the butcher of Lyons - as Ezra mentioned in his letter. Are you sure you want to hear this? It's horrible and I may repeat something you already know."

"Uncle Shlomo, don't spare us. Ignorance has its own consequences as I, your nephew, know all too well. Not having a father led me to fantasize everything from my own ugliness and unworthiness to his extreme Narcissism. We must learn the truth. Neither Sarah nor I believe truth comes free of mental pain. We want to know what you know."

"Ezra and I found out about Madeline from another survivor. She was brutally beaten and tortured. It left our family in total shock. That was followed by another horror. Our parents, Ezra and I were tattooed. Nazi Storm troopers were very efficient. They first interred us at Drancy. Then we were placed on a packed cattle car for Auschwitz - seventy people in a space that should hold no more than twenty. Hitler said we were animals in his 1925 book; we were now treated as such. When we arrived through a gate proclaiming that Work Leads to Freedom (Arbeiten Macht Frei), our mother and father were separated from us. That evening we saw the smoke stacks belching forth the incinerated remains of our parents. No words can express the utter depravity of it all. I was age eleven and Ezra was thirteen . Both of us were capable of solid physical labor so we were saved for awhile. In our bunk house my brother took the top bunk of a four bunk bed making sure I was okay on the third tier just below him."

"So that explains his high bed" Sarah muses quietly to me.

"Maybe only a month went by … who was counting? … and we went on a work detail outside the camp. Soldiers with machine guns and large dogs accompanied us. At the other end_of our detail which was working on railroad tracks, an inmate almost decapitated a German soldier with his shovel. Chaos broke out. Prisoners were running in every direction. The soldiers and dogs went there - a minor massacre occurred.

"One parenthesis. All four of our family had jewels hidden in our clothes when we were arrested. The S.S. found mine; Ezra realized what was happening and swallowed one of his jewels, a very valuable black opal. He sifted through his excrement later, washed it carefully, and kept it for an emergency. When the chaos occurred on the work detail, he gave the opal to a kapo in order to buy us some time and give the SS no directions to where we fled. The kapo, a prisoner who got extra rations for cooperating with the Germans while being a supervisor, lived up to his bargain and did not point out the direction we ran."

I muse, "We found a black opal in his overcoat."

"I have one too. Before moving to Abilene, Ezra, who rarely shared, once held up a black opal and said 'This is a jewel, but it's also a metaphor. When I swallowed it at Auschwitz, it traveled on a journey through my body, was doused with acids, and ended up covered with shit. Then I cleaned it and used it for our freedom. Schlomo,' he said to me, 'our lives have been like that. We go through gut checks and are battered by acids. We can either clean ourselves up or stay mired in shit.'

"That was probably the longest he'd ever spoken to me. That's why I remember it. He startled me. But back to our flight from the work detail. Ezra grabbed my hand. We ran in almost the opposite direction of the disturbance, crossed a stream and ran on a hard-packed snow-filled gully for awhile and then hurriedly crossed a frozen field. The Germans came looking for us.

"They searched. Fortunately, the dogs were busy on the other end of the work detail with the chaos there. We hid in a large snow-covered haystack. Not sure where we were, the Nazi's, set the haystack on fire and riddled it with gunfire. Ezra covered me with his body and his back got horribly burned. He also was hit several times with bullets. I was unhurt. When they left, we crawled under a rocky outcrop, and packed Ezra's back and wounds with snow. Why he didn't go into shock, I'll never know. The Germans had moved to search in a different direction, and over time, we very carefully made our way back to France. Catholic Jesuits helped us greatly in our escape. They kept Ezra alive with salve for his burned back and bandages and medicine on his wounds. At great risks to themselves they helped him heal. Later they sneaked us through the countryside. I will always be grateful to those priests.

"I'm growing a bit tired. You are the first people to whom I've told this story. It is mentally wrenching to me. Elie Wiesel once said that silence is the only way survivors can cope with the horror of the death camps. The horrific reality has been branded in my mind for over sixty years. As I tell it to you two, I feel like it is all being experienced once again in my body. Several times I've felt my heart race."

"Uncle Shlomo, please rest a few moments. You've added sizable amounts to our understanding of my father and the original family. How can any human brain process the cosmic evil of it all? Because Sarah and I grew up in sheltered times, we're stunned. We can visualize a four year old boy with the devastating news of his grandmother's death - said news that had him surrender play - and even childhood itself. We've heard about Madeline and knew, without actual information, of the deaths of my grandparents. Now we understand Ezra's scars. It seems he received one major blow after another - as did you. How do you adjust?"

"In a major way, there is never adjustment. We adapted. Ezra adapted with revenge. We both joined the French Resistance. My job was to steal food and sneak it to the men and women hiding in the woods. Did you know that Jews were only one per cent of the French population, but fifteen to twenty per cent of the Resistance?"

"Uncle Shlomo, if you were to catalog all the ignorance we have of that period of time, you'd be able to write an encyclopedia."

"My brother became an incredible shot with a long sniper rifle. There is no putting it in nice terms: he became a cold assassin, getting back at the Germans for Madeline, our parents, and the entire insanity of the concentration and death camps."

"Uncle, his letter told me this part of the story. The letter we e-mailed told of his path of vengeance and the murders at Oradour."

"Oradour branded his brain even more with consuming hatred. He did change one of his tactics. He no longer concentrated his shooting in one area. Ezra would leave our encampment with bullets, cheese and bread and create havoc over a large range. He shot German soldiers on trains, one showing himself in the top turret of a tank, a sentry ... it made no difference. He was on a one man mission to kill them all. It marked him deeply. The only softness left was when he related to me. Even here, though, there were no smiles, no touches, no camaraderie. Protectiveness, yes. I also know there was love somewhere deep in the marrow of his bones. As soon as he got more bullets and food and was assured I was safe at one of our Resistance camps, he was off again. And that is the way he lived until the end of the war.

"You can say that both Ezra and I were reamed out … hollow … men without emotions. We appeared alive; we were dead inside. When the opportunity came - or was it Ezra, once again, who arranged it? … we came to Ellis Island and America.

"I left out something. Our parents had hidden a packet of jewels in our Paris home. We went back and retrieved them. They were hidden in a unique place - the ceiling molding in their bedroom. (Sarah and I exchange glances.) We sewed them into our clothes like we learned from other Jewish prisoners. So, when we came to New York, we were not poor. We had enough capital to start a business. We did not continue the business in jewels because we had been too young to be trained by our parents plus we had no international contacts. We did have contacts with émigrés from the old country that helped us establish a new business. I'm good with numbers; Ezra was good at research. We entered the world of finance and made our way, a very good way, I might add. The passage of sixty years allowed us to build up quite a fortune. We've lived minimally.

"I never married. It was a shock when Ezra became intrigued by your mother, Daniel. I'm afraid to say it, but I think she did all the wooing. She saw something in him and would not let him go. It was like he was trying to reach deep and find some shreds of long ago love in his core and … I believe this fully … whatever he discovered was translated into what he felt for your mother. He loved her. And, in the beginning, not just protected her like his wont was. He loved her as much as he was capable. Man to woman. As time went by, she became an obsession - like he was reviving Madeline and making sure she was alright. His love became possessive. Ezra finally caught what he was doing and realized he was choking the life force out of her in a strange, all-consuming manner. He knew he had to end the relationship and left when you were born. I never understood until I read the letters and the will you faxed me. I knew only that he went even more into a cave of silence and pain. He focused on work. Work. Work. Accruing capital. As did I."

"Then, in 2000 - he was 71 - Ezra was restless and wanted to try something different. We had both researched through Holocaust sites in search of pictures. He began to be intrigued by Abilene and the Eisenhower Center. I wasn't interested. I'm pure New York. I haven't left since we arrived and do not ever want to leave. This is my sanctuary. Ezra decided to move to that small town in Kansas. When I asked why, he said that he wanted to shuttle from the bucolic to the barbaric, from looking at the horrors of World War II and the Holocaust to something like he experienced in the woods with the Resistance, from the darkness of the thirties and forties to the light sleepiness of rural Kansas. I didn't understand it. I still don't. He said that Eisenhower knew the violent cruelty of war and the death camps and had somehow been able to mentally assimilate it all and become President of the United States. He admired the man, as do I. I have no idea how successful Ezra was. Over the years of his time in Abilene we only contacted each other about financial exchanges and the information about you, Dan, and some about you, Sarah."

"Rest a moment, Uncle Shlomo. Allow us to tell you about the months preceding my father's death. Near the Eisenhower Center is a playground. Ezra began to watch the children in all their spontaneous play. Then, one day an inspiration hit him (an archivist was observing.) Ezra went in a private area where no one could ostensibly see him, and sought to imitate the children. He sought to renew himself, to gain back what he had lost on that day in Germany when he was four years old. He tried to dance."

Shlomo stares at me in disbelief. "I'm having a hard time believing you. My brother never smiled, never played. He was seventy something … 77 maybe. And you are telling me that he was seeking to come alive again as a normal child? That's the most amazing thing I've ever heard in my life."

"It's true, Uncle. It's amazing to us also. The old archivist who witnessed it saw him from a very covert window. My father was breaking his body armor and tried to happily move. He was seeking to run and play and dance."

Shlomo looks at us still in the mode of disbelief. "It will take some time for me to assimilate that thought. It brings to mind my favorite sculpture: The Dancing Hasid. It captures a moment when a man with a very harsh Superego breaks through, raises his arms, claps his hands in celebration and then kicks his legs with joy. That is a picture I will seek to attach to Ezra in my mind. A lifetime of experience with the man makes this very difficult. Still, you've given me a blessing with that story. Thank you."

Uncle Shlomo pauses before continuing. "Which brings up another matter: finances. There is a lot of wealth you two will inherit. You not only get his share, you get mine when I die because, when I read what he did in his will, I followed with a will of my own. Sarah will receive forty per cent and you, Daniel, will get sixty. Ezra and I have been so work oriented that we never gave anything away. I hope you two break that mold in a philanthropic way. I don't want to intrude on what either of you do. But if you choose to create a foundation, the money will still grow because each year you only have to give away five per cent. I have already sent a substantial amount to join that of Ezra's at the First Bank of Chicago in each of your names. You have no obligation to me, to Ezra or each other for that matter: do with the money what you will."

Sarah speaks up: "It's all so strange. Everything. The story of Ezra. The money. The journeys we all have taken. The Holocaust is stone cold insane in the light of looking out the window and seeing a beautiful Central Park out there. I don't want money; I don't even like money. There is no way that I am going to live like a wealthy heiress walled off from normal people. Suddenly, my life in Abilene looks very good to me."

Uncle Shlomo wisely responds: "Sarah, don't be hasty. You can do a lot of good with money. You can still live as a pauper if you so choose. There must be a way to honor the craziness Ezra and I went through. It's up to you, though: you are free."

With tears in my eyes, I say, "Uncle, my mind seems to continually be in a whirl recently. I'm at a loss for words. Sarah and I need time to sift through what all this means. Sarah knows patience much better than me. She'll help me assimilate. I will ask you, Uncle Shlomo, to re-consider one decision of yours, namely, about always being here in New York. Next Autumn, on the first anniversary of my father's death, I will have a memorial service at my father' and mother's graves in Chicago. I ask that you come and stand with us at that time."

"I will. I must honor my brother and you two. I'll be there."

Sarah and I head toward the door. Sarah pauses and suddenly asks: "Did you enjoy the peaches, green beans and tomatoes?"

Uncle Shlomo looks confused. "The peaches …?"

"....green beans and tomatoes. Ezra sent them. They were sealed in Ball jars."

"Oh. Oh, yes. They were excellent. Thank you."

Sarah smiles triumphantly. I shake my head as we leave my Uncle's apartment. "I'm relieved, Sarah. At least you didn't ask him if he made marinara sauce."

****

Therapeutic Analysis

It may sound harsh to say it, but Shlomo lives in denial of most feelings, his traumatic childhood, and any need for relationships. I immediately add that I do not want to appear judgmental because it is understandable for some - if not many - to live in a kind of personality darkness, a closed secure world where basic needs are met while emotions are avoided. In order to accomplish the ruling out the past, the person needs to narrow interests down to a very small area. In addition, he or she needs to control their world and rule out erratic situations. I do not particularly like this option. Again, I repeat that, for some, it's necessary. Therapy is not for everyone.

Shlomo's obsession with accruing money provides him a measure of happiness and excitement, two key emotions. He thinks money, but not in the sense of Midas who loved it. Shlomo just loves numbers. Ezra's brother is uninterested in fame or power. Making money is a big fun game to him. That's all. He simply wants to raise his numbers every week. It probably never occurs to him that he's lacking emotional vibrancy. The man has security and is comfortable. To him, after a rough childhood, that is enough.

Analytically trained therapists - in the unlikely case that a person like Shlomo were to show up for sessions - happen to think differently than this honorable old survivor. We note the small personal signs that show remnants of sadness, scare, and anger as well as the missing element of tenderness. Therapists note, for instance, body shrugs when questions of personal history arise. It would also be clear that he does not experience awareness, spontaneity, or intimacy. Those would be quaint notions to the man. In therapy sessions, Shlomo would be antsy because he'd want to get back to his numbers and avoid all the discomforting considerations of psychotherapy.

Again, is Shlomo's choice OK? The answer is "Yes." It is fine if one can do it and does not want to encounter the ugliness and beauty of existence, does not want to expand freedom, is oblivious to natural experiencing, and is uninterested in intensely close or even casual relationships. For some terrifically bruised individuals, a life in a convent, living in the wilderness, or, say, a hidden condo in a major city is not only acceptable - it makes ultimate sense. Remember that the first task of analysis is a secure identity. There is no cosmic imperative to move to an expressive free Identity or Identity-in-Relationship. That is a longer road, one that offers greater rewards. Some will not go in that direction.

In terms of evaluating Shlomo's life, it's to be remembered that his money will eventually be used for human betterment. That is, if Sarah keeps her compassionate stance and Daniel continues to contribute in regard to his Board memberships and architectural firm that builds schools. Is there any question that either Dan or Sarah will lose their value centers?

***Script**. There is some complexity that I have avoided in my explanation of Scripts. It is clear, from this chapter, that Ezra's began with a terrific trauma when he was four years old. There is a developmental aspect to Script that demands more information than this book can legitimately deal with. In terms of Ezra, he had a shade of four year old psychology that added a dimension of seriousness that kept him from spontaneity. His grandiosity was twisted to think himself the cause of other's suffering. Dan's four year old issue with grandiosity was switched into Narcissism - a different option than that of Ezra. In a similar fashion, others may have a birth trauma, a problem with attachment as a baby, an exploratory issue during the crawling phase, a stubborn two year old component, or the magical years of three to six that are so primary in Freud's Oedipal formulations.*

For deep therapy, developmental clues are quite significant. What about Shlomo? He has the dimension of the two year old in his personality. Remember that he had a traumatic move when he was two years of age as the family fled from Hitler's Germany to France. If you want to know precisely how the issue affects him, think anal retentive. He gets money and saves it. His clothes are buttoned up. He lives tight.

Some readers may wonder how their early childlike trauma fits with Script. The developmental problem provides the ***style*** *of the Script. It determines the flow of the personality. Shlomo lives tight like a kid learning to hold it in for the potty. Solving the issue introduces massive new freedom to the personality.*

Ezra's black opal metaphor*: It provides an image for all who have experienced heavy traumas. You can choose to live like a cold stone, staying in darkness while being battered by your own self-produced acids and mired in crap. Or, you can travel through the necessary miles of darkness until you eventually wash the shit off yourself. For polite readers the grimness of the images may be shocking. It is to be remembered that psychotherapy is not a polite church stroll; rather, it is marked by fierce emotions that need straight confrontation and, yes, tough language and images. Sessions are frequently quite rough. They are not for the timid.*

The Bible metaphor matching that of Ezra is that of Jonah who, due to his bad choices, was contained in the belly of the whale. He eventually was vomited off on shore and had to wash the filth off of himself and pursue a meaningful path. Jonah was a tough case. His narcissism extended to the end of the book. He never caught the lesson that others are valuable. He was lost in himself and stayed locked in his own selfish image.

The moral in all metaphors of the kind of Ezra or Jonah are ever the same: work for freedom or stay stuck in your shit.

Chapter Sixteen

The Psychoanalyst

Back in Chicago several days later at the scheduled therapy session, I observe Sarah and Dr. Sidney Rabinowitz exchange polite words, shake hands firmly, and look much longer in each other's eyes than is customary. The good doctor covertly notes the incredible personality change in me as well as how I relate to Sarah. After seating ourselves in comfortable leather chairs, Dr. Rabinowitz speaks: "I've studied Ezra Loew's two letters, the will, your report on the interview with Ms. Hocking, and the accounting of your meeting with Shlomo Loew. How can I be of help?"

Sarah, not me, speaks up. "Dr. Rabinowitz..."

"You may call me Sid."

"Sid, we want to understand the psychology of Ezra. We also want to learn about the psychology of traumas. Are you familiar with PTSD and Survivor Guilt?"

"Forgive me Sarah if a bit of smile occurs around my eyes as you phrase your question. My name, Rabinowitz means 'son of rabbi,' We've had rabbis in our family since the Twelfth Century. Despite family pressure, I broke the mold and went to medical school though, the entire time, my plan was to continue eight centuries of rabbis who listened to people who hurt. Do I know anything about Survivor Guilt and the Holocaust? Since the late 1950's I've had patients from the Old South Shore, the Near North, Highland Park, and Skokie who have the tattoo and struggle with the Holocaust."

Sarah continues, taking charge as I sit amazed for my previous picture of the session was that I'd ask all the questions. "We are interested in your professional opinion regarding extreme traumatic situations like the Holocaust. If you will, please tell us about the therapy of major traumas and what works to heal people."

"That's a tall order. I can see this time will be different from the normal route of listening for 45 minutes followed by five minutes of my interpretations and counsel."

"That's right. We are not interested in that."

Sid looks startled. "Okay, I'll give you a professional assessment of Ezra Loew and how others have healed, to the extent anyone heals from such extreme situations as human brutality at its worst. Are you in agreement with that, Dan?"

"I am" ... the only words I speak prior to the end of the session.

"Guilt itself is an internal dialog. The Superego, that is the part of the mind that says 'should,' berates another part of the personality, the Id - the little child part. Inside the person a continued talk goes on ... as in ... 'You should have done more. ' 'I'm sorry.' 'You should have helped more.' ' I'm sorry'. This internal dialog continually beats in a person's mind. That is the first major source of Survivor Guilt. It is followed by mental visuals where the individual sees or fantasizes the gruesome (example Madeline in the cruel hands of Klaus Barbie), and feels shame that he or she was incapable of righting the wrong, healing the pain, stopping the suffering. Shame has a component of thinking that others mind-read your failures. This is projection, thinking others are judging you harshly when it is actually going on in one's own mind. Survivor Guilt (internal dialog) and Shame (hurtful mental images) are like twin worms eating away at the brain. Analysts like me de-construct those two until a person has a grasp of, and can control, the internal mechanisms."

"Does this also apply to PTSD and other major traumas?" Sarah inquired.

"Yes. Post-Traumatic Stress Disorder is simply the latest name for post-war Combat Fatigue. It has happened in every war since time immemorial. True enough some soldiers do not have it. The ones that do are usually those with a greater moral conscience (one aspect of the Superego.) In the war, the soldier had a continuous case of body tightness as a result of the constant uncertainty of what might happen. He or she might get shot, wounded or killed at any moment. Thus, they are on constant guard and cannot be loose and relax. They may kill in war and that may, unfortunately, include killing innocents.

"When they come home after the conflict, that tight scared stress is locked in their bodies. Sometimes a little sound or a surprised touch sets them off. Some call this paranoia; I do not. The reason is that I'm not interested in the least in diagnoses that put complex people in simple boxes. I'm interested in empirical detail opening paths to cure. I know deep suspicion to be a perfectly natural reaction to the craziness of war. This is treated by de-sensitization techniques where a patient hears the same noise or is touched when not on guard so many times that the old 'bell' no longer rings. The idea is to get rid of the feared surprise touch or sound that remains from those extreme situations.

"In addition, returning soldiers (or those going through catastrophic traumas) look around and see a different world than was just experienced. Everything seems shallow and unreal. War was real; ordinary life seems phony. In a way they are correct because much of life in a consuming culture is, indeed, trivial and meaningless. PTSD is tough to solve without talk therapy. Drugs may help during phases but, alone, they won't do it. People need to re-orient their bodies by learning how to breathe and move without stress. They need to re-acquaint themselves with what is moral and meaningful in the light of the vast amount of human hatred and tragedy they know all too well. That takes time.

“Many have nightmares that shake them and others around them in the wee hours of the morning. Freudians like me are usually good with dreams and nightmares. One way we treat returned soldiers is to have them go over the dream with us and give it a new ending. Another tactic is to have people keep journals and bring in appropriate anxious thoughts to share. Talking is cathartic and healing in and of itself.

“Now, Sarah and Dan: am I getting too particular and technical here?”

“You’re doing fine. Continue please,” Sarah said. Sid nods and goes on.

“The real task is re-learning emotions. Traumatized people must learn to authentically feel. Returning soldiers are afraid that if they feel sadness they’ll cry forever. Feeling anger scares them because they fear they may become violent and hurt a loved one. During conflict situations overseas, they often deny scare so their buddies will not see them acting ’chicken.’ That leaves them with the residue of denying a normal emotion like ordinary fear. Happiness, excitement and tenderness seem totally foreign because that leaves them vulnerable. They may have lost those emotions when a friend was killed. To regain ordinary feelings is no easy matter to accomplish. Further, along the way of learning emotions, each individual discovers that some blocked emotions not only come from problems of war, but from difficulties of childhood. Analysis is a re-training of emotions and takes a great deal of mental concentration and commitment. Achieving tender vulnerable love is both the greatest scare and the greatest accomplishment. It is invariably the last step of analysis." (Sid looks knowingly at me. Neither of us speak.)

"Going back to the Guilt matter, Ezra was typical in terms of seriousness. Part of Survivor Guilt is that the individual feels he (or she) is betraying the deceased loved one if there is the slightest sign of personally feeling happiness or excitement. For some, play of any kind is a failure to keep in mind the tragedy they experienced."

"I know that one" Sarah interrupts . She and Sid exchange long unblinking looks that speak unspoken volumes.

Sid continues "So they do not smile, laugh, play, and are rather emotionless. They are frequently morbidly serious. They carry personal mourning and pictures of loved ones in their eyes and in their bodily carriage as did Ezra. To repeat, they are rather terrified of loving again. Even ordinary excitement is threatening. Joy is gone.

"There is also grandiosity and unfortunate mind-reading in fearing to be real again. Certainly, no beloved deceased person would want their family survivor to imprison themselves in a coat of armor. Rather, if the deceased could speak, he or she would want surviving family members to laugh, play, and celebrate all the more. In a sense, the living are to honor the deceased by celebrating life even more fully. It is okay to fully experience life in honor of those who've died. In the case of the Holocaust, living a full life is a way to spit in the face of the demon, Hitler. This is a hard lesson to learn. Gestalt therapy developed by Fritz Perls helps here. He set up mock dialogs between the deceased and the survivor. That is dramatically beneficial to people. It relieves their tortured minds.

"Ezra did have a unique form of grandiosity due to the incident when he was four years of age. He held himself responsible for the death of his grandmother, as did, possibly, his father. In addition to death , there is nothing worse for a small child than for a parent to act shocked and horrified about something the child has done. That freezes a kid. It is a very serious parental mistake. At age four grandiosity reaches its peak. Ezra carried that all his life, unfortunately.

“Before I continue Sarah, understand that my profession is bent on removing negative remnants from childhood or later traumatic events that unconsciously damage adult options. That’s our main task. All day long we confront patients to be here and now and not carry old traumas that ruin the present. So if my words seem too confrontational, please tell me and I’ll slip into my more nurturing Rabbi pose.”

Sarah quickly responds: “Not in the least. In fact, if you minimize what you know according to your professional opinion, I would be disappointed in you. We want the truth as you see it and understand it: nothing more, nothing less.”

“Hmm. You are tough.” I shake my head in silent agreement.

“You are also from a good family with a loving father and mother. I can also see that you have experienced great suffering and have come back from it in one piece - exceptionally well, in fact.”

“That’s right, but this is not about me. Continue.”

Sid studies her with amazement. “Ezra assumed that he was responsible for the death of his parents. That is most likely not the case. Once the four year old grandiosity problem sinks in, it colors everything the person sees and does for the remainder of life unless there is serious therapy or extraordinary circumstances that show the person the limit of his or her power. Otherwise, the person assumes responsibility for everything and every one. It is a very difficult problem to solve and takes time.

Stacked on to his four year old developmental trauma was an additional three years of killing Germans as retribution for his sister and parents." Dr. Rabinowitz pauses.

Nodding her head, Sarah says, rather authoritatively, "Please continue."

Again Sid looks a bit surprised. He's not accustomed to office visitors pushing him. "I believe that, without therapy and transforming himself, Ezra was right about not raising Dan here. He'd unconsciously transmit his incredible sadness to his son - and his wife over time. According to Shlomo, his wife began to squelch her life force energy around her husband. If he had stayed, the family would have become enmeshed in guilt, shame, and mournfulness - though there'd be no conscious understanding of what was happening. To laugh would be frivolous; to play, forbidden. Dan would not have had a normal childhood because Ezra's dreadful seriousness would pervade everything."

"I agree." Sarah responds. Sid looks at her with pleased wonderment.

"The most arresting thing to me is Janet Hocking's story of Ezra identifying with children and seeking to imitate them. I confess that I've never seen or heard of any survivor using that route to healing. Well, I take that back. I had one highly successful businessman client who was totally ashamed when he had a severely retarded son. I told him he had lessons to learn from his son. Sure enough, he learned about happiness as his retarded son became this brilliant father's teacher. That is the only person I can think of who even partially took that route. I confess that I'll employ Ezra's discovery with future clients. I accept his wisdom. My future instructions to clients about emotions will be coordinated with sending clients to playgrounds in order to identify with children who are actually expressing spontaneous and free emotions."

Looking at the clock, Sarah remarks "Is there major psychological material to add?" She looks at Sid full in the eyes for a long moment.

He ponders deeply and says: "I've given you some of the psychoanalytic approach to the Holocaust and major traumas and how they affect people like Ezra. I focus on the pathological side, but that is not all I have to say; psychology is only part of the story.

"As to whether I would have killed Nazis like Dan's father, the unqualified answer is 'You'd better believe it.' I, too, lost family in Death Camps. As to whether Ezra was more obsessive than I'd have been, probably. But it makes no final difference. Analysis has to do with how people heal after the traumas, about what can be done to have a normal life. That's what_Analysts concentrate upon. If Ezra Loew had been in therapy for a number of years prior to the birth of his son, things might have turned out differently. He wasn't; things happened and that's that. We deal with what is real, not wish-filled illusions. As to my own personal response to the Hitler period and the camps, I shudder from deep within at the mere thought of it. I bow my head in honor of the deceased and in bewilderment at what humans wrought. I do not ascribe the horror to just a militant people; I'm too Freudian and Darwinian for that. I know that people, all people, are capable of violent sadistic acts. Any human can commit inhuman deeds or experience major traumas. That's life as it happens, not as we wish it."

Noticing the clock showing nearly the end of the hour, Sarah thoughtfully considers Sid's words and says "I thank you for your honesty in sharing your own reality as well as thoughts on traumas. Is there something else to add before we go?"

Reflecting for a moment, Dr Rabinowitz said "Yes, I guess there is another thing. It will be addressed to my patient Daniel Michelson. Dan, as long as Sarah is around, you won't be needing my services. She will not allow one flicker of pathology to occur in your personality. While I confront for an hour per session, she'll be confronting twenty-four hours a day. You will not get away with anything, any piece of victim thinking, grandiosity, shallow materialism, power ploys ... ANYTHING. So, I repeat: as long as Sarah is around, there's no need to call or make an appointment. Be authentic or you'll be in trouble. She will handle your therapy."

"Well, thanks, Doc. I notice you are not saying the reverse to her," I say, acting as if my ego has been bruised.

"All I can say to you, Sid, is that I hope she will be around forever ... and , as you will easily understand, she has never heard me say these words. You must be amazed since you've heard me dally around with women issues for hundreds of hours ... and many thousands of dollars, I might add. I will not completely disappear from your life though, because, Sid, you've been important in my life. This session has been mind freeing and I ... we ... thank you. I'll drop you a line now and then. And, if Sarah ever leaves me, count on my returning for five days a week for as much time as you can spare."

We shake hands all around, Sid staring deeply into Sarah's eyes once again. His final words are these: "And thank you, Sarah, for coming. If I need a Rabbi, I'll give you a call because you will be it."

Sarah and I leave the office with much deeper understanding than we had upon entering an hour earlier. It all makes so much sense if one telescopes time and views the problems in a holistic manner. Sid's counsel does have the touch of ancient rabbis. The Doctor's wisdom causes me to add new measures of forgiveness for my absentee father. And love for him, also. I take Sarah's hand and find myself so grateful for my new partner. Nothing is said.

We are both absorbing what we just learned.

****

Therapeutic Analysis

An explanation of Dr. Rabinowitz' training is in order. At the time he became a psychoanalyst, the procedure was to first get a B.S. degree from a university. That was followed by medical school, a year's internship in psychiatry and three years as a Resident in psychiatry. To become a psychoanalyst, there were an additional six or so years on the confessing couch - five days a week, one hour a day. The idea is to sift through the remnants of childhood like an archaeologist at an ancient human settlement site. The training is thorough. When that is added to the rabbinical heritage and decades of listening to clients, Dr. Rabinowitz happens to be very learned and wise.

At times in these italicized chapter additions I've mentioned how people can be therapeutically aided by identification with healthy figures. Maybe one of the best identifications is that of copying children at play. For those who have hardened armor, move slowly, and are lost in their minds rather than bodies, the advice is - to re-phrase an old poetic phrase - "Get thee to a playground!" Over many decades I've employed that counsel with clients and have been thoroughly pleased with the results. So, too, have those who re-learned from natural children.

I've also explained how analytic therapists see through surface presentations by noting every mannerism while having such deep rapport that they can actually discern what the client feels. In Dr. Rabinowitz' encounter with the depths of Sarah he knew, without listening to her story, that she was a person of remarkable integrity and integration. In my estimation, he is correct.

Since Rabinowitz was thoroughly impressed by Sarah, it's time to re-consider her psychology. We know a few things on which to base an analysis: she was an only child, the 'Princess' of her home, and married with a belief structure of creating the 'perfect' home with the 'perfect' husband and the 'perfect' children. Analysts think developmentally. Sarah's historic remembrances indicate that she was originally fixated at about the four year old phase. She probably could wrap her father around her finger and, with Electra separation from her mother (a competitor for dad's love), probably got her spoiled way thru the entirety of childhood. This is another way to say that she was, most probably, a female Narcissist who expected to automatically win with others. If there was opposition, she'd probably do the flirty seductive thing anticipating that men, especially, would fold. Cinderella beauty worked, if works meant that she got her way. If crossed by someone who did not buy the Beauty Queen story, Sarah probably became vengeful either overtly or with passive aggressive ploys. If her husband did not fall in line, for example, she'd punish him with no sex.

The Dream Narrative guiding her life was destroyed by the death of George, Lance, and Laura. The entire Doll House fantasy of the perfect home and life was demolished. Again, the mental software of everything being wonderful according to a little girl's projected movie was irreparably broken. The illusion was dead. Properly so, she was devastated and began her bus journeys. Psychologically speaking, when a person loses their narrative, they are viscerally lost. Normal paths of thinking, acting, planning, and even being no longer make sense. Cute manipulation of others ended bluntly by the deaths of the ones Sarah loved.

So, she wandered mindlessly, taking a bus in any direction and ending up, as she described it, 'dry empty' in Abilene. Forced to start again, she began building a new narrative where she was not the main character. Rather, there was literature, music, nature, and an awareness of the pain of others. She was no longer a grown-up child; she became a mature person whose life was built on awareness. Accepted by Ezra, Sarah had also learned, obliquely, about the value of compassionate care.

Adding all this together, she no longer is obsessed with her looks. Sarah lost the idea of being seductively cute in order to get her way. Certainly, it would not work with Ezra nor does she even try it with Dan Michelson. She has accomplished a cataclysmic re-orientation of values. Reality, not appearance, is her focus. Having solved the basic human fear of abandonment, she knows what she wants and will not adapt in order to please. Consuming has been replaced by wanting to be a contributor.

In sum, Dr. Rabinowitz' evaluation is right on. She merits being looked upon as the therapist's therapist because Sarah Anne Bannock has become a full human being. My conviction is that those on the other side of childhood fantasies, those who know about death and tragedy - those who have re-done their values according to human hurt are the redemptive people so needed by a sick world. They've used personal hells to spend the remainder of their lives giving back.

* * *

I'll end this chapter's analytic notes with a comment about therapists. Just as with plumbers or auto mechanics, there is tremendous variation. Some know what they are doing; some do not. Many have never examined their own personalities and pass on some of their own unfinished neurotic issues to clients. Some follow the fad of a given therapeutic rhetoric and simply spout supposed truisms.. Some freely dispense pills. Others give matronly or paternal advice ex cathedra. Sill others convey a prejudice of a given authoritarian rhetoric passed on by a charismatic founder. Some get lost between what is and isn't (the am and the ain't), get confused as to what to do next, and then nod wisely as if they know what they are doing, when the reality is that they are passively ignorant. Some know absolutely nothing about the dynamic unconscious with its power to continually flood childhood issues into present-day life.

It is unfortunately true that even a brilliant innovator like Freud failed to solve his own Script of being a spoiled son of a doting mother who thought him "golden" (her word.) Freud thought himself 'above' and frequently failed to listen to other brilliant companions. Another Analyst, Carl Jung, never grew beyond his magical mother and presented many non-empirical hysterical ideas that simply further religious mumbo-jumbo.

I've met Analysts who are passive aggressive Narcissists, others who are control freaks, many authoritarian know-it-alls, one or two sexual predators, and others who are manipulative gamesmen. In Indiana there was a psychiatrist who popped every client with electroshock treatments and then bragged to peers about how high his electric bill was. Some therapists just herald the latest drug, while receiving benefits like free travel and expenses to a workshop in a distant fun city by a pharmaceutical company.

To find a good car mechanic or plumber is often difficult. It may be problematic to pierce through a therapist's academic degrees and inquire about his/her own path through mental suffering. It becomes necessary to check out a therapist's humanness to see if she or he is up-front and real. If they are evasive and pull the curtain down to hide their oneness with ordinary people, get the hell out. You want someone with a bit of humility who is still growing; not someone who is scared of being an ordinary human who has traversed the halls all of us must travel in order to gain mental health.

As for Dr. Rabinowitz he qualifies. He's part rabbi, part Analyst, and most, of all, an honest human being. He's also wise about Sarah.

Chapter Seventeen

The Ezra Fund

The next day Sarah and I leave First National Bank of Chicago utterly stunned. Neither of us speaks for a long period of time. We just filled out papers and checked to see the inheritance each of us received from Ezra with additional funds from Uncle Shlomo. Our accounts are separate. The sums are astronomical.

Taking a gulp of air, Sarah manages to say " When I saw the numbers on my ledger, there were far more zeroes than I ever anticipated. It's a good thing Shlomo did not mention the amount when we were in New York. I'd have fainted. I thought I had reamed out of my soul the last drop of materialism. The amount in my savings now has me scared. My breathing is shallow. I fear that I will be seduced by money and begin the luxury route. Why Dan, if I want, I can buy the whole town of Abilene Kansas!"

"I sure hope you don't do that. I've done my share of ladling out macaroni and cheese and if you buy several restaurants, I'm afraid you'll put me on the line again. One thing is sure: you won't be marrying me for my money."

"Is that a proposal?"

"Sarah, I'm on the precipice of asking you but, as strong willed as you are, I'm afraid we'll have to make the decision at the very same moment. No macho proposals, no man on bended knee - none of those - are in order. Anyway, we need to come to terms with this money. I, like you, am shocked. I'm wealthy! I don't have to work or do anything but travel and play for the rest of my life. I can buy a yacht to sleep on in Lake Michigan. I might just buy a high rise and look out at the world."

"Get real, Dan. Neither of us can live the wealthy lifestyle. We're not made that way. We didn't grow up and go through all we have gone through in order to be wealthy, luxury-seeking swells. Neither of us can live without some kind of work and creativity. That's who we are. As to some kind of married union, I at least know that you are not looking for a hired nanny, cook and housekeeper."

"No housekeeper, please. Cook maybe. As to our newly arrived wealth, I agree. Money can be choking. It can replace one's identity with appearances. As hard as we've worked to be ourselves, we cannot surrender to a life of consumerism buying more and more expensive things. Wait a minute: did you say Nanny!? I'm interested."

"Just kidding. I'm too rich to pamper a spoiled Cubs fan. Dan, I'm so glad we are one on the subject of wealth. My thinking is that we need to figure out a way to honor your mom, Ezra, Shlomo, the Loewi family, and both of my families. That's priority."

"I love it when you say 'we' and have us mutually figuring this out. Shlomo mentioned philanthropy. Do you have any thoughts?"

"Right now my first priority is food. I suggest we walk over to our favorite deli, get a sandwich, catch a cab, and have a picnic by the Children's Zoo at Lincoln Park."

"I couldn't agree more. Hey! It's your time to pay," I say laughingly.

When the counter man takes a single glance at us, he said: "Okay, I get it. Corned beef and pastrami on rye divided exactly in half. Pickle the same way. Two bottles of water. Next!" We laugh and think it so Chicago typical.

After the cab ride to Lincoln Park, Sarah and I are silent for about an hour during and after lunch. It's one of those beautiful Autumn days in Chicago. We quietly watch kids at the petting zoo. A boy and girl run by who were the ages of Lance and Laura when they died. Sarah suddenly bends at the waist in her grief and is racked by deep sobbing. I get on my knees in front of her and hold her tightly as she weeps.

"Dan, there is no way I'll ever be free of missing my children. They were so beautiful and precious. There'll always be a chapel in my heart where I retreat in silent meditation to be with them. I hope you understand."

"I know, Sarah, and would not have it be different. I respect your pain. I'll be outside the chapel when you visit your children and honor you with respectful silence. Please hear me: I love you so much."

She sobs all the more. I gently press on her back encouraging her to peal forth her tears just as they come forth from her natural bodily reactions. People passing by seem to understand and give us respectful space.

Silence then reigns for perhaps an additional hour. We sit absorbing the park's beauty and the thrill of kids enjoying themselves at the petting zoo.

I suddenly have an inspiration.

"We are on the same wavelength about money and philanthropy. There is so much need in the world that I am lost how any person can make a decision one way or another. Starvation, medical needs, education, poverty ... the list for suffering humanity boggles the mind. Maybe, Sarah, we can go back to our own tragedies and get a hint from what we've experienced. With a wave of sadness, I think of how your children did not get to finish childhood and play freely like these children around us here at the zoo. Ezra stopped his playing at age four. The breakthrough of my father's frozenness came when he began to copy children. Somewhere in all that pain is a clue as to how we can invest money wisely… in the souls of people … maybe in children at play."

Having recovered from her healing catharsis of sadness, Sarah speaks up: "Dan, you may have hit upon something. Let's stick with it. Philosophically, it makes no difference where you attack the problem of human suffering. There are vast oceans of need. Each gift only accomplishes a smidgeon of what is needed. Pain, suffering and evil are like runaway tanks and helpers like us only have the equivalent of a cotton ball to stop their erratic paths. We must narrow our focus and see exactly what we can accomplish. The play idea is intriguing. I love the idea. Still, I question: Is it too trivial? Should we, instead, think of helping poverty, medical issues or starvation … in Africa, for instance?"

I reply, "What a metaphor Sarah! A runaway tank and cotton balls. That is disheartening in one way; nevertheless it is true. All we have is a cotton ball even with all our money. Any effort seems so paltry, so utterly worthless. And yet: hurl we must!

"Sarah, it's like you frequently say, we must focus. Rather than simply throwing our money at insurmountable problems, ones that demand the wealth of nations to solve, I think we need to concentrate all our energies on one narrow issue. As you know, my firm builds schools. Do you realize how many times we've encountered school systems who will build a school and then get argumentative about our plans for neighborhood playgrounds attached to it? Let me tell you that the number is close to seventy per cent. They'll build buildings and sports fields; they ignore the crucial significance of play for normal growing younger kids in the neighborhood."

I'm feeling very excited. "On our walk last week north of our home in Abilene, I remember looking at the school and playground. They added swings and slides; that's basically it. If I were to mention a petting zoo or a concrete play pool to a school committee hiring our firm, for instance, they'd scoff with peals of laughter. Committees we meet with usually think childlike play not worthy of their considerations. I don't. Of course, I understand difficulties in using tax money, but it bothers me greatly that children are slighted. If Ezra is to be my mentor besides my benefactor, I think he also passed on clues about the preciousness of children spontaneously expressing themselves."

"Dan, this is exciting. With our huge funds, we can become the Carnegies of playgrounds. Carnegie built libraries. We are able to research and become authorities on spaces and equipment that will keep alive the wonder of children at play. I'm thinking we might concentrate upon playgrounds for kids, toddler age through twelve. I love it. "And," she adds, ""I've never thought about how limited most parks are in Abilene. You're right. There was little color, no playhouses, not much in the way of large jungle gyms: just a few swings and an old slide out in the sun that must be scorching in the summer."

"Are we going too fast here? I know one thing, Sarah. I am independent enough and you are the Archetype of Independence so neither of us will submit our philanthropy to a committee. We either figure it out and carefully follow up or it won't be done."

"I have a name, Dan: The Ezra Fund. If we are going to be wild here and really throw around ideas, I just came up with a dilly of a symbol for our foundation also: The Dancing Hasid. I'm building on Shlomo's idea which captivates me."

With tears in my eyes, I say, "That image makes me so happy, Sarah. It's like dad's resurrection also. It's done: We'll become champions for children."

Sarah looks at me strangely. "Oh my. Is not this the man who threw girl friends away if they even mentioned children? What a switch! Do you realize that this may mean we have thousands upon thousands of sons and daughters?"

"The more, the better. I'm a changed man. Ezra, truth and you have transformed me. I know what is valuable now: people. Not things, success, power or whatever. That junk is so illusory. And to think those were my goals before the Sheriff's phone call!"

The day at the children's zoo seems to hang on. We sit close and touching on our bench. A vendor comes by selling popcorn for the pigeons. We buy some and throw it out without thinking. With minds engrossed in fantasies about the Ezra Fund and the utter joy of being able to release spontaneity and play of children with our philanthropy, Sarah and I feel totally complete. We're content. We have a mission for the remainder of our lives. Occasionally one of us taps the other on the arm and points out a child feeding a lamb at the petting zoo, a delightful little girl excited about a balloon, or a little boy imitating a monkey.

"Our children," Sarah says. I nod affirmatively. Hours go by. This is forever time.

Nearby Sarah notices old men playing checkers and chess on concrete tables with small benches on each side. "In addition, we can add those tables so grandfathers and grandmothers will have places to play also as they watch over their grandchildren. Dan, do you realize how creative we can be? We can research toys and playground options on the Internet and come up with some grand ideas. This is so exciting."

More time passes with both of our minds teaming with ideas.

I suddenly say somberly "I propose..."

She smiles, "Oh my, here we go again ..."

"Not that, Sarah, although I'm ready. You and I are so independent, any proposal of marriage had best be said aloud mutually. Anyway, the marriages I've seen boil down to either the man or the woman ending up being the boss. I'm too old and stubborn to be a wimp and you'll never be a traditional wife. We'll have to decide the Big Issue at the same time. Now, what I was saying is that, I propose, since November has arrived in Chicago, that we fly to Abilene and stay for a day or so. Then we'll fly to San Diego, and on to cruise around the Mediterranean. That's what I propose. Are you game for some travel?"

"Yes to all you just said. Hold my hands, look into my eyes and, on the count of three, pucker up and say 'Yes'. I laugh uproariously. Holding hands and looking into her eyes as she counts ... one, two, three ... we say together "Yes."

I add: "On the count of three say 'I do". She laughs. "One, two, three." We say together "I do" and our relationship is sealed. We become spiritually married right at that moment. My heart glows. I've found my soul partner.

More time passes. "During our silence just then, Sarah, I had architectural insights like I've never had before. I decided that I want the schools my firm develops to be more artistic and less boxy. I want morning light coming in through upper windows that show different images on a large school symbol on the wall. Do you know that there are software programs showing how light hits on a building at all times of the year?"

"No, I didn't. Tell me more of your ideas, Dan."

"I want more light in the halls, light cascading down from skylights. I want the school administration with glass all around so kids can see their principals working for them. I want more color splashing around in the rooms and a general sense of openness. I want kids to feel a sense of community in the midst of structural beauty, beauty that teaches them to love art, science, history and all the disciplines."

"Dan, you're virtually glowing with creativity."

"Of course, I am: I just got married!"

We laugh and squeeze hands. "Sarah, part of education is inspiration. As an architect, I want to inspire kids to be creative and innovative. I want my buildings to communicate that. All this is new to me. Further, guess what?"

"Okay, I'll bite: what?"

"I know I can convince school boards to go for these new innovative structures we are going to build!"

I suddenly stand, throw my arms upwards, clap my hands, kick my legs, and begin dancing like my image of the Dancing Hasid. We both laugh freely. It's all so wonderful. At that very moment we began to think like children and for children.

It's such a memorable day. The bank. The Deli. The cab ride to Lincoln Park. Our meal. Sarah's catharsis. The exchanges about The Ezra Fund. Realizing that freeing joy in children will be Ezra and Shlomo's heritage, a fitting tribute if there ever was one. Our soul union. My breakthroughs in terms of architecture. We both feel complete.

The Ezra Foundation is still another step in soul togetherness. I sense a new spiritual quality as we hold hands and walk to our North side home. I know inside that I love this woman with all my heart. The old me is gone. The new me is starting a journey with the finest human I've ever met. I'm the most fortunate man in the whole world.

****

Therapeutic Analysis

It is worthwhile to recall Sigmund Freud's combating dualism. He pitted the Life Energy principle (libido) vs. the Death Energy principle. He pointed out that some give themselves over to mortido and spend their existences lying, cheating, stealing, robbing, killing, etc. In other words, their Narcissism is turned inward to selfish ends and they do whatever they deem necessary to fulfill their goals. Freudians also pointed out that mortido wins when a person pursues self-destructive pursuits such as drug, alcohol or food addiction and other similar tissue destructive options. In the same mode, personal surrender to psychological issues like despair or rage all represent mortido victories.

Luckily and fortuitously for the future of people on earth, some give themselves to libido - Life Force Energy options. These redemptive people hallow life and work for its continuance in manners ranging from ecological matters to working for peace, justice and love. Their numbers may be few but their efforts are powerful.

Just as an objective spectator, one might conclude that mortido wins. Things deteriorate. Metal rusts. Wood rots. People grow old and die. Nature, as the poet says, is "red in tooth and claw." The second law of Thermodynamics is that things wear down. All life forms, from microbes to humans, eventually die. (This is one reason Freud kept emphasizing sex because it keeps the earth renewing itself.)

Still, it is fair to ask "What is the apex form of Life Force Energy? When does it appear that libido is definitely winning?" The answer is: "Children at play." They run, squeal, laugh, mimic, throw and catch balls, slide, swing, climb, etc. Free expressing children breathe deeply, move freely and make joyous sounds. None of these expressions were allowed at Ravensbruck where Ezra's grandmother was killed; none were heard at Auschwitz where Ezra and Shlomo's parents were incinerated. The sounds of children at play is the music of renewing humanity. This is Life Force Energy released, the herald of life's unwillingness to surrender to mortido.

This leads to the second point.

Spending one's energies for others while minimizing self happens to be one of the most important growth steps in terms of trauma and redemption. The greatest solution from history for those who have been on destructive get-nowhere paths or been on the receiving side of ugly tragedy, is to become a contributor. Several times across the decades of doing therapy, I saw clients who had been by the bedside of their own children when death occurred. Parental grief was appropriately massive in therapy sessions. Eventually they came to the position that it's necessary to spend a good portion of the rest of life helping kids. My thinking is that this may be necessary, also, for soldiers who unwittingly kill innocents in a home they just riddled with 50 caliber bullets. The old therapeutic proverb is that "human hurt demands human healing' meaning by that one needs a human, not a pill, to mentally recuperate from major trauma. So, too, if one finds himself or herself on the destructive side of the ledger, it is necessary to switch and be on the constructive side: It's now time to concentrate on human healing, nor hurt.

Living the giving life actually provides a most wonderful unplanned gift for the giver. To say 'giving feels good' is to be trite. To sit by someone dying of cancer and holding her/his hand provides a sense of meaning beyond understanding. Providing a coat for a cold homeless person just plain feels right. To take food to a Food Bank and then see someone who is hungry walk out with your gift provides a sense of having really helped. Giving can even be extended to public service where, though salary is rather poor, you institute programs that benefit others where students get college educations, the unemployed find jobs, or the homeless receive housing help. All in all, it is better to give than receive as the old book has it. There's no question about it.

I'm hesitant to say more on the subject of giving because it may appear too moralistic. Quite the contrary, my belief is that giving is essentially moral. Can you imagine Sarah and Dan using their immense resources to buy luxury homes in Cannes, Ireland, Italy, or Acapulco? If so, their lives would revolve around changing formica counter tops to granite, then marble, then, surprisingly, concrete - as the modern trend has it. Their wine rooms at each place would be temperature controlled. They could go to wine auctions and buy cases of only the best fruit of the grape in the world. Time could be spent buying the latest and greatest of cars. They could have large entertaining cocktail parties inviting the rich and powerful.

Ask yourself: Does that sound like the desired lifestyle for a man whose grandparents were incinerated in a Nazi crematorium, or a woman who sat pinned in a car while hearing her two children take their last gasping breaths in life? It is unfortunately true that some wealthy people take Narcissism to absurd heights. They never learn the lesson of Midas that fascination with gold leads to hardening of the bodies and the hearts of those you love.

Sarah and Dan - both of whom want to expand their own souls to the very end - know that their reward is one that honors the silent and almost invisible Ezra. Like his silent viewing of his son … after a playground is established and functioning … they want to hide in the shadows, hold hands, and watch the spontaneous activities of children at play, children who won't notice the couple watching them expressing unleashed joy.

Some say the ultimate wealthy never get enough. Enough, for Dan and Sarah, is watching one child freely be and laugh from the heart. That is a way to honor Lance and Laura, Shlomo, and Ezra. That honorably keeps beloved dead very much alive.

In this sense, then, life is payback. Others have loved us and provided. Now, it is our turn. Redemptive history marches to that tune. Again, is that moralistic? No. It is life with a mission.

Chapter 18

Identity and Teamwork

The day begins in Chicago where I eat twice the number of scrambled eggs and toast than usual. Sarah looks at me a bit puzzled. I catch her look and confess that I do not want to stop and get a meal on the road between where the plane lands and our home in Abilene. "Let's make a run to the grocery store on the way to the place and eat at home," I say innocently. She smiles knowingly, and packs crackers and cheese lest we get hungry en route. For fun, she makes a show of putting a box of macaroni and cheese in the sack.

We fly to Salina where a rented car is available to take us to our home in Abilene Kansas. Sarah and I are accustomed to long periods of loving silence and we both, in fact, relish it. While driving along, Sarah suddenly speaks

"Dan, I've got a sudden inspiration. You put 65 per cent of your money in the Ezra Fund and I'll put in 35 per cent."

That makes me laugh with a very deep belly laugh. "There you go. Women! This money we inherited is so huge it is like playing with fake Monopoly dollars. So you want to start the game with my giving away Broadway and Park Place. That seems odd, but fair. Why not? I'll go sixty-five per cent. Now, my wealthy friend, what will you do with the money that leaves you better off than me?"

"I'm thinking ... I'm thinking ... but I don't want to be too forward."

"That's a switch" I say smilingly while shaking my head.

"Let's say that we really develop a deep partnership, something beyond the marriage thing ... a union of souls, bodies and futures. Ceremonies don't mean much to me - been there, done that. I'll have to work with an accountant (or a mathematician) but I'm thinking that with my extra money I'll buy half of your business, half your house and match you in per cent of the Abilene home. I want to make sure we both end up with the exact same amount of money in the bank. I'll be President of the Ezra Foundation and you'll be President of the architectural firm. How's that one, my Pigeon love?"

"I'll still be ahead, my love."

"How's that?"

"You've forgotten one of our quests in Abilene. If there is a stash of cash or jewels behind the crown molding near Ezra's bed, I'll get sixty per cent and you get a measly forty per cent. That seems correct to me, actually. The man should be in charge."

"Don't count on it, Daniel. Don't forget that you are paying for our European vacation. I want to stay at five star hotels and eat lobster twice a day. Since I'm your guest, I'm also taking only my purse so you can buy me clothes as we travel along. If you are ahead when we return, I'll catch up fast. I can eat on ten dollars a week while you spend thirty bucks on one meal. I like macaroni and cheese. Also, I can wear my sweats every day because I don't have an image problem. I'll pass you by in months."

"Are you implying that you'd bring boxes of that yellow powder and elbow macaroni into our home just in order to match my wealth? That's a spiteful form of getting even. You ought to be ashamed, Hayseed."

"Don't cross me. I have womanly wiles."

"You sure do, Sarah. We'll perfectly divide in half anything behind the molding, okay?"

Upon arrival we hurry to Ezra's old room. I crank up the bed and study the crown molding until I figure it out. Carefully removing the board, I discover a blue velvet pouch whose contents are the size of several billfolds. I carefully put the molding back in place, crank the bed down and hand the unopened bag to Sarah.

Going to the kitchen we carefully study the booty. Among other valuable jewels there is a single beautifully cut diamond. There is also a large black opal which is almost a perfect match for the other one. "It doesn't take a lot of figuring to know what the diamond is for," I say as I hold the sparkling jewel up to the light. "Do you really think my father was that far ahead of me … of us? I want this put in a ring for your finger, Sarah. That must be what Dad intended."

"I don't go in for big rings, Daniel … maybe in a necklace that I'll covertly wear. Only you and I'll know about it. I don't do ostentation." Looking at the opal, Sarah adds, "Interesting. We now have matching black opals. We could hide them in our clothes so we always have a fallback option."

I smile at her. I'm surprised about something else. It's nice to be home.

In fact, the house in Abilene seems just right. It's a place to become mindless, absorb nature and the rural life, and rest. For a few days, all Sarah and I want is the mood of the place to sink into the marrow of our bones. Loving silence is normal. The peace of the place takes us over. Occasionally, we just sit quietly and close on the porch. We occasionally touch with mutual love when we hear children at play several houses down the street. Our mission. Ourselves. Us.

Abilene is a small town with less than seven thousand inhabitants. Like all towns, there's a poor section and a more well-to-do section. As the location for the first venture of the Ezra Fund, we search for a place where a new playground for young kids might be located. My architectural firm has always been insistent that schools should match the community and Sarah and I have the same standard for the proposed playgrounds. We also examine existing playgrounds. Are they modern with many options? No. Do they have the same facilities for young kids as the ones for older, more competitive teenagers? No. Save for swings and slides, young children are ignored except at the Eisenhower Park where there are nice facilities.

We drive around in order to analyze where kids play in their own backyards due to no close playground. We consider what equipment will work, how important it is to provide benches for parents to be close and keep watch, and other safety matters that are highly significant. Everything is a learning experience. Sarah suddenly notices kids playing with a garden hose as they shoot water into the air and on each other. This causes her to think how neat it will be to figure out a shallow pool with water shooting up. Such a feature would provide cascading water children could run through and under. Ideas are flowing in the minds of us both.

Understand, this is not a Save The Children campaign; it's a plan to provide resources so future generations have the possibility of an enjoyable childhood. Joyful freedom for kids, in and of itself, is the goal. Sarah and I find that richer neighborhoods west of Buckeye have park space, but the section east of Buckeye - which is more middle class - is mostly devoid of playground facilities. "That doesn't seem right and we'll do something about it," Sarah firmly states.

Our minds spin with options. I work on drawings on the kitchen table. Sarah surfs the computer in order to research playground materials. At city hall we investigate available land east of

Buckeye and obtain regulation information. This provides loads of fun for both of us; it's like we both are re-doing childhood. There is a virtual flow of childlike excitement in our bodies. Sarah and I hustle around checking on this and that. It's all so immensely creative. Certainly, we have more work to do on the Ezra Fund, but the basic goal is set. We'll develop playgrounds honoring natural expressions of children. That's solid gold in our minds. Our work future (and love future) is set.

After several days of research, we begin making plans for a European vacation. It is not just Chicago that has rough winters; so, too, does Abilene Kansas. It's time to go to warmer climes overseas.

"Dan, I confess. I want to see how children are being treated in the various countries. I want to see how they provide playgrounds for toddlers through twelve years of age. Do they let kids be kids? I'm not interested in testosterone bullfights in Spain, getting a tan in a seductive bikini on the Riviera, or sipping sauces on elegant food in Paris. That stuff has a measure of value to it. I won't deny it's appeal. But I confess: the tragedies we've been privy to does not allow me to be selfishly frivolous.

"I may have caught a case of seriousness from Ezra, a seriousness that does not allow me to be narcissistic while ignoring the suffering of others. With the enormity of the money in our Fund, let's tour European playgrounds. These are my thoughts about our vacation. Therefore, count on me to not go crazy over things. If that is bad of me to program what I'm interested in on our travels, know it now before we cross the ocean."

"Sarah, you amaze me. Your confession calls forth one of my own. I haven't made a mental movie of what we do as carefully as you have. I simply want to be with you and flee to warmth, avoiding brutal cold Lake Michigan winds or those whistling across the Kansas plains. You've taken me aback. Now that I've had a half minute to think about it, I know you are exactly right. We cannot flee meaning. We cannot simply blot out the Holocaust and my father and uncle's struggle. We cannot forget Lance and Laura. We'll make this a journey of learning. I want to add one other thing, Sarah. Are you always going to be ahead of me? Is my future to be a follower?"

"You slay me, Daniel. If I remember correctly, you had the first thought of how to spend the money in the Ezra Foundation. Our relationship is going to be mutual energy, mutual sharing, mutual love. I teach you; you teach me. You already have. When Ezra died, I may well have stayed in Abilene and simply become a comfortable country girl taking care of a garden. You offered options, the chance of a new life. When you arrived, I blossomed and unleashed loads of creativity I didn't know I possessed. Evidently, truth and life energy held to earth will rise again. So don't tease me about being 'The Leader'. We're a team. I'll keep my private identity, sure. In many ways though, we're one. We'll choose moments and not go for some ugly symbiosis where we merge and lose our private selves."

"Hmm,"I murmur, "Symbiosis. Are you talking dirty again? Okay. Okay. I may teach you some business skills and have a few ideas, but you're teaching me Life. We're mutual teachers. That's the way it has been and always will be. I love our union; I love our separateness. I'll do the architecture; you do the playground equipment. I'll do the site planning; you handle people. I'll have my private time where I do my thing like squash; you - without my even saying it - will certainly do your thing. This is a model I've never thought of before. I bet that, obliquely, we will have grand soul union for the remainder of our lives. I love you Sarah. You are the inspiration for a whole new world for me."

"I love you, too, but I have another confession, Daniel."

"Okay. Let's hear it."

"I'm still only taking a small purse so you can buy me appropriate clothes in Europe."

"Is this another ploy to make sure that I don't have more money than you?"

"Maybe."

****

Therapeutic Analysis

First a word about partnership in a marriage. It is highlighted in this chapter in terms of money, in terms of how both contribute to creative innovations, and in terms of dividing management responsibilities. One key to a successful marriage is making sure that there is cooperation at all levels. During our decades of doing therapy, my Analyst wife and I seldom experienced a week without a couple arguing about money. Our solution was ever the same: split the income and divide the responsibilities with transparent accounting at the end of each month. Guess who would resist that? Men. They frequently had the idea that they were the providers and should keep the money under their control. The problem is that scheduling one's self as the caretaker and the woman as the dependent wife leaves a bit of resentment in each - him for her spending and her for his doling the money out from on high. Further, it was our experience that, if divorce proceedings were instituted, the forty plus year old man who had controlled family finances inevitably sought to hide some assets. At the level of people we saw, the number hidden was often upwards of two hundred thousand dollars. Sometimes more. Sometimes much more.

So we pushed both married partners to assume responsibility for financial matters. Men were very hesitant about transparency regarding finances. We stood firm with our recommendation. For couples who made the switch there was a growth in terms of open communication. Once that is established, love blossoms.

Therefore, I think Sarah's emphasis entirely logical. It gives a foundation. Each is responsible. Each is accountable. Openness is the standard. In other words, each little step - be it money or transparent sharing of emotions - adds to mature love.

* * *

Anyone courageously plowing through this book dealing with painful human realities is now ready for the final great lesson:

Life without a mission is a hollow existence indeed.

For some the mission is to provide for their own family and getting the kids through school. That is very honorable. For others, the goal becomes more expansive. They look around and discover how their stubborn ounces of power can help. Narcissism fades when one joins with contributors, that is, those who, across the centuries, have gradually pushed the human venture into more loving and just paths.

The lesson is clear. All those scarred by personal tragedy can either crater or they can find a way to help someone else. As quickly said in a previous italicized section, even negative concentration upon the self happens to be Narcissism. If you think yourself the ugliest, the weakest, the most helpless, the one closest to death - with those negative superlatives - you just went wading with the Greek god Narcissus. There comes a time when it's necessary to forget yourself and join the band of those, throughout history, who had a vision and worked for, a better world. The familiar shibboleth has it: It's not about you. Every Analyst can mark this positive change in direction when a client finally takes a radical bend in the direction of benefitting others, rather than just self.

As for fulfilling love, a very subtle matter is occurring in the relationship of Sarah and Dan. Each happens to be creating the other. Yes, creating. It automatically happens when two people live together. The choice is to either let it occur unconsciously where actions and words simply influence the partner in a sloppy or negative fashion. Or, the reverse, waking up to the reality. The trick, for the fully aware partner, is to actively take charge of the creating phenomena, surrender passivity as an old childhood relic, and initiate activities that transform their mate. The plea of this author to readers is to continually create beautiful transformative moments. Again, passivity is for babies.

Transformative behavior begins, of course, with knowledge of what you want in life, something that was partially explained at the end of Sarah's Day. Let's say that one discovers he or she likes touch. The passive remnant from childhood is to silently wait, hoping against hope, that the partner will finally awaken and touch. That does not and will not work. Taking active charge of 'creating' one's partner means an array of tactics ranging from initiating hugs, initiating skin-to-skin closeness (with or without sex), snuggling on the couch, reaching out and putting one's arms around the other on a walk, lightly 'bumping' into the partner in, say, the kitchen, etc. Daily language of an aware partner includes words about touch emphasizing it as a present reality in the other's conduct. Giving means you receive. Receiving prompts giving.

'Creating' is the apex option in terms of partner relationships. Golden presuppositions exceed gold bracelets studded with diamonds. Anticipations in eyes, face, breathing, arms, legs - all bodily expressions for that matter - happen to shape (create) the other. There are few escapes for a partner from this option when it includes everything from everyday encounters to trusting faithfulness. Hopefully, both engage in this option. If one refuses and stays passive, it may be time for therapy. Or worse.

Still, one must ask "Having established the creative shaping approach after awareness at mid-life, what if infidelity occurs?" My belief, and that of my wife, is that there will be no forgiveness in the face of such. Why? Because, when one mature partner fully trusts and goes full force in creating a vital spouse, a betrayal of trust does not allow a marshmallow response. Marshmallows are for roasting. Working for vital love is too serious and too much a full investment of heart and mind and actions and being to be toyed with.

Getting back to our story, can any reader imagine either Dan or Sarah blinking if there was a breach of faith by the partner? Really! That is unthinkable. What if Dan became an alcoholic or Sarah became a meth addict? Would the other hang around? No.

Still, some think my wife and I too harsh in this matter. Our forty years of doing therapy - which can be stretched to eighty plus years if it is realized we frequently worked separately in sessions - neither of us saw a legitimate exception to what is being said here. Trust broken was never trust renewed. We saw some who tried; none succeeded in gaining back the beauty of true love. Life is short. One need not waste it with a kind of half life. Remember: we are talking about mature mid-life love as described above and also in the lives of Sarah and Dan.

Deep intimacy strangely revolves around the issue of abandonment and its consequences. Cessation of relationship can mean hard times if there is minimal financial resources. Thus, the above comments may seem facile. Divorce is a wrenching traumatic experience. Again, please understand that I'm talking about mature love that usually comes about in the late thirties and beyond when resources are usually better.

My thinking is that all relationships - including relating to adult children - must contain the tension of abandonment. Parents, for instance, who keep helping a child hooked on drugs is not being loving: they are enabling a habit. Love does not mean one is to graciously watch someone you love destroy him or herself. This leads me to say rather categorically that the tension of abandonment needs to be an unspoken background reality or even the best relationship is in trouble. Without hesitation, I see that as an essential part of love. This may sound ironic; my experience says it's true.

This chapter should not end grimly. With Dan and Sarah lost in the flowering of their love, it is only natural to ask how that vitality can continue until death does them part. The last two paragraphs support the reality of long lasting love.

Now, as to finding redemptive solutions to major trauma, a deeply loving relationship can provide the real bonus in life. Independently, one can be happy. A partner to share life with is a huge bonus. Is it worth working for? I say "Absolutely."

Final Therapy Notes:

Analysts basically have five tools to use in doing therapy: one's personality based on compassion and logic, the surgical use of questions, a concentration upon emotional clarification, a generous supply of metaphors and the intelligent use of presuppositions.

***1. Rapport.** I started to write "Hopefully the therapist has studied his own personality and has removed most of his neurotic issues." On second thought, it is necessary that the therapist has examined himself. The reason is that an understanding of one's own errant modules provides both self-understanding and compassion when the patient reveals similar personality failures. Knowing one's self also allows patience and honesty; not phony commiseration. An Analyst is not a critic from on high. He's a fellow human being who has stepped into the holes of the road years before the client's missteps and therefore knows the phases along life's way. Self-knowledge also provides what is popularly called "a bullshit detector" since you've already mastered your own labyrinth of rationalizations to avoid the truth. The idea is to be straightforward.*

***2. Questions.** Doing therapy is unlike ordinary conversation. Having someone relating his personality issues allows the Analyst to be totally nosey and inquire down to incredible* *specificity. You cannot guess or act like you understand when you do not. If someone says she hates "Chicago" you ask what pictures come to mind when she says "Chicago." You never assume. The idea is to pierce the person's deep model of the world and people. This is not just idle inquiry; the point is to get to the heart of how the person constructs values, behavior, emotions, and thinking.*

3. Emotions. *The text has already supplied an abundance of information about emotions. It should be clear by now that emotions form the heart of therapy. They are the fundamentals whereby one either fails or makes progress in personal growth. They provide the fundamental unit, also, of Psychoanalysis and allow that discipline to be clearly empirical. (Is anyone listening?)*

As is clear in all four major characters of the novel, each, early on, failed at the point of being Tender - the vulnerable feeling issue that marks success or failure in therapy. People often are confused thinking that sad depression is real when it is often masked anger, that scare is not masculine, that excitement is sexuality, or that happiness is naivete. The six emotions are clearly understandable when their polarities are pointed out: sadness is the opposite of happiness, excitement the opposite of scaring one's self, and tenderness is the opposite of anger expressions. To be human, all six are real.

The subject of emotions merits a book in and of itself and I've done that elsewhere. For now, let it be said that something appearing simple such as sadness becomes incredibly profound (masked anger? True grief? Manipulation of others? Actual Narcissism? Etc.) Just the use of ridiculing laughter, like Dan Michelson in Chapter One, offers many sessions where he is taught to be real and not haughtily act above other people. While the subject of emotions is complex, mental health depends on authentic expression of them. Or, why else would the term "emotional disturbance" be used?

4. Metaphors. *Great religious leaders often told stories. Buddha was good at it. Jesus told parables. (The first half of this book is a story about trauma and redemption.) On occasion the story told by the therapist appears odd and out of context. Imagine a patient ashamed of facial scars who listens to this story. "I once went to a local fair in South Bend Indiana and was fascinated by clocks made by a man in his eighties. Each of the clocks were a narrow cross-section of a tree. He picked up one walnut slice, holding it lovingly, and told me its story: 'This clock face shows that a sprig of a walnut tree was fallen on by a rotten old tree when the walnut was quite young. As the older tree rotted, the young tree kept growing. Look at it. See how it is not symmetrical. It has beauty to it because the sap wood grows more to one side.' The old man went on and on telling me about the clock he had made from the old bent slice of walnut. Of course, I bought the clock. There it is on the wall. The old man honored experience; so do I."*

I find it helpful to have a supply of stories from literature, poems, and even music lyrics to use during sessions. Example: "This reminds me of the seven stages of the cross as a person works his way through crises until victory is achieved."

5. Presuppositions. *This is rather a unique field that I inadvertently developed. I was studying linguistic material about transformative language and was wondering how it could be used in therapy. It suddenly hit me that many clients would unfortunately not go the whole distance in re-orienting their lives with straight emotions. A shortcut had to be developed. At first I thought it arrogant, but I finally decided that therapists and other people given the mantle of authority (ex. Clergy, Teachers and Doctors) can actually tell questing clients (students or parishioners) who they are. My first principle, therefore, was to gain what I termed The Authority Transference. My partner and I wrote a little book on how grandparents can significantly add to a grandchild's self-understanding through chosen words. The idea is that you tell them who they are and what capabilities they* *have. Presuppositions make all the difference in terms of teaching. (Is anyone listening?)*

Later I developed what I called The Presuppositional Process. It has three steps:

First, determine the outcome you want. Second, declare that outcome as real and operative in the present moment. Third, any derivations from that outcome by the person you are presupposing are to be treated as momentary tangents; not the real truth. An example: My outcome is that the reader of this work learns how to free himself from Script. My second step is to assume that you get the message and have imbedded it in your personality right here and now. If, in the third instance, you sway away and show lack of having the lesson internalized I say: "Hey! You've got it and you will be discovering that the material has sunk in as you move along in your life." Is it any wonder that my Aunt Mildred told me a half century ago that I would someday write a book?

Now, is that manipulative? Here I become more pragmatic rather than moralistic. My goal, as therapist and as a person intent on redemptive outcomes, is to use my little cotton ball of strength to good ends. To avoid some of the manipulation I develop a long list of desirable goals: mental health, the ability to love, to think logically, to feel cleanly, to value yourself and others, to be intelligent, to have a good attitude, to work for the good, etc. Please recall that I did just this in my italicized notes with Dan in the first chapter. I am definitely not using presuppositions to sell a used car.

I can guarantee you that I've seen incredible results from intelligent use of presuppositions. So, too, can the hundreds of people I have trained across the years. In therapy, I found that I was able to sow in wonderful seeds in people's minds, seeds that defined, in many good and beautiful ways, who the person is and will be.

So, you decide. Are presuppositions worthy to be used? I defy anyone to have a grandchild look up at you with love and semi-adoration and you refuse to tell that child that she has a good soul and will always seek to do her best in life.

It certainly beats being passive and watching a child follow some meaningless Script for the remainder of life.

Final Thought

Doing therapy - sitting there hour after hour with honest searching souls who desire full lives - is an honor beyond explanation. Being a talk therapist is a spiritual vocation, one that allows you to accompany a person through the Valley of the Shadow of Death to the Mount of Victory.

As I end these reflections, an array of clients pass by my mind's eye. I see Janet who died with cancer at a Chicago Hospital; Carl - long gone - who told me about 'jungle juice' and his closeness to death in Okinawa; Ernie who died too early due to wounds from the Battle of the Bulge; on and on I proceed in my mental scrapbook of them all. They are all heroes in my estimation, pilgrims who refused to give in to despair and kept forging ahead to have meaningful success in their lives.

I love them. One and all.

EPILOGUE

Two Grateful Letters

On the first anniversary of Ezra Loew's death, a memorial service at the Chicago Jewish Cemetery is held by Sarah and I. It is a gloriously beautiful Autumn day. A somber group gathers out of respect for a man of honor, a man tattooed by sadists, a man who responded in the only way he knew to re-establish a good rational world. Mourners are Uncle Schlomo Loew, Dr Sidney Rabinowitz, Mr. and Mrs. Daniel Michelson Loew, a Cantor, a Rabbi and the Minyan - ten adults from a local synagogue who also join with respect for the deceased.

A small discrete hole is apparent in the funeral mound that holds the casket of Ezra. A slender open brass capsule is on the grave. Once receiving several contents from Sarah and I, it will be lowered to touch the casket The opening will be sealed securely.

The rabbi begins reciting the Shema........ In Hebrew.

Hear O Israel, the Lord is our God, the Lord is One.
Blessed be the Name of His glorious kingdom for ever and ever.
And you shall love the Lord your God with all your heart and with
All your soul and with all your might.

And these words I command you today shall be in your heart.
And you shall teach them diligently to your children

And you shall speak of them
When you sit at home, and when you walk along the way,
And when you lie down and when you wake up.

And you shall bind them as a sign on your hand,
And they shall be frontlets between your eyes.

And you shall write them on the doorposts of your house
And on your gates.

- Deuteronomy 6:4-9

Sarah then opens a letter she holds in her hands and reads aloud the following:

Ezra Loew, my friend, mentor and spiritual father, I stand here in great gratitude for what you gave me - no less than a new awakened life. You gave me the gift of accepting silence and the nurturing warmth of solitude. Ezra, my Ezra, you gave me appreciation of the free Kansas wind, the blue sky and driving clouds, a bedroom and a window with a view of blue spruce trees and a lovely garden. You taught me simplicity by providing me with the job of cooking and cleaning which allowed me to be thankful for those who do menial tasks. Your foundational trust let me find myself at my own speed. You possessed, when you looked at me, the golden belief that I could and would heal. My gratitude ripples from the beat of my heart throughout my whole body and brain.

Ezra, you also gave Dan and I the resources to follow a meaningful path for the remainder of our lives. As you appreciated children next to the Eisenhower Center and allowed them to become your teachers, we will build many, many playgrounds that will pass on the message of life to observing aware adults. To honor you, we will provide a place to play for as many children as possible. In their spontaneous releases of joy, they will have - in their generation - what was refused to members of your family - your parents, Madeline, you and

Shlomo, my children Lance and Laura - and the many millions who died during the dark days of the thirties and forties.

I also thank you, Ezra, for trusting me with your son. Words are lost in my tears. I will watch over him as you did during your life.

With all my heart,

Amelia.
Sarah Anne Smith.
Sarah Anne Bannock.
Mrs. Daniel Michelson Loew.

Sarah hands her letter to the Rabbi, who covertly and respectfully places the letter in the brass canister that is to be lowered over Ezra's coffin.

Then, I open my letter and read with faltering voice:

Ezra Loew, my father: I, who felt so sorry for myself for so many years, so empty, have discovered, with gratitude, that I have a loving father. Right now I wish I had the lovely words of a poet or the thrilling melodies of a composer. I have neither, but I know that my heart is full. I am glad to place you beside my mother who always respected you and passed on to me the words, now golden, that you were a good man.

Sarah's letter has expressed so many of my thoughts. I echo her completely,with the underline of gratitude that you provided us with a mission for the remainder of our lives. Children, all children, will be part of your heritage.

I … we … vow that we will never forget and that we will bear witness in the unique way of seeing that children may express joy without fear.

I thank you especially for my beautiful and strong wife and your wisdom in bringing us together. That is the greatest gift. I love you my father. Goodbye.

With great appreciation and love, Your loving son, Daniel Michelson Loew

Wiping tears from my eyes, I give my letter to the rabbi who places it next to Sarah's in the brass canister. He seals it carefully.

* * *

The Cantor standing beside the Rabbi chants the Kaddish in Hebrew:

May His great Name grow exalted and sanctified.
(everyone say AMEN)

In the world that He created as He willed.
May He give reign to His Kingship in your lifetime
and in your days
And in the lifetimes of the entire Family of Israel.
Swiftly and soon. Now say Amen.
(everyone says AMEN)

May His great name be blessed for ever and ever
Blessed, praised, glorified, exalted, extolled,
Might, praised, and lauded be the Name of the Holy One.
Blessed is He beyond any blessing and song.
Praise and consolation that are uttered in the world,

Now say Amen.
(Everyone says AMEN)

May there be abundant peace from Heaven

And life upon us and upon all Israel, Now say Amen.
(Everyone says AMEN)

He who makes peace in His heights,
May He make peace,
Upon us and upon all Israel. Now say Amen.
(Everyone says AMEN)

The brass capsule is carefully lowered to its position, slightly touching the six foot deep casket of my father. Each member of the family picks up a handful of earth and drops it carefully in the hole.

Everyone waits expectantly, not knowing what comes next. I seize the moment. Looking down at my mother's grave, I say firmly and lovingly: "You were right, mom. He was a good man." Everyone hears. Everyone understands. Everyone agrees. With that, I nod to the assembly signaling that the memorial service is over.

The service now being concluded the family and friends head toward their cars with the sobriety funerals demand and the honorable life of Ezra Loew deserved.

After a few moments of appropriate silence, Schlomo and Sid glance at each other with mutual understanding and then begin to move their bodies and legs like the Dancing Hasid. They laugh as they dance, arms aloft, hands clapping and legs freely kicking - kicking in a protest against death and with an affirmation of life. Sarah and I look with great pleasure at these two old men who know full well the message that life energy is irrepressible, and that, even in the face of death, one must celebrate the miracle of joyous life.

With my right arm around Sarah and Sarah with her left arm encircling me at the waist, we walk together as a loving team.

Then, with in an impulse born of deep respect for Ezra Loew and with a respectful glance at the graves of my mother and father, we erupt in free joy as we skip and dance to our waiting limousine..

****

Therapeutic Analysis

It seems almost sacrilegious to add analytic comments to the above, but I must because there are several key lessons for those struggling with major traumas, those desirous of redemptive options. It is appropriate given the ceremony we just experienced.

Death is the final destiny of every form of life. Therapeutically speaking, some take that end destination as justification to live with a strange bent on freedom. It is as if they say: "Since I'm going to die anyway, I'll do anything I damn well please." That is followed with tissue destructive paths such as alcohol and drug addiction, or the treatment of others as 'marks.'

They follow spirit-destroying approaches to life. Others may follow reality-denying wish while dreaming their way through meaningless existences. In sum, they allow deep anxiety and persistent trauma defeat their souls.

Joining courageous clients, artistic greats, literary masters and those serving humanity (nurses, doctors, social workers, etc.) I believe the actuality of death can impel each of us to re-double our efforts by creating moments of love as well as providing redemptive options for others. The Great among us address the Grim Reaper thusly: "Yes, Death, you will be the ultimate winner but your victory will only be for a second. Until that slender micro-moment, I will defeat you. The victory is mine. I choose to be happy. I will fully live life with excitement. I will dare to love fully. I will encourage life in others. I will exercise my freedom every day. I choose to contribute. So, poor Death, you are the ultimate loser, not me."

That speech arises from every song and symphony, every poem and great book, every soul that refuses to give in to despair - no matter the traumatic occasion.. And that is why the Dancing Hasid is an apex symbol, a symbol also extolled in exultant spontaneous children bursting with joy on a playground.

* * *

During my days as a psychotherapist, there was a magnificent array of beautiful moments occurring each day. While it is difficult to choose one exquisite moment, I shall do so. My hesitation is caused by an onslaught of other memories, mental pictures of individuals dying of cancer, clients wrestling to win against long-term sexual abuse by a parent, physical traumas of all manner of description, and, of course, war. I honor them all even as I necessarily must choose one illustration.

The instant I choose was while working with an elderly Irish priest (now deceased) who served a church in an abjectly poor and crime-ridden ghetto. This man was remarkable. Week after week he told me stories of his personal tragedies, stories that plucked my heart strings like a harp. He overcame his torturous past by being a supremely good and loving Catholic father. Those who had little hope were comforted and encouraged by this kindly man. He was a superb representation of full humanity.

On the occasion that springs to my mind, this wonderful priest halted his normal narrative and studied me closely as if piercing my soul's center to see if I was trustworthy of something quite precious to him. I must have passed his test. "Frank, the greatest poem ever written is Fern Hill by Dylan Thomas." Then, without hesitation and with an Irish brogue he quoted it from memory:

"Now as I was young and easy under the apple boughs
About the lilting house and happy as the grass was green,
The night above the dingle starry,

Black Opal

Time let me hail and climb
Golden in the hey-days of his eyes,
And honored among wagons I was prince of the apple towns
And once below a time I lordly had the trees and leaves
Trail with daisies and barley
Down the rivers of the windfall light.

And as I was green and carefree, famous among the barns
About the happy yard and singing as the farm was home,
In the sun that is young once only,
Time let me play and be
Golden in the mercy of his means,
And green and golden I was huntsman and herdsman, the calves
Sang to my horn, the foxes on the hills barked clear and cold,
And the Sabbath rang slowly
In the pebbles of the holy streams.

All the sun long it was running, it was lovely, the hay
Fields high as the house, the tunes from the chimneys, it was air
And playing, lovely and watery. And fire green as grass.
And nightly under the simple stars
As I rode to sleep the owls were bearing the farm away,
All the moon long I heard, blessed among stables, the night-jars
Flying with the ricks, and the horses
Flashing into the dark.

And then to awake, and the farm, like a wanderer white
With the dew, come back, the cock on his shoulder: it was all
Shining, it was Adam and maiden,
The sky gathered again
And the sun grew round that very day.
So it must have been after the birth of the simple light
In the first, spinning place, the spellbound horses walking warm
Out of the whinnying green stable
On to the fields of praise.

And honored among foxes and pheasants by the gay house
Under the new made clouds and happy as the heart was long,
In the sun born over and over,
I ran my heedless ways,
My wishes raced through the house high hay
And nothing I cared, at my sky blue trades, that time allows
In all his tuneful turning so few and such morning songs
Before the children green and golden
Follow him out of grace,

Nothing I cared, in the lamb white days, that time would take me
Up to the swallow thronged loft by the shadow of my hand,
In the moon that is always rising,
Nor that riding to sleep
I should hear him fly with the high fields
And wake to the farm forever fled from the childless land.
Oh as I was young and easy in the mercy of his means,
Time held me green and dying
Though I sang in my chains like the sea.

"That final line, Frank, 'As I was young and easy in the mercy of his means, Time held me green and dying, though I sang in my chains like the sea' - that line, Frank - is the ultimate in poetry and in life: Don't forget it."

I haven't.

It was a holy moment.

* * *

Now you tell me, my reader, who was the therapist, who the client?

Attached Paper

THE ANATOMY OF A TRAUMA

I've introduced many therapeutic ideas in the course of this book, chief among them my explanation of children as playwrights who compose three character dramas I term Script. While I call this idea psychoanalytic, it's true that my particular interpretation will not be found in Freudian literature. I still hold to the term "psychoanalytic" because Script is a great grandchild of the theories of Sigmund Freud.

There are other fresh explanations. Guilt as an internal dialog between Superego and Id is a clear descendant of psychodynamic theory. Shame, understood as a projective belief that others can mind-read one's own internal movies (eg. Mother's extreme fatness, a father's drunken scenes, poverty in a roach-infested home, etc.) is a result of my own observations with slight hints from older interpretations.

Among the new ideas is the primacy of six emotions (Sadness, Anger, Scare, Happiness, Excitement and Tenderness – SASHET.) I have been convinced for four decades that emotions provide the empirical basic unit so necessary for any legitimate science. I'm also convinced that a failure for psychoanalysis to provide an emotional basic unit will spell the end of the discipline. That's a shame in the light of empirical data that is so easy to verify by an analysis of just one person's life showing the primacy of feelings - nevertheless the whole of humanity (a much larger study.)

Other innovations introduced in this book come to mind: rationalization and transference as everyday phenomena; the necessity of real abandonment in the background of deep intimacy; the fear of tenderness as the source of Defense

Mechanisms as well as the fear of vulnerable Tenderness being the main barrier to real soul love; the extraordinary power of Presuppositions once one is given the mantle of authority; the avoidance of passivity by taking charge and creating vital 'moments' in marriage; the use of children at playgrounds as a learning situation for those frozen with traumas; etc. It was no idle comment in the Preface when I said that psychotherapeutic theory has been my lifelong obsession. I think it a cardinal avenue to deeply benefit others.

With the sole goal of being an effective psychotherapist, my practice throughout the decades was to study any and every writer who might offer clues on how to help people. There was a wealth of resources available. Particularly powerful were writers, mainly Jewish, who had struggled with the absolute insanity of Hitler and who wrote in the late forties, the fifties, and sixties. Those writers not only analyzed the psychological reasons people followed the madman, they also developed grand systems of therapy to thwart future destructive dictators. Every aware therapist is in their debt.

In my readings, I discovered brilliant solutions to personal difficulties. I'd clone the option in therapy and usually find the idea to be quite beneficial to clients. Trying out the next author's insight, I'd experiment with it and discover it to be equally valuable. This practice of gaining an insight here and there went on for a long time leaving me partially satisfied as I filled my therapeutic quiver with a large number of arrows.

Something, however, was missing. Each solution seemed partial. While each idea worked for awhile, it failed to offer the larger good that I (and my patients) desired. One day - perhaps in 1978 or so - I came up with the idea of combining all the ideas into what I termed "The Anatomy of a Trauma and its Resolution." During the following decades I taught this to an array of therapists - individually, at training sessions with groups and upon the occasion of speaking engagements. I received consistent feedback that the Anatomy was quite powerful in terms of therapy.

How can it be used by ordinary readers of this book? Let's take the first step, that of gaining a 'God's eye' view of the precipitating event - that is to say, the original trauma. Please know that a person having experienced a transforming negative event views it so personally that objectivity does not occur. Everything is highly subjective and rules out the view of, say, a journalist or historian recording the occasion.

Imagine that you are told of a trauma by a friend, family member, or close acquaintance. Utilizing the first step, you phrase sentences like the following: "Tell me about what happened as if you were describing it as a writer." Or, "If you were God looking down on what happened, how would He look upon it?" (Hear also a covert note that Freud believed that all people have remnant traumas leftover from childhood because freedom is diminished in every home by every parent in every situation. In other words, parents have Scripts that have them occasionally act like overgrown children.)

As the person relates the old situation in an objective manner, something dramatically and secretly changes. The traumatized have gained a viewpoint never before considered. The objective story cauterizes some of the old wounds. The personal intensity, heretofore held, loses some of its intensity. The entire event is given new context. This happens to be quite healing in and of itself. Therapy begins in the re-telling from an objective viewpoint.

Enough prolog. As writer, I'll seek to give small therapeutic questions as the following larger scheme is provided. One need not fear using these in everyday occasions as long as they are said in an offhanded, almost casual, manner where you are not probing, not seeking to be a shrink, not being a sterile critic, and not being a psychological smarty-pants. The idea is to be a friend. Soft questions are best. I well recall asking these questions on a dilapidated porch of a country store in Kentucky while I was drinking a Dr. Pepper with peanuts in it. A plumber who worked on my vacation home had just told me of a trauma he experienced as a child.

Step One: The Original Situation. The client is to provide a perspective from 'on high' rather than as a participant. This allows new objectivity. Question: "Will you describe that old scene as if you were viewing it from afar?"

Step Two: The Subjective Experience. Question: "Will you now tell me the experience in terms of your own five senses?"

Step Three: The Catastrophic Fantasy. Question: "What wild thoughts came to mind when the event was occurring and when you look back upon it?"

Step Four: The Frustrated Need. Question: "What did your really need back then that was not available?"

Step Five: The Denied Emotion. Question: "On the occasion of the trauma, were you able to express sadness, or anger, or scare or were any or all of them held inside? What about happiness, excitement and tenderness?"

Step Six: The Body Armor. Question: "Do you tighten up some part of your body when you think of what went unexpressed?" "What color is it?" "Change the color."

Step Seven: The Unfortunate Decision. Question: "Did you decide anything in that situation that remains with you?" "How can that decision be changed?"

Step Eight: The Continuation. Question: "How has that old situation continued in your relationships?"

Step Nine: Life in the Present. Question: "What do you need to change in order to shake off the negative past?"

Step Ten: Particularity. "Will you tell me exactly what behavior you'll start changing?"

Each of those ten steps are greatly abbreviated because it is anticipated that only a few readers will follow the entire sequence. My intent is to provide sufficient information so that anyone who experienced a major trauma, or, has a friend who is open to change will know a path to change. Ask the questions gently. Do not pry.

OTHER BOOKS

by

FRANK R. MORRIS

may be obtained from:

HTTP://STORES.LULU.COM/MORRIS-MORRIS

2007 - **Liberation Psychotherapy**, a system with five emphases:
Modularity, Emotions, Life Force Energy, Abandonment, Presuppositions

2008 - **The Freudian Labyrinth**. This book updates Sigmund Freud's system by closely analyzing the author's life.

2009 - **Black Opal.** This combination novel with an accompanying analysis allows the author to illustrate what therapy can accomplish.
The sub-title is **On Trauma and Redemption**.

2010 - **The Therapy of Toxic Ideology** (in process). This book will explore fundamentalist ideologies and what they have in common with Narcissism.

www.ingramcontent.com/pod-product-compliance
Lightning Source LLC
Chambersburg PA
CBHW060342030726
47497CB00003B/565

* 9 7 8 0 5 7 8 0 0 8 0 3 5 *